A Locket for Maggie

CAROLE GIFT PAGE

A JANET THOMA BOOK

THOMAS NELSON PUBLISHERS
Nashville

Published in Nashville, Tennessee, by Thomas Nelson, Inc.

Library of Congress Cataloging-in-Publication Data

Page, Carole Gift.
    A locket for Maggie / Carole Gift Page.
      p. cm. — (Heartland memories ; 6)
    ISBN 0-7852-7673-4 (pbk.)
    1. Indiana—Fiction. I. Title.

PS3566.A3326 L63 2000
813'.54—dc21

00-025548
CIP

Printed in the United States of America

1 2 3 4 5 6 QPV 05 04 03 02 01 00

To my beloved grandchildren—
Lucas "Luke" Anthony Page, Lauren Ashley Page,
and brand-new Alyse Destiny Bunch

1

Christmas Day, 1967
Willowbrook, Indiana

Any other year Maggie would have found the towering Christmas tree in the parlor comforting, reassuring, a beauty to behold with its silver garlands, silky angel hair, and bubble lights. Any other year. She fingered one crimson candle as silent bubbles percolated mysteriously up its narrow glass stem. "I love these," she told Jordan, averting her gaze, lest he read more in her face.

Even to Maggie her words sounded more accusing than affirming, as if she had said, *You were there yesterday, but tomorrow's another story.* She gazed again at the ornaments. It was not memories they stirred but feelings that Maggie couldn't articulate, even to Jordan. These were strong, heartfelt, urgent emotions, deep as the roots of the gnarled oak trees surrounding her parents' home—this timeworn Victorian mansion on Honeysuckle Lane where she had lived forever, where life was wonderfully, infuriatingly predictable. Try as she might, she could never get far from her roots.

The memories flooding over her today, the sudden sweep of feelings, were like that exactly. Their roots were deep, untouchable, unseen. One knew they were there, felt their presence, saw the result of their work—the sturdy tree with its limbs flowering everywhere—but one didn't see the roots.

With a sharp breath she turned at last and looked at Jordan, tears dancing in her eyes. *Please, God, don't let him see what's really there.*

"You're in a mood." Jordan was standing by the love seat, arms crossed over his crisp new navy uniform, his pilot "wings of gold" gleaming on his left breast pocket. He was a tanned, strapping man, more than six feet tall, with the hardy, stalwart face of a warrior—high forehead, straight, distinctive nose, generous chin. But he still had the jovial, mischievous eyes of a boy eager to please. Even now, a curious expression crossed his face, a mixture of love and wonder and pride, as if he'd just climbed a mountain or won a race and was waiting for her to congratulate him. She couldn't, wouldn't. She was losing him. He was just back from the Naval Air Station at Pensacola, fresh from the rigors of flight training, a grueling regimen that crushed lesser men. Now, in his mind he was already half a world away . . . in Vietnam. He hadn't even gone off to war yet, and already he looked like a hero, like a man who'd tasted victory.

"Did you hear me, Mag? You look sad. What's wrong?"

"Nothing. I'm fine. Better than fine."

How could she tell him? She wasn't like Jordan, nothing like Jordan. He was so filled with passion and energy he always lost himself in the moment, gave himself wholeheartedly, holding nothing back. She thrived on his energy, admired and envied it. But she was the opposite, a person who analyzed everything, who thought things through to the point of tedium. She rarely acted on impulse, never jumped in headfirst; she weighed her options, contemplated her actions until nothing seemed spontaneous.

Even now. She wanted nothing more than to throw herself into his arms and pour out her fears. Instead, she remained stone still, hands clenched at her sides, her face an inscrutable mask. Or did he read her better than she knew?

"I know it's hard, Mag. Just say it."

"Say what, Jordan? What is there to say? It's too late."

She heard herself and cringed; she could have been reciting lines in a play. Why couldn't she say what she really felt? Like a demanding stage director or a ruthless umpire, she always stood outside herself, watching, observing herself, skeptical, judging. Did she measure up? Was she behaving like a dunce? Did people find her lovable, acceptable? Would the masterful, strong-willed Jordan Barrett love her if he knew the real Maggie Herrick?

Did he guess what a coward she was? Even when she willed herself to act, when she stepped into the milieu of life, she toed the waters gingerly, careful not to get her feet wet or her hands soiled. She never threw herself in with such passion and zest that she forgot herself, like Jordan did. He seized the moment, became the moment, triumphed over the moment, and caught everyone else up with him in a delirious, spontaneous joy.

"Maggie . . . Jordan. Soup's on."

They both turned and gazed at Jordan's younger brother, Chad, in the doorway—a shorter, leaner version of Jordan, but with the same square jaw, aquiline nose, and striking blue eyes. Chad still wore the thick, wavy brown ducktails Jordan had forfeited for a military crew cut. Chad flashed an awkward, lopsided grin, his cheeks ruddy, his eyes crinkling at the corners. "Guess I should say the turkey dinner's on, with all the trimmings, compliments of your grandmother Anna. Smells good, huh, Magpie?"

Maggie nodded. She hated that name. Chad had called her that all her life, since the days he had tied her pigtails in knots and convinced her mud pies were good to eat. "Mud pies for a Magpie," he'd teased. She was six, he, seven. But eight-year-old Jordan had rescued her and made his brother eat the mud. The brothers had maintained a friendly rivalry over Maggie ever since. Not that there was any real question about where Maggie's loyalties lay. Nor Chad's. They both looked up to Jordan, counted on him, fed off his energy. They were like spokes, with Jordan the hub; mere shadows of Jordan, pale moons revolving around his heat, his light, his energy. His brilliance.

"So how about it? You two coming? Food's getting cold."

"We'll be right there," said Jordan, an edge in his voice.

Chad held up his hands. "Okay. Take your time. But your dad won't say grace, Magpie, until everyone's around the table."

"I know," said Maggie. "We're coming."

Chad gave her a lingering look, as if he, too, were trying to read her emotions. It was enough that she couldn't express herself to Jordan; she wouldn't have Chad playing his own guessing games. "Tell Daddy we'll be there in a minute, okay?"

Chad shrugged and said, "Will do." But his eyes looked wounded as he turned away, and Maggie felt a pinch of guilt.

When he had gone, Jordan pulled her into his arms and pressed her cheek against his sturdy chest. She could feel his heart beating under his uniform, a strong, steady beat. He didn't say a word. Nor did she. She had no words.

A teacher once told Maggie, "Still waters run deep." She was stunned, awed by his comment. What did it mean? Was it a casual, throwaway remark? Or had his solemn, all-wise eyes noticed what no one else saw? Had he surmised something important about her, gleaned some vital truth she in all her painful, self-conscious ruminations had missed? Had he seen that she was like a cautious skater on ice, always fearful of breaking through, of sinking deep inside herself, swallowed by dark waters, vanishing forever?

So much of who she was lay below the surface, beyond reach, even beyond Jordan's reach, in the dark waters of her own subconscious. Her father once told her, when she was eight and cringed at facing the crowd of rollicking children at her own birthday party, "Just go out there and be yourself." But how could she when she had no idea who she was? She had buried her face in his coat until ten-year-old Jordan Barrett strolled over and took her hand and drew her into the party. Dear Jordan. Always her rescuer, her hero.

From that day on, she and Jordan and his brother Chad were

inseparable. The Three Musketeers, someone called them. The name stuck. Through junior high and high school their motto was, "All for one and one for all." When it was time for college, they had all enrolled at Willowbrook University, Maggie and Chad a year behind Jordan, following comfortably as always in his sure footsteps.

It had all been perfect, until this year when Jordan, with the ink still wet on his diploma, had enlisted in the service, his head filled with visions of winning the war single-handedly.

"Are you ready to go to dinner?" he asked, relaxing his arms around her waist.

"Give me a minute."

"Alone?"

She nodded. "Do you mind?"

"Not if that's what you want." He took her face in his large hands and kissed the tip of her nose, then kissed her on the cheek—a circumspect kiss, nothing like last night. After all, his parents and hers were in the next room. "I'll do better later, when we're really alone," he whispered, his breath warm and minty on her face, his aftershave sharp and pungent as sliced limes. His blue eyes crinkled like merry half-moons, his white teeth gleamed in the wide arc of his smile.

He drew her back into the warm circle of his arms and as always, she was enraptured, bedazzled as a lovesick schoolgirl. He ran his fingers through her straight brown hair, letting the long, burnished strands cascade over her shoulders. "I love your hair, your face, everything about you, Maggie. I'll carry a picture of you like this in my memory forever—your velvety eyes, the roses in your cheeks, your skin like cream. You'll always be with me, Mag, no matter what happens, no matter where I go."

"You'll always be with me too," she murmured, refusing to think about where he might go or what might happen to him.

Finally Jordan released her and turned, shoulders straight, and strode out of the room. Already walking tall . . . like an officer.

Maggie sat down in the cherry wood rocker beside the Christmas tree and gazed at the white, swirling ice scrolls on the windowpanes. She couldn't face her family and Jordan's yet. She was trembling and didn't know why. Was it because Jordan was leaving in the morning? Shipping out for Vietnam? Yes, it was that, and more. So much more.

All day she had felt as if she were standing on a precipice, as if her entire life had somehow led up to this moment, and after today nothing would ever be the same. Since early this morning she had gone through the motions—eating an ordinary breakfast of bacon and eggs and toast, opening the gifts with her parents and her younger brother, Jon Knowl. Careful not to tear the paper, folding the wrappings neatly, so they could be used again. Making small exclamations of pleasure ("I love this sweater, Mama; it's exactly the right color!"), all idle conversation, silly chitchat.

She was going through the motions, seeing herself from a distance, watching herself moving in slow motion, sometimes the sound turned down, the words so rote, so inconsequential she didn't hear them. She heard something else in her head, the low hum of a disturbance, a warning. *Nothing will be the same. After today nothing will be the same. Especially you. Whoever you thought you were, you aren't. Someone else will emerge, someone you never imagined in your wildest dreams.*

A ripple of fear went through her. Who would she become? What would happen to change her so drastically? Surely it had to do with Jordan. Everything began and ended with Jordan. He loved her. Had told her so just last night, on Christmas Eve. That should have been the most glorious news on earth. Should have sent fireworks of joy exploding inside her.

Instead, the elation somersaulted into panic, into a tight knot of apprehension, a sense of white-knuckled urgency. She had to hold on to him, feel the solid reality of his strong arms around her, for soon he would be gone, a memory. And she would be alone, empty-handed, her loneliness spiraling into plummeting despair to match this moment's crescendoing joy. A harrowing thought emerged from the dark waters of her soul. *This is the best thing that has ever happened to me, and the worst!*

How ironic that just when he had pledged her his love, Jordan was stepping out of her life, leaving her alone to swim without a lifesaver. Chad would still be here, of course, but what were they without Jordan? They would be lost without him, rudderless, incomplete.

But we will survive, she told herself. *We have no choice.* They would hold on to each other and keep their heads above water until Jordan returned. Then their lives would right themselves and everything would be as it had always been—safe, sane, and predictable. She had to believe that, or she couldn't go on.

She reached out idly and traced the ice swirls with her fingernail, scratching her own design. Without thinking she wrote Jordan's name on the frosty glass. It was time to join Jordan and Chad and their parents in the dining room for Christmas dinner. After all, the two families had gathered to give Jordan a magnificent send-off, and who was she to spoil the party?

With a sharp intake of air, she slipped out of the rocker, smoothed her red velvet dress, crossed the room, and headed down the hall. As she approached the dining room, she pressed her cold fingers against her lips, willing a smile in place. Regardless of her misgivings, she would make a grand entrance in honor of the man she loved.

2

Maggie paused in the doorway and gazed around the dining room, savoring the enchantment of the moment—a homey scene straight out of a Norman Rockwell painting. The chandelier cast a rosy glow on the two families—the people Maggie loved most in the world— gathered around the long, linen-draped table for a Christmas feast. Everything was perfect—the silver antique candelabra, Grandmother Anna's best china and crystal, and the delectable centerpiece, a plump golden turkey. To make the picture complete, sweetly scented evergreens and blood-red poinsettias graced the cherry wood buffet; snow flurries danced against the windowpanes; and from the record player in the parlor came the languid strains of "I'll Be Home for Christmas."

It would have been the best Christmas ever, if Jordan weren't going away.

Maggie felt everyone's eyes on her as she took her place between Jordan and Chad. "Honey, your father was just about to say grace," said her mother softly. Even at forty-seven, Annie Herrick was the most beautiful woman Maggie had ever known. Perhaps her chest-nut brown hair was flecked with gray and her ivory skin etched with faint lines, like aged, expensive china, but her gray-green eyes were as bright and luminous as the sea. And nothing rivaled her inner beauty—her quiet wisdom and confidence, her gentleness, her unshakable faith.

"Let's pray," said her father in his deep, resonant voice. As everyone joined hands and bowed their heads, Maggie stole a sidelong glance at her father. He had always been the only man in her heart . . . until Jordan. At fifty, Knowl Herrick was both handsome and distinguished, with sharply chiseled features, a ruddy complexion, and wire-rim spectacles over his crinkly brown eyes. His wavy, honey-brown hair had receded slightly and his jowls had thickened a bit, but otherwise, the years had been good to him.

"Our Heavenly Father," he said in the quiet, companionable voice of one accustomed to speaking often and intimately with God, "we thank You for this delicious dinner Annie and her mother have prepared. We're especially appreciative that You made them such great cooks. And we thank You for letting our good friends, the Barretts—Daniel and Clara and their two fine sons—join us in celebrating Your birthday. We pray You'll be with Jordan as he heads for Vietnam to serve our country and fight for freedom in our troubled world. Bless Maggie and Chad as they graduate from college next June. And help Jon Knowl get through another year of high school. Lord, we don't know what the new year will bring, but we pray we will be faithful to You in 1968." He paused, and with a wink at Maggie, added, "We especially thank You, Lord, for all the love we feel for one another around this table. It warms our hearts."

Jordan nudged Maggie as her father said amen. "Guess he's talking about us, huh? All that love . . . ?"

Maggie's face warmed. Of course, her father meant them. It was his little joke, his playful way. Lately their romance was their families' favorite topic of conversation. Maggie's brother, Jon Knowl, added fuel to the fire by drawling, "Yeah, some of us are feeling the love around this table a whole lot more than others. Right, Chad?"

Chad eyed Maggie and made a mock grumbling sound as he passed the mashed potatoes. "Yeah, some of us have been left out in the cold when it comes to all that love around the table."

Maggie teasingly slapped Chad's arm. "Don't be a spoilsport. You know I'll always care about you too."

Chad handed her the green bean casserole. "But my big brother, the navy pilot, has won the fair maiden's heart. It must be the uniform."

"Face it, little brother," Jordan bantered, "the best man won."

"Best? Come on! That uniform's gone to your head."

"No chance. My cover fits just fine. But don't worry, little brother. I'll leave Maggie in your safekeeping until I return."

Chad gave Maggie a knowing wink. "And I promise I won't let her out of my sight."

"Hey, man, I saw that." Jordan looked over at Maggie's brother. "Jon Knowl, you keep an eye on those two until I get back, okay? Don't let my brother make any moves on my girl."

Jon Knowl frowned, as if he didn't want any part of this age-old Barrett rivalry. "Yeah, I guess I can keep my ol' eagle eye on them," he said at last. At fifteen, Jon Knowl was clearly his father's son, minus the receding hairline and the spectacles. Maggie could see it, even though Jon Knowl would deny it hotly. His winsome, oval face and wide-set hazel eyes still possessed the soft innocence of youth, but the skeptical, downward curve of his mouth suggested troubled waters ahead. "But, man, Jordan, I still don't see why you have to go off and fight that dumb old war."

"That's just the way it is," said Jordan. "I've got to do my duty."

"Says who?" Jon Knowl slammed back.

Grandmother Anna spoke up. "Knowl, as soon as you have that turkey carved, you pass some to Jon Knowl. He looks awfully hungry."

Maggie's father smiled knowingly. "What you mean, Mother Anna, is that with some turkey in his mouth, Jon Knowl won't be so apt to put his foot in his mouth."

Jon Knowl scowled. "Shucks, I'm the only one around here who's honest enough to speak the truth about the war. Why should Jordan go fight for a country nobody can even find on a map, with names nobody can pronounce? Why should he risk his life for a bunch of foreigners?"

"Because if we don't fight the Communists over there, we'll be fighting them over here," said Jordan. "And I promise you, I'm going to kick those Commies so hard in their big, fat behinds, they won't dare show their faces over here."

Jordan's mother put her hands to her lips, as if her appetite had fled or she were silencing herself. She was a small, frail woman with a narrow face lined beyond her years. Her face had a pinched look, with small, fretful brown eyes and thin, pursed lips. She wore her short gray-brown hair in a casual, unadorned style, straight on each side with a shock of bangs on her forehead. Maggie had never seen her wear even a dab of makeup.

"Clara, what's wrong?" demanded her husband, his chair creaking as he swiveled his torso toward her. He was a big bear of a man, solid as a lumberjack, with large, calloused hands and tanned, leathery skin and the start of a potbelly under his checkered flannel shirt. Maggie had always found his gruff, no-nonsense manner painfully intimidating. With his dark brown hair and sharply sculpted profile, he had surely been a handsome man in his youth, but age and appetite had deepened and broadened his features and puffed out his jowls, so that his face had a mottled, distended quality. "Did you hear me, Clara? Are you okay?"

"Yes, Daniel," she said, craning her neck slightly, "it's just, you know, thinking of Jordan leaving, going so far away, thinking of what could happen." She rubbed her hands together, her long fingers moving with a quick, nervous energy. Clara Barrett had always reminded Maggie of a mother bird; she flitted rather than walked, fluttered her hands when she was anxious. She was always twittering, puttering, fussing. "You know how it is, Daniel. Sometimes it's just more than a mother can take."

"I'll be fine, Mom," said Jordan with a little scoffing sound.

Clara's hands fluttered. "That's easy for you to say, Son."

Jordan sounded exasperated now. "Mom, you've been worrying about me since the first day I crossed the street to go to kindergarten."

"This isn't kindergarten, Jordan. It's war, and you take it entirely too lightly."

"He does not, Clara," Daniel shot back. "He's worked hard to prepare himself to be a good soldier."

"Of course, he has, but . . ."

Daniel cut her off. "Look at me, Clara. I fought in the big war. On the front lines. You think it was easy? I busted my back for my country and came home a hero. Jordan will do the same thing. Fight the good fight, the way we've trained him. He'll be just fine. I'll tell you this, the Second World War makes Vietnam look like child's play."

Clara's face blanched. "But it's not child's play, Daniel. You were lucky. You came home. Lots of men didn't."

Grandmother Anna spoke up, her voice tremulous. "My son Chilton didn't come home. He died at Pearl Harbor. Twenty-six years ago this month. Hard to believe. He's been gone more years than he lived."

"He was a real hero, Mama." Annie reached across the table and patted her mother's arm, but the gesture seemed hapless, as if she knew consoling words weren't enough. It seemed strange to Maggie to see her mother step out of her maternal role and become a daughter again, groping for words. "And, you know, Mama, Chip will always live in our hearts."

"But I wanted more than that. So much more."

Everyone was silent for a long, awkward moment, busying themselves with the food. Maggie scoured her mind for something wise and comforting to say, but no words came. Even her mother, who usually always knew what to say, was silent now.

To Maggie's relief, her father stepped in and saved the moment.

"Jordan," he said, adjusting his glasses and clearing his throat, "I haven't heard much about your experiences at Pensacola. What was it like becoming a naval aviator? Can you fill me in?"

"Sure, Mr. Herrick." Jordan flashed a smile at Maggie and straightened his shoulders, as if the mere mention of Pensacola reminded him he was a naval officer. "I started with Pre-Flight, like all aviation cadets, Mr. Herrick. Training was divided into academic, physical fitness-survival, and military. For over three months I studied aerodynamics, aviation science, navigation, the whole ball of wax."

"And he came through with flying colors," Daniel Barrett interjected. "I'm a proud man. My boy was commissioned an ensign in the U.S. Naval Reserve."

"But first I underwent a whole lot of military training and discipline by tough marines, and exhausting days of marching and learning formations. They transferred me to Saufley Field, ten miles west of Pensacola's pre-flight school, for flight training. Started me on the prop-driven T-34. I had to spend endless work hours on the ground for each hour I spent in the air."

Maggie's father sat back and tented his fingers over his plate. "Sounds like you took to military life quite well."

"I did, sir. In ground school I learned cockpit procedures, engineering, and flight characteristics of the various aircraft. It was grueling."

"Has to be," boomed Daniel Barrett. "Aviators have to understand every phase of their assigned missions."

"When it was time to fly, Training Squadron One at Hangar 809 became my home. Man, I couldn't wait for my first solo flight." Jordan's voice grew more animated as he relived the moment. "It was the most breathtaking event of my life, knowing the control of that plane was in my hands alone. Within weeks I was doing all sorts of aerial maneuvers—the loop, the full Cuban eight, the wingover, the barrel roll, the spin. I felt like an acrobat in the air, but it was all dead serious; I swear, Mama, no monkey business."

"I should hope not," said Clara, her hands fluttering again.

"We had some Vietnamese in our squadron. Straight from the University of Saigon. Funniest thing. When they'd have a problem in the air flying, they'd get all excited and start spouting Vietnamese, and no one could understand a thing they said. But they did okay. They made good pilots."

Grandmother Anna passed the turkey around again. "Goodness, Jordan, I didn't realize the Vietnamese came over here to train."

"They wanted the best training they could get to defend their country, Mrs. Reed."

Maggie's father took a slice of white meat and handed the platter to Jon Knowl, who waved it on. "No better place than Pensacola," her father agreed. "Right, Jordan?"

"That's right, sir. After my training in the T-34, they transferred me to the bigger, faster T-28 Trojan trainer; it's a heavier aircraft, with more power. Climbs and cruises a whole lot faster than the T-34." He chuckled. "Like driving a Cadillac after plugging along in a Volkswagen."

Maggie sank down in her chair. She didn't want to think about Jordan in the air, flying alone, risking his life. Why couldn't they talk about something else? She cast a sidelong glance at Chad. He was poking listlessly at his green beans. The more excited Jordan sounded, the more downcast Chad looked. Maggie knew the reason. Right after Jordan had left for Pensacola, Chad had enlisted in the army, but he'd been rejected. Something to do with an irregular heart rhythm, nothing serious, but it kept him from qualifying for the service. He refused to talk about it, but Maggie knew it had been a keen disappointment. He had always felt like a failure in his father's eyes, and the army's rejection seemed to confirm it.

"Son, tell them about landing on a carrier," prompted Daniel Barrett, sounding nearly as excited as his son.

"Yeah, Dad, that was my biggest thrill of all. Landing on a real carrier. Talk about precision flying. On my first landing I held my breath, scared out of my wits my tail hook wouldn't snag the arresting cable, but it did. I learned basic instrument flying and night flying too. And radio instruments and formation tactics. My final training was in air-to-air gunnery in the North American T2A 'Buckeye.' I completed my carrier qualifying aboard the USS *Lexington-CVS 16.* After that I moved on to advanced training and, to make a long story short, I finally got my commission and my wings of gold." He fingered the gold wings on his left breast pocket. Maggie had never seen him look so proud.

"And tomorrow's the big day," said Maggie's father. "You take the train to Chicago and catch a flight overseas."

"That's right, sir. I'll be flying to the South China Sea and joining the Seventh Fleet in the Pacific. I've been assigned to the aircraft carrier, USS *Independence.* I'll be flying bombing sorties into both North and South Vietnam to support the army and marine ground action there."

Jon Knowl spoke up, an undercurrent of scorn in his voice. "And pray to God you don't get blown to smithereens while you're dropping those—"

Maggie's father cut him off. "We all pray that God will protect Jordan while he's serving his country, Jon Knowl. We're all proud of him and wish him well. Isn't that right?"

"Sure, Dad. I'll be praying like the dickens." Jon Knowl looked earnestly at Jordan. "Man, don't get me wrong. You know how much I look up to you. You're the greatest. But that doesn't change how I feel, or how a whole lot of other guys my age feel. We know our turn's next, and we're not sold on this whole give-your-life-for-your-country bit. Maybe I shouldn't speak my mind—"

"No, that's okay," said Jordan. "You have a right to your opinion, just like the rest of us."

"Okay, so I think you're crazy to get sucked into this whole Vietnam mess. It's not like you were even drafted; you volunteered! Most of the guys I know are talking about going to college or joining the Peace Corps so they can beat the draft. It's not college or serving humanity they care about; it's staying alive. Some guys are even running off to Canada."

"They're lily-livered cowards, plain and simple," said Daniel Barrett. "I never raised my sons to be cowards. Jordan will do his duty. Chad would have, too, if . . . if . . ."

Chad bristled. Maggie could feel the air suddenly charged with electricity. "What you mean, Dad," said Chad thickly, "is I'd be serving my country, too, if the recruiting office hadn't rejected me."

"Chad, that's not so," cried Clara Barrett. "Your dad is just as proud of you as he is of Jordan."

"Proud? How could he be, Mom? I'll never fly a plane and shoot down the enemy. The only thing I'll ever shoot is a camera." Chad threw his napkin in his plate, shoved back his chair, and strode out of the room.

Maggie started to push back her own chair, but Jordan put a restraining hand on her arm. "Let him go, Mag. My brother just needs some time alone. Nothing anybody says will change things."

"How do you know? Maybe I can . . ."

"He'll be back, Mag. Don't make a big deal of it."

Jon Knowl tapped his fork on his plate. "Dad, is that what you'll think of me if I don't enlist? That I'm a coward?"

"No, Son. But if you're drafted, I hope you'll go and do your best to make your country proud of you."

"And if I don't?"

Maggie caught a look of vexation on her father's face. "What about standing up and being a man?" he challenged, his dark eyes flashing behind his spectacles. "What's happened to character and courage, to loyalty and commitment, to duty to one's country?"

"Those are just words, Dad. They don't mean anything anymore."

"Are you telling me, if your father or brother or son was in a fight he believed he had to wage, you'd walk away and let him fight alone until you figured out whether he was right or wrong? If he needed your help, you'd better help him! If your country needs you, you go. Because it's like family. You support your family. You fight your family's fights. You protect your father, your brother, your son. You fight for your country like every generation has before you. I'd hate to think I haven't trained you well enough to instill in you a desire to protect your own country."

Jon Knowl's voice took on a surly edge. He sank down in his chair and crossed his arms on his chest. "I don't see any Vietcong running around the streets of Willowbrook with their bayonets."

"See what I'm talking about, Knowl?" said Daniel Barrett, thrumming his fist against his palm. "It's a sign of the times. These wise-guy college kids are filling your son's head with this stuff. Thank God Jordan and Chad didn't fall for it. Most young people today aren't committed to anything except their own comfort. Nothing matters to them but sex and drugs."

"That's not so, Mr. Barrett," said Jon Knowl hotly.

"Then why are kids today so afraid to be flag-wavers, afraid to love their country?" questioned Barrett. "Sure, our country has its faults, but America's still the best place on earth. You try living in Russia or China or some other Commie state and see how much freedom they give you."

Maggie broke in, but no one heard her. "Listen, everyone, this is Christmas . . ."

Jon Knowl was speaking with an impassioned urgency. "I love my country as much as anyone, Mr. Barrett, but I don't agree with what they're doing. I'm not a pacifist, but I think the Vietnam War is wrong. I hate having the draft hanging over my head, just waiting for me when I turn eighteen. Why should I fight a war I don't support?

I don't want to kill people. But the minute I'm out of high school I'm expected to make a decision that will affect the rest of my life. Will I fight or not? Will I give up my life here at home and run to Canada? It's not fair. What if the Commie I'm supposed to kill is just a kid like me?"

"That's sentimental hogwash," declared Daniel Barrett, his ruddy nostrils flaring, his temples throbbing. "That's exactly the mentality the Communists want our boys to have. That way they'll win the war hands-down."

"Daniel's right," said Clara Barrett, pressing her fingers to her face. "The world is so topsy-turvy these days. Did you read in the newspaper—what was it, Daniel, a couple of weeks ago? About the antiwar protesters in New York City who tried to shut down an induction center? Over a thousand protesters. And would you believe Benjamin Spock, the pediatrician, was among them? I was so shocked. Why, I raised my children on his book—"

"Didn't we all!" said Annie with a grim smile.

"—and now he's leading a whole generation of our young people astray with his radical ideas."

"Maybe Spock's just following his own conscience, the way I'm trying to do," said Jon Knowl. He sat forward and stared across the table at his father. "What about it, Dad? All my life you've taught me to think for myself, to do what I thought was right. So okay. Now I'm thinking for myself, trying to follow my own conscience, and Mr. and Mrs. Barrett say I'm being influenced by Communists . . . or Dr. Spock! How does a guy know what's right? I'm not even old enough to fight yet, and already it's tearing me apart inside, not knowing what's right."

Maggie's father was silent for a long moment. She could see the conflict playing out in his face. When he spoke his voice was low and controlled. "Jon Knowl, if there were easy answers to your questions, our country wouldn't be experiencing such torment these days. All I can tell you is, if the draft board calls you and you refuse to be inducted, you risk a possible five-year prison sentence and a $10,000 fine. Is that what you want to be? A draft-dodger? An expatriate? Branded as a traitor to your country?"

Jon Knowl gave Jordan a sidelong glance. "Okay, so maybe the truth is I'm not brave like Jordan. I'd be plain scared to be heading for Vietnam tomorrow. Man, I'm already scared to death for him. Don't you all feel it—the fear? Don't you feel it in the pits of your stomachs?" His voice broke on a sob. "Man, what if . . . what if Jordan doesn't come back?"

Jordan reached over and squeezed Jon Knowl's shoulder. "Don't you worry, man. Like I said, I'm going over there and making mincemeat of those Commies. I mean, how long can it take for the most powerful nation in the world to rescue a little backwoods country like Vietnam? I'll be back when the job's done. Before you know it. Don't you doubt it for a minute."

"I know you believe that," said Jon Knowl, "but—"

Grandmother Anna broke into the conversation as Chad came back into the room. "Children! Like Maggie said, it's Christmas, and this is hardly dinner-table conversation. We're together and we have so much to be thankful for. Let's talk about something pleasant and enjoy the holiday while we can."

"You're right, Mrs. Reed," said Clara Barrett. "Annie, why don't you tell us about the book you're writing—you are writing one, aren't you? You're always working on a book."

"Yes, I am, Clara. It's about a Christian's response to America's changing society, but I'm still in the research stage, so I won't bore you with it."

"Oh, you wouldn't be. Daniel and I are always interested, aren't we, Daniel? It must be so exciting to be a published author, to see your words in print."

"It is. It's very satisfying."

"And you, Knowl, owning your own publishing company, printing your wife's books. It's all so perfect, isn't it?"

"Not perfect exactly, Clara, but I must say life is never dull."

Chad nudged Maggie's arm. "What about you, Magpie? You like to write. You're about to get your degree in literature. Are there going to be two authors in the house?"

Maggie felt her face grow warm. She stared down at her plate, her heart suddenly racing. "I don't think so."

"Come on, Maggie," prompted Jordan. "I bet you could write a best-seller like your mother."

"No, I couldn't."

"Sure you could, Magpie," said Chad. "It's what you want. I know it is. Your name on a book cover just like your mom's."

"Is that so, Maggie?" asked Clara Barrett. "Why, dear, I didn't know you wanted to be a writer."

Maggie's heart hammered. "I never said—"

"So someday your father may be publishing your books too," said Daniel Barrett. "Wouldn't that be something, Knowl, publishing your daughter's books?"

Maggie stole a glance at her father. A faint smile played on his lips. "Well, Maggie has written some nice little stories and poems," he said, "but books? I've never heard her mention writing books."

"Margaret's a very good writer," said her mother. "Who knows? Maybe someday . . ."

"No, Mama," Maggie said through clenched teeth, her embarrassment mushrooming. "I'm just a small-town girl with nothing to say. I'll never write important books like you."

"Well, my wife, Annie, is a one and only original, that's for sure," said her father. "I have a hard enough time keeping up with her myself, and I'm her publisher."

"But first of all, dear, you're my husband."

Maggie watched her parents exchange a private smile, seemingly forgetting the rest of their guests. They were right, of course, about Maggie's talent . . . or lack of talent. She would never measure up to her parents, never carve her own significant identity in their eyes. How could she? She had never experienced life. She had nothing of consequence to say.

But how she yearned for them to reassure her that someday she would write important things and be every bit as good as her mother. *Nice little stories*, her father had called her efforts. Why had those words torn at her heart, stung like a slap? *Nice little stories* . . . Why couldn't she let it go, this dream of tapping into some secret part of herself and releasing a fountain of words that would capture some essential truth about herself, about life?

Maggie steeled herself, shut out her father's words. No matter what anyone else said, she wouldn't always be a sheltered, inexperienced Indiana girl with nothing to say. Her life was changing, just as Jordan's was. She could feel the changes coming, sweeping over them already, even as they sat around the table eating their Christmas dinner. Her hero, her protector, the love of her life, was going to war, leaving her to fend for herself, alone. Already, in the quiet center of her heart, she knew nothing would ever be the same again.

3

As a pale pink sun groaned over a gray, frigid horizon, blustery winds whipped through the red brick Willowbrook depot, whistling a ghostly lament. Maggie and Jordan, clad in heavy wool coats and scarves, stood on the sagging platform amid freshly drifting snow, clinging to each other for one last time. His parents and brother had stepped away, giving them this moment together. With glistening eyes and a wavering smile, he cupped her face in his gloved hands and gazed deep into her eyes. His voice was soft and light, nearly lost in the wind. "Maggie, my girl, I love you, darling."

"I love you, too, Jordan." The cold made her teeth chatter. Tears ached behind her eyes; when she blinked, the wetness escaped from under her lids and turned to crystals on her lashes.

"Don't cry, Mag, or you'll have me bawling." He kissed the wet spots under her eyes, gently, tenderly, his lips lingering, warming her skin.

"I don't want you to go," she whispered, the words breaking over a tightness in her throat.

"Me neither, sweetheart." His eyes burrowed deep into hers, his gaze so riveting she flinched. "Maggie, listen. It'll be okay. I promise. I'll carry you with me everywhere, in my pocket, in my heart, in my head. No matter what happens, you'll be with me. I'll see you when I close my eyes, hear your voice in the silence of the night."

"Me, too." The words hardly escaped her lips.

"You just wait for me, okay?" His breath came out in little white puffs that faded in the icy air. His leaving would be like that, here one moment, gone the next. "I'll be back before you know it," he said, his voice ringing with courage and conviction, "and then our lives will really begin. We'll have that storybook life we've always dreamed of. The whole 'happily ever after' routine."

She choked back a sob. "Promise?"

"Promise." He fumbled for something in his coat pocket. "I got this for you, Mag. A little gift. To help you remember me."

She shook her head, baffled. "I don't need anything to help me remember. I'll never forget you, Jordan."

"I know, but I wanted you to have something to hold onto, besides memories."

"You shouldn't have. Christmas is over. You've already given me my gifts."

"But this is something special. I want you to have it to hold onto when my train pulls away."

"What, Jordan? Show me."

He held up a small, shiny object—brass or gold, with a long gold chain. "For you, Maggie. My heart. Yours for safekeeping while I'm gone." He dropped a heart-shaped locket into her gloved hand. It looked antique, delicate and lovely, with tiny rhinestones around the edge.

"Oh, Jordan, it's beautiful."

"There's more, Mag." He pulled off his right glove with his teeth and snapped open the locket with stiff fingers. "See inside?"

"Oh, Jordan!" Inside the locket were two tiny pictures, his and hers, one on each side. Last summer, on a lark, they had taken the photos in a booth at Woolworth's. Four sepia-toned poses for a quarter. Two together, two apart. The camera had captured something timeless and extraordinary in their faces; they were laughing, unposed, natural, joyous. It had been a perfect day, the bond between them growing into the kind of delicious camaraderie only true soul mates could experience. It was the first time she realized how much she loved him.

He loosened her scarf and fastened the locket around her neck. "Even if we can't be together now, Maggie, we'll be together in the locket. Wear it always, over your heart to remind you of my love. And someday when this war is over and I come home, I'll give you a ring to show the world you're mine forever."

He pulled her against him and kissed her with a smoldering intensity that made her forget the wintry chill. Then he stepped back, shoulders arrow-straight, and saluted her, his hand tapping the brim of his cover. "God be with you, Margaret Kate Herrick, until we meet again."

"God be with you, too," she whispered.

He embraced his parents, wiped his mother's tears, and bear-hugged his brother, then pivoted and strode across the snowy platform to the passenger car, his steps already falling with a military cadence. He slung his duffel bag over his shoulder, greeted the conductor, and boarded, with one final backward glance at Maggie and his family. With his free hand he made a victory sign, then disappeared inside.

Desperately Maggie scanned the frosty windows for a glimpse of him. Surely he would sit by the window. Already she missed him, hungered to see him just once more. Then, there he was, taking a seat, waving to them through the smudged glass, smiling, mouthing words. She could still feel the warmth of his kiss on her lips, and yet he already seemed a million miles away.

She waved frantically, like a frightened, excited child. She heard the explosive whoosh of the mammoth engine, followed by a shrieking whistle that fractured the frosty heavens. Diesel fumes invaded her nostrils; under her feet the platform rumbled. The train was moving, so slowly at first she hardly noticed. She began walking along the platform, her eyes fastened on the window that framed Jordan, her boots slipping on the icy places. Then she was running, the frigid air snatching her breath away, her tears turning the world into a surreal looking glass. She ran until Jordan was out of sight.

As she broke into desolate sobs, strong arms enveloped her. Her beloved Jordan? No, it was Chad. He held her close, letting her weep against the nubby fabric of his overcoat until no tears remained. "I'll take care of you," he whispered against her windblown hair. "Whatever you need, Magpie, I'll always be here for you."

But no one, not even Chad, could give her what she needed now.

The letters came, three and four times a week at first. Newsy, cheerful, written in Jordan's robust scrawl, packed with detailed accounts of his extraordinary new life at sea.

> *Maggie, darling, life aboard the USS* Independence *is like nothing you ever imagined. We call her the Indy. What an aircraft carrier—a proud and regal lady coursing through the choppy waters of the Pacific! Her deck is as flat and barren as the plains of Kansas, but when you're coming in for a landing, it still doesn't look long enough.*
>
> *When we passed the equator, we had to endure a revolting initiation ceremony called "Crossing the Line." We lowly pollywogs had to bow to the mighty shellbacks, and it wasn't a pretty picture. I'll spare you the painful and humiliating details, except to say there was a lot of groveling before King Neptune's court before the crew was permitted passage into the "solemn mysteries of the ancient order of the deep." The rites were pure misery at the time, but now most of us are chuckling over the whole bizarre experience.*

It's been a long crossing, but I haven't had a chance to get bored. We've had boxing matches in Hangar #1, and a terrific variety show, with the crew performing songs from Hello, Dolly! *and* South Pacific. *One of my new buddies, Sam Kelso, dressed up like Sophia Loren, in a black wig and two-piece bathing suit, with grapefruit in the top. We nearly laughed ourselves sick watching him strut around the stage. If this is the navy, no one warned me there would be times like this. But, of course, as we head for the troubled waters of Vietnam, we all realize the laughs will soon be behind us . . .*

My darling Maggie, it seems I've been away from you for months. Has it only been two weeks? Already I've discovered that the most important time of day is mail call. You should see all the guys scramble for letters from home. It puts a lump in your throat to see grown men reading their mail with tears in their eyes. I know what you'd say, Mag. We're all little boys at heart. So, okay, I admit I feel as excited as a kid when I get your letters. Keep them coming, sweetheart. They're my lifeline . . .

Well, Maggie, activity on the flight deck has increased dramatically since official flight operations began. It's quite a sight to see—a gleaming Skyhawk being moved from the shelter of hangar bay onto the giant elevator and up to the flight deck. The plane is taxied into position on the catapult, where it glistens like a silver bird in the sun, high above the rolling seas. Flight deck crews race around like mad, ducking under wings, signaling with their hands, preparing for launch. The various crews wear different colors; yellow shirts get the planes on and off the deck; blue shirts put the blocks and chains in place; everything's done to precision.

Finally the deck is spotted for the launch, and it's my turn to perform. My heart is hammering in my chest so hard it hurts, and my mouth is dry as sandpaper. As I await the signal for takeoff, I know there's no room for error. The jet engines scream and the catapult officer raises his arm high, then drops it and squats down, his signal to go. And suddenly I'm on my way, roaring along the deck and lifting off into the clouds like a powerful eagle. It's a terrifying, exhilarating sensation, Mag.

Our planes are flying bombing sorties over both North and South Vietnam. Four huge catapults fling planes into the air as often as every thirty seconds; within 250 feet the jets are already going well over a hundred miles an hour over the South China Sea. Once launched, the planes fly in formation to their assigned targets inland—radar sites, troop concentrations, barracks, bridges, highways, sampans, missile sites . . . whatever it takes to destroy the Vietcong's war-making ability.

Mag, yesterday was a red-letter day for me. My first real bombing mission. On earlier missions they had me dropping supplies by parachute to the marines in the trenches at Khe Sahn, but now our commanding officers have ordered us to step up the shelling and give the North Vietnamese a real "baptism of fire." We've begun tactical air strikes with a twenty-four-hours-a-day bombardment, our planes flying from midnight till noon or from noon till midnight, with another carrier taking the alternate hours. We're really giving it to them, Maggie, shelling enemy fortifications and mountain strongholds with a steady barrage *of bombs, rockets, and napalm. At the rate we're going, this crazy war will be over before you know it.*

Anyway, like I said, yesterday was my first bombing raid, and I don't mind telling you I was scared. White-knuckling it all the way. But, thank God, it went without a hitch. For security reasons I can't give you a lot of details, but let's just say a petroleum storage facility at Nam Dinh, east of Hanoi, won't be producing much petro for a while, and a port facility south of Vinh is temporarily out of commission.

On the way back to the ship after our bombing run, the pilots in our strike group checked one another's aircraft for damage from antiaircraft flak and fire. Talk about being on a wing and a prayer, we were all clean. Not even a scratch. But we still faced our greatest challenge—a night landing. Landings are the most dangerous few seconds of an entire mission.

It was nearly midnight when we returned to the carrier. I was dead tired, my nerves tight as high-tension wires. There was no moon, and in the pitch blackness I could hardly distinguish between sky and sea. Finally I spotted her on the horizon, the Indy, a shimmering phantom of eerie, floating blue lights in a vast, rolling darkness. For a minute I was seized with a terrifying attack of vertigo. I was hurtling toward the flight deck at a shrieking speed and couldn't tell if my wings were level or not. My heart started pounding, and my mind went blank. I thought for sure I'd do a bolter and have to go around a second time. Or maybe I'd really mess up and land in the briny deep. A naval aviator is only as good as his last landing, and I was beginning to think this might be my last.

With my heart in my throat, I started some delicate

maneuvering to make sure my plane's tail hook snagged
one of the four wires that protrude a mere six inches off the
deck. If I missed the wires I'd have to shove open the
throttle, blast off the bow, circle around, and try again. But
God must have been with me, Maggie, because I made it on
my first try. I hit the deck at over 130 knots, and my hook
caught the wire. You should have seen the sparks fly when
I touched down. It looked like a million sparklers on the
Fourth of July.

While the crews connected the tie downs, I clambered
out of my jet, my sweat turning my green flight suit black
and my hair matted and damp under my helmet. All I could
think of was getting through debriefing and collapsing on
my bed with a steaming cup of coffee . . . and with a picture of you next to my heart, Maggie . . .

My dearest Maggie, it's awful hard for me to write this letter tonight. I'm not the kind of man to shed tears, but
they're falling now even as I write. Remember me telling
you about my buddy, Sam Kelso, the guy who dressed up like
Sophia Loren at the variety show a couple of months ago?
Now it seems like years since we were laughing and joking
around together.

Maggie, I'm still in shock, numb, my head reeling. My
buddy Sam was shot down on a bombing mission today.
We were in the same attack squadron, flying in formation,
his plane just ahead on my right, when artillery fire hit his
fuselage. He went into a nosedive, and his Skyhawk
exploded on impact in some blasted rice paddy. I watched
it happen, Maggie, and there wasn't a blessed thing I could
do to help him.

When I returned to the carrier, I was trembling like an

old man with palsy. Didn't think I'd even be able to land. Somehow I got down, but I was so sick in my gut I could hardly stumble across the flight deck. Several crewmen tried to help, but I pushed them away. I was like a crazy man, Maggie. I just kept sobbing and saying Sam's name over and over, like maybe if I called out to him long enough he'd be there, safe and sound. Only, he won't. He's gone forever, Maggie, and he took part of me with him—a big chunk of my spirit and my blind faith and optimism.

To tell you the truth, Mag, I'm beginning to wonder if this crazy war will ever be over. It seems like we take one step forward and two steps back. Since January the Commies have been coming on stronger than ever. North Vietnamese troops have launched a massive, unrelenting attack throughout South Vietnam, seizing several major cities.

The siege at the marine base at Khe Sanh has gone on longer than anyone expected, with several bunkers taking direct hits and scores of American soldiers killed or wounded. The air force has even unleashed their powerful B-52 bomber on the Vietcong, but nothing seems to flush them out of their mountain strongholds. The constant bombing has denuded the countryside around Khe Sanh, leaving a landscape of desolate craters. Like the dark side of the moon.

Rumor has it that the Communists have made such a large-scale offensive in honor of Tet, the Vietnamese Lunar New Year holiday. Whatever the reason, they're giving us a run for our money . . . and they're costing us lives. That part of it didn't hit home for me until I saw Sam's plane go down. It's a messy, bloody war, Maggie, with no end in sight. Just a lot of small, personal, agonizing endings as we hear of buddies going down, their planes or choppers blown to smithereens.

It was the end of March, and a raw wind was blowing through Willowbrook, cutting to the bone, whipping across a bleak white landscape, stirring dead limbs on desolate trees. Maggie was convinced winter would last forever. Winter was like the war—harsh, mind-numbing, no end in sight.

On the last day of March, as Maggie helped Grandmother Anna set the table for dinner, her father called her into the parlor, where he and Jon Knowl were watching the evening news. "Listen to this, Maggie. President Johnson is making an announcement."

Still holding the china salad plates, she sat down on the sofa between her father and brother and gazed at the president's weary face. His droll, ungainly features sagged in defeat as he said solemnly, "I shall not seek, and I will not accept the nomination of my party for another term as your president."

"Just as well," said Jon Knowl, "after the mess he's got us in."

Her father gave him a scrutinizing glance. "You mean Vietnam?"

"What else?"

"What more do you want, Son? He said he's calling for a partial halt to the bombing in North Vietnam, and he's opening peace negotiations."

"If you ask me, it's a lot of empty talk. Jordan's still over there risking his life every day in bombing missions. Right, Maggie? He's seen his buddies die, right and left. I'll believe Johnson means business when he brings our troops home."

Maggie ran her fingers around the smooth edge of a china plate. "Jordan is proud to be serving our country, Jon Knowl. He's defending our freedom with his life."

"I never asked him to defend my freedom."

Her father spoke up, an edge in his voice. "Son, freedom is one of those things no one fully appreciates until they've lost it. It's a precious privilege that too many countries in our world have never experienced. If the Communists had their way, we'd lose that freedom in a minute. Surely you can see that."

Jon Knowl stood up and loped to the doorway, his eyes dark and inscrutable. "All I know is that a country that forces guys to die in a hellhole like Vietnam doesn't feel like freedom to me."

"You don't think we should defend the freedom our fathers and grandfathers gave their lives for?"

"You didn't go to war, Dad."

Her father adjusted his glasses, his face scarlet with indignation. "I would have gone eagerly, Jon Knowl. Heaven knows I wanted to go when your uncle Chip shipped out to Pearl Harbor, but my eyes weren't good enough."

Jon Knowl pushed his own glasses up on his nose. "Maybe my lousy eyesight will save me, too, huh, Dad?"

"I never looked for an excuse not to serve, Son. And I hope you won't either."

"I don't need an excuse, Dad. If the draft calls, I'm just not going. I'll go to Canada first."

"Canada? What kind of crazy nonsense—!" Before her father could spill out his rebuke, Jon Knowl kicked at the fringe on the oriental carpet and ambled out of the room without a backward glance.

"He doesn't mean it, Dad," Maggie assured him. "He just likes to talk big."

Her father reached over and patted her arm, his expression crestfallen. "I wish I could believe that, honey. Your brother's a very angry young man, and I don't even know why."

Maggie cupped her palm over her father's sturdy hand. "Don't you know, Daddy? All the guys his age are angry these days."

4

April should have brought the promise of spring; instead, it ushered in a new torrent of tensions and troubles for the nation, for Willowbrook, and for Maggie. But, on the afternoon of April 4, troubles were the last thing on Maggie's mind when Chad Barrett stopped by after class with a letter from Jordan.

"My mother said you'd want to read this," he said as Maggie invited him inside. He was wearing a rumpled leather jacket and faded jeans, his collar-length hair windblown, his cheeks ruddy with the cold. "Mom knows how eager you are to hear any word from my brother."

Maggie nodded, anticipation prickling her skin. "She's right. I devour every word. I have some letters from Jordan you can take home for her to read, too, but you've got to give them back to me tomorrow."

"So you can put them under your pillow?"

She smiled coyly. "That's none of your business."

Chad swiped an unruly thatch of brown hair back from his forehead and flashed her a teasing smile. "Really? Well, I'm surprised you're even willing to share your letters. I figured anything my brother wrote you would be for your eyes alone."

She eyed him skeptically. "You mean mushy stuff? Come on, Chad. You know your brother's not like that."

His lip curled slightly. "Well, I would be if I were him."

"But you're not him. Besides, I can't imagine you writing mushy stuff either."

"I might. If I were writing you, Magpie."

She gave him a quizzical glance. She could never tell when he was joking. It was best just to change the subject. "Want to stay for dinner, Chad?"

"Sure. I love your grandmother's cooking." He followed her into the parlor and sat down beside her on the love seat. While she read Jordan's letter, he turned on the television set. After a minute he said, "Listen, Maggie. They're talking about the peace talks."

Her ears perked up immediately. A peace settlement would mean her beloved Jordan would soon be coming home to her.

In a smooth, professional, slightly detached voice a network newscaster was saying, "In Paris today, Premier Pham Van Dong of North Vietnam warned that Hanoi will take a tough and uncompromising line in peace talks with the United States. The premier was quoted as saying, 'We will be as firm in negotiations as we have been on the battlefield.' The premier went on to say that Hanoi is in no hurry to achieve its ultimate objective—a reunified Vietnam under what he described as a 'truly original' Communist government."

Maggie and Chad exchanged disheartened glances. "With Hanoi spouting that sort of contemptible rhetoric," said Maggie, "it doesn't look like Jordan will be home any time soon."

Chad turned down the sound and sank back on the sofa. "You know the old saying, Mag. When the Communists say they want peace, they mean a piece of this and a piece of that, until there's nothing left for anybody else."

"In other words, they're up to their same old tricks."

"Exactly."

Maggie spoke over a painful lump in her throat. "I was so hoping this war would end and Jordan would come home to me."

Chad sat forward and cracked his knuckles, first his left hand, then his right. "I want him home too. More than anything. My house is a lonely place without him. My mom mopes around like it's the end of the world. He's all she can talk about." He flexed his fingers and cracked them again. "Jordan's the one who kept all the rest of us going. Nothing will be the same until he gets home."

"Sometimes I feel like my life is in such limbo, Chad," Maggie admitted. "I feel like I'm just sitting around and doing nothing but waiting for him."

"Not so, Maggie. Look at us. We're finishing college. Getting our degrees. When Jordan gets back we'll both be graduates. That gives us something to work for."

"He talks about that in his letter," she said, scanning the tissue-thin pages again. "He says we'll all go out and celebrate. Drive to Chicago. Or Lake Michigan."

Chad swiveled around and looked her full in the face with such earnestness that she smiled in spite of the ache in her heart. "It'll happen just like he says, Magpie. We'll go anywhere he wants. We'll order his favorite food—pizza with sausage and mushrooms, even though I hate mushrooms. Detest the little rubbery, tasteless things; they always look like toadstools to me. But I don't care. For Jordan I'll eat them and pretend I love them. We'll do all the things he loves to do, and I won't even be jealous when he puts his arms around you, because I'd give just about anything to see him home safe and sound. I'll even pretend I'm happy he's got you, because I know how he adores you. We'll all be together again like when we were kids. The Three Musketeers. All for one . . ."

". . . And one for all," she finished with a tearful smile.

Chad sprang forward and turned up the sound again on the television. "We'd better listen, Maggie. A news bulletin's coming on. Might be about the war."

They watched, holding their breath, as the news anchorman appeared on the screen and said in a solemn voice, "We have just received word from Memphis that Dr. Martin Luther King Jr. was fatally shot by an unknown sniper today. The 1964 Nobel Peace Prize winner and champion of nonviolence in the civil rights movement was standing on the second-floor balcony of the Lorraine Motel talking to aides in a parking lot below when the fatal shot was fired. Police suspect the assassin fired from the brick building across the street. Dr. King was rushed to St. Joseph Hospital, where he was pronounced dead of a bullet wound in the neck.

"An all-points bulletin has been issued for the assassin, described by witnesses as a Caucasian man about six feet tall and in his late twenties or early thirties. A five-square-block area of the city surrounding the motel has been sealed off by police. Tennessee Governor Buford Ellington has ordered 4,000 national guardsmen into Memphis, and all police and sheriff's deputies have been called to patrol duty. Memphis Mayor Henry Loeb announced a curfew at nightfall, but already reports are coming in of violence, including shootings and fire bombings . . ."

For a full minute Maggie and Chad sat, speechless, unmoving. The anchorman was still talking, but, for Maggie, his words had faded into the background and ceased to have meaning. Chad stirred, reaching for Maggie's hand. His fingers were as cold as hers. "What next?" he murmured under his breath, anger and disbelief shading his tone.

Maggie shook her head ponderously. She could feel her heartbeat pounding in her temples. "Isn't there enough violence in Vietnam, enough men dying? Why does it have to happen here in our country too?"

Chad rubbed the back of her hand with his thumb, pressing so hard it hurt. "I don't know, Maggie. It's like the whole world's gone crazy. The insanity just keeps spreading."

Grandmother Anna appeared suddenly in the doorway, wiping her hands on a dish towel. She looked painfully frail, her wrinkled face blanched. "I just heard on the radio," she said in a small, stunned voice. "Someone shot that Negro leader, Dr. King. He was on the news just the other night in that protest march in Memphis. I saw him. Big as life. Just a few days ago. He was a minister. How could they shoot a minister?"

"It's on the TV right now," said Maggie. "Listen."

They all listened, then lapsed into a heavy silence.

Chad was the first to find his voice. "I don't even want Jordan to know all the crazy things going on here while he's gone. He'll wonder what he's fighting for."

Grandmother Anna twisted her dish towel, her knobby knuckles white as marbles. "The world's not like it was in my day. We had Hitler and the world war to contend with, but our enemies were over there, not in our own backyard. We all hung together. Didn't turn on one another like folks are doing now."

"It's going to get worse," said Chad, thrumming his fingers on the arm of the sofa. "Can't you feel it in the air, Maggie? Everybody's stirred up. The blacks and whites. Those for the war and those against. Everybody's choosing up sides, like it's us against them, like it's not enough to be fighting a war on foreign soil. Like we've got to fight it at home too."

"Maybe so," said Grandmother Anna, her voice tremulous. "Maybe the whole world's going to end tomorrow, but there's supper to eat tonight. The table's set and the food's piping hot. Come and eat. Forget about all the mischief and shenanigans for a little while. At least long enough to let your food digest in peace."

But there would be no forgetting. The news bulletins kept coming from the television in the parlor, loud enough to catch the sonorous tone but too muffled to hear the actual words. Maggie didn't want to hear any more. Not tonight. Not when her heart was filled with such nagging anxieties.

Everyone was subdued as they gathered around the dining room table—Maggie and Chad on one side, her parents arriving home from the publishing house just in time to sit across from them, Jon Knowl on one end, and Grandmother Anna on the opposite end.

As they clasped hands for the blessing, her father gazed around from face to face and said, "Let's remember the King family tonight . . . and our nation."

"And Jordan," Maggie whispered.

"Yes," said her father. "Jordan. Always."

After his prayer, as Grandmother Anna passed the pork chops and scalloped potatoes, the conversation turned inevitably to the assassination. "How come things like this keep happening?" said Jon Knowl. "President Kennedy a few years back. Now Dr. King. Who's next?"

"The world's gone crazy," said her grandmother as she handed Maggie the biscuits. "It's like the Bible says. The last days. If Jesus doesn't come back soon, He won't have anything left to come back to."

Maggie's mother expelled a small sigh of dismay. "There must be more we can do as Christians. Somehow we've lost our voice, our influence. The world isn't listening to us anymore."

"Did it ever?" said her father. "The world has always been blind to the claims of Christ."

"But at least Christian values and moral standards were respected by the majority of people. Lately it seems that dissident voices have taken over, that violence and ungodliness are the norm."

"It's all predicted in the Bible," said Grandmother Anna, "but I never expected to see it happen in my day."

"Not everything that's happening these days is bad," said Jon Knowl as he spread strawberry jam over his biscuit.

"I didn't say it was, Son," said Knowl.

"It sounds like it to me."

Chad broke in. "So what are you talking about, Jon Knowl? You have something specific in mind?"

"Yeah. Students protesting the war. They're standing up for what they believe. I think that's good."

Chad's tone took on a hard edge. "You think so? Even though they're condemning the very thing my brother's over in that putrid jungle fighting for?"

"That's my point," said Jon Knowl, his hazel eyes flashing. "If more people stood up against the government, maybe Jordan wouldn't be over there risking his life for nothing."

"It's not nothing," snapped Maggie, her fierce gaze meeting her brother's squarely. "Jordan's fighting for his country, and there's nothing more noble than that."

"Yeah, and I bet that's what all those guys thought who are being shipped home in body bags."

"That's enough, Jon Knowl." Knowl's voice silenced everyone. "Children, we can't solve the ills of the world tonight. We can't bring Dr. King back, nor can we bring Jordan home from the battlefield. All we can do is pray and be faithful to God in our own lives. Now let's see if we can find something pleasant to talk about." He pushed his spectacles up on his nose and added, "Mother Reed, will you pass the pork chops please?"

After passing the chops, Grandmother Anna got up and put one of her favorite 78 rpm records on the old Victrola beside the cherry wood buffet. "Maybe a little Guy Lombardo will help."

"I'd rather hear the Beatles," said Jon Knowl.

"When you cook the dinner, Grandson, you can decide on the music."

Knowl nodded. "Fair enough, Son."

For a while they ate without speaking, the mellow tunes sounding distant and scratchy in places but setting a wistful, nostalgic mood, as if they were back in the war years Maggie's grandmother knew so well, the years when everyone seemed to know what they were fighting for.

"Save room for dessert," Grandmother Anna said between songs.

"Mind if I ask what it is, Mrs. Reed?" asked Chad.

"Cherry pie. Fresh from the oven. With vanilla ice cream."

"Sounds great. I'm ready."

"Me too," said Maggie's father, forking up the last morsel of potato from his plate. He looked around the table, trying on a smile. "Say, kids, how about a game of Scrabble after dinner?"

Annie's lyrical voice rang out. "I'll play, darling, but you know I always win."

"Do not."

"Do so."

"That's because you're an author. Words are your stock in trade." He looked at Jon Knowl. "Son?"

"You know I'm not much for games, Dad."

Maggie toed her brother's ankle under the table. "Come on, Jon Knowl. Don't be a spoilsport. Chad and I will take you on, right, Chad?"

"Sure, but spelling's not my forte."

Knowl chuckled. "Don't worry, Chad. It's not who wins or loses. It's the fun of the game."

Annie added her own laughter to the merriment. "I'll remind you of that, darling, when you're losing."

"But first we have pie to eat," said Grandmother Anna as she collected the soiled dinner plates. "Jon Knowl, you come help me scoop out the ice cream. It's always hard as a brick."

As they ate pie and listened to Guy Lombardo's orchestra on the record player, Maggie thought about how deceptively peaceful the evening seemed. Like any other cozy evening on Honeysuckle Lane, with the family gathered around a bountiful dinner table, laughing and chatting about nothing in particular. Safely tucked in for the night, the doors locked, the curtains drawn, the lamplight glowing. The family safe from all harm. Walled off from the disquieting darkness beyond their door. With nothing more to worry about than who would win at Scrabble.

But the world wasn't like that anymore, no matter how much they pretended it was. Somewhere on the other side of the globe, her beloved Jordan was dropping bombs on steamy jungles in Vietnam and American soldiers were bleeding and dying in anonymous trenches and bunkers.

Tonight Martin Luther King Jr. was lying dead in a morgue, and his wife and children were beside themselves with grief. In Memphis, national guardsmen were rallying to stop riots and violence in the streets.

How long, Maggie wondered, *could her family enjoy their idyllic life before the tranquillity was shattered and their familiar world inundated by tides of darkness?*

5

The tides of darkness came more swiftly than Maggie ever could have imagined. They came on May 3, a warm, sunny day in Willowbrook, the air fragrant with blossoming lilacs, the scudding clouds overhead a vast cotton field ready to be picked. Maggie finished her classes early and returned home to study for final exams. Chad was coming over for dinner, and they would study together afterward. They always did better on tests when they studied together and held each other accountable.

The household buzzed with its usual dinnertime rhythms. Pleasant. Harmonious. Grandmother Anna was in the kitchen whipping up a meatloaf and creamed potatoes. Maggie's mother was setting the table, and her father and Jon Knowl were watching television in the parlor. While waiting for Chad, Maggie paused in the parlor doorway and listened to the newscaster. The United States and North Vietnam had agreed to hold peace talks in Paris, but Maggie wasn't going to get her hopes up yet. Such peace talks had fallen through before, and they could fail again.

Maggie listened a moment longer as news footage cut to the Capitol. Rev. Ralph Abernathy was leading the Poor People's March on Washington. The camera scanned thousands of people surging like a slow, determined river down Washington's streets. "An amazing sight," intoned the newscaster. "Dr. Martin Luther King Jr. had planned this march before his death, and these men and women are eagerly carrying on his legacy."

The newsman moved on to sports, announcing that the Boston Celtics had won the NBA basketball championship, defeating the Los Angeles Lakers four games to two. Before Maggie could hear any more, the doorbell rang, diverting her attention. That would be Chad. She was always eager to see him, hopeful that he would bring the latest letter from Jordan. With a spring in her step she strode over the marble entryway and threw open the door. She blinked in surprise. It wasn't Chad; it was his father.

Daniel Barrett was a big, swarthy man, with a larger-than-life personality and the imposing, intimidating stance of a general. But today he looked smaller than usual, almost fragile. His tie was loose and his white shirt unbuttoned at the top. His face was a doughy gray, his piercing brown eyes red-rimmed and glazed. His sturdy face seemed somehow ajar, his features strangely contorted. His mouth twisted as he said, "Hello, Maggie. May I come in?"

"Of course," she said quickly, stepping aside. "Where's Chad?"

"Home with his mother." Barrett entered the foyer, massaging his calloused hands as if they were cold.

"But why?" asked Maggie. "He was coming for dinner."

Barrett looked around, his pale lips sagging at the corners. He had never looked older, the creases around his eyes and mouth deepening even as he gazed at her. "Are your parents here, Maggie?"

She nodded. "Mom's in the dining room. My dad's in the parlor watching the news. Why?"

"Would you get them please?"

She hesitated, a silent alarm going off in her head. She felt a dampness on her palms and under her arms even as her mouth went dry. "Is something wrong, Mr. Barrett?"

His shaggy brows furrowed over his eyes. "Get your folks, Maggie."

She couldn't bring herself to move. "Is it Jordan? Have you heard from him? Is he okay?"

Something in Barrett's face seemed to crumble. His lower lip trembled as he fought for control. "Your parents. Get them!"

Maggie pivoted like a reprimanded child and nearly ran down the hall to the parlor. She was breathless as she reached her father, not from running but from something else. A dark, mushrooming terror had snatched her breath. "Daddy," she said haltingly, "Jordan's father is here. Something's wrong. He won't tell me. He wants to see you and Mom."

Her father got up without a word. Jon Knowl stood up, too, and called their mother from the dining room. Grandmother Anna heard his call and bustled out of the kitchen and gave Maggie a questioning look.

"It's Jordan's father," Maggie said, as if that explained everything, and yet it explained nothing. But it was enough for her grandmother to toss aside her dish towel and follow the rest of them to the foyer.

Daniel Barrett was standing exactly as Maggie had left him, his expression grim and dazed, his mind many miles away.

Maggie's father beckoned him into the living room and offered him a chair. "Sit down, Daniel. You look like you've got the weight of the world on your shoulders."

"I do, Knowl." Barrett sank down on the sofa and sat forward, his hands splayed on his knees. He looked rumpled, distracted, edgy, his eyes dark and desolate. He inhaled deeply, as if he couldn't quite catch his breath, as if his ashen lips couldn't articulate the words trumpeting in his head.

"Tell us," Maggie begged. "It's Jordan! I know it is!"

Barrett pulled a handkerchief from his shirt pocket and mopped his brow and blew his nose. "We got word today . . ." His voice broke. A muscle twitched at the side of his mouth.

Maggie felt a hard sob rising in her throat. "Is he——?"

Barrett barely uttered the words. "Jordan's plane went down."

"His plane?" she echoed numbly.

"It took a hit, Maggie."

She swayed. "No!"

Her father helped her onto the sofa and kept his arm around her. "What happened, Daniel?"

"I don't know exactly." Barrett rubbed his hands as if trying to stir feeling into them. His voice quivered. "Another pilot saw him. Saw the plane go down."

Maggie shook her head. "Not Jordan. It couldn't be Jordan!"

"Maggie's right," said Jon Knowl. "Jordan wouldn't let those Commies shoot him down."

"Where is he?" cried Maggie, her heart thundering in her ears. "Did they rescue him? Is he wounded?"

"I don't know," Barrett rasped.

A sob broke in Maggie's throat. "How . . . how could you not know?"

Barrett straightened his shoulders and rubbed his palms on the knees of his trousers. "All I know is two men came to the house—naval officers. I don't even remember their names or faces now. They sat Clara and me down and said they regretted to inform us . . . I knew the minute I saw them at the door. Knew it was Jordan. Knew it was bad. Can't even remember their words now, because my mind was already racing ahead, filling in the blanks."

A wave of nausea spiraled up from Maggie's stomach. Her voice came out shrill and desperate. "Is he alive? He's got to be alive."

"They don't know, Maggie." Tears glazed the older man's eyes. "They said . . . the official word is . . . my son is missing in action . . . and presumed dead."

"Dead?" Maggie reeled. Her mind stalled. Heart paused in mid-beat. The room spun. Walls turned a vivid white. Sound stopped. "He's not dead!"

"I pray to God you're right," said Barrett.

Instinctively she fingered the locket around her neck. "I would know, wouldn't I? If he were dead, I'd know it. The world would feel different. I would have known in my heart the minute it happened."

"You bet he's alive, Sis," said Jon Knowl. "Jordan's tough as nails. He wouldn't let anyone get the best of him. You know that. He's okay. I know it in my gut."

"I pray to God!" said Barrett.

Maggie's father squeezed Barrett's shoulder consolingly. "Start at the beginning, Daniel. Tell us everything you know."

He held out his hands helplessly. "That's just it. I don't know anything. No real details. Just that Jordan was on a routine bombing mission."

Maggie's mother broke in gently. "But how can that be? Didn't President Johnson call a halt to the bombing a few weeks ago?"

"A partial halt in North Vietnam," said Barrett, his voice grave, subdued. "No bombing north of the twentieth parallel." Barrett's chest heaved as he drew in a shuddering breath. "Jordan was flying a search-and-destroy mission to expel National Liberation Front forces from the demilitarized zone. Flying an F-4B Phantom at 30,000 feet when a surface-to-air missile hit. Not a direct hit, according to a pilot in a nearby reconnaissance plane. He saw the missile explode near Jordan's wing. Says shrapnel must have punctured the fuel tanks because the plane caught on fire and started to disintegrate."

Maggie covered her mouth with her hand. "Oh, my poor Jordan!"

"The pilot couldn't tell for sure whether anyone ejected from Jordan's plane," said Barrett. "He thought he saw a parachute open as the plane spiraled down, but he says it could have been clouds or debris."

"But if he ejected in time, he could still be alive and okay," said Jon Knowl. "I bet he's just sitting somewhere cooling his heels and waiting for his navy buddies to rescue him."

"I suppose that's possible, Jon Knowl," said Barrett doubtfully.

"But Jordan's plane crashed in dense jungle terrain. So far the search-and-rescue teams haven't found the crash site. And there's been no word from his survival radio. So they don't know if he's dead or alive." A tremor caught in his voice and he swiped his eyes with his handkerchief. "But I'll tell you this. I swear to heaven. If my son made it out alive and ended up a prisoner of the VC, he'd be better off dead."

They were all silent for a long moment after that. What was there to say? "I'm sorry?" Sorry wasn't enough. Sorry couldn't begin to touch the deep, lacerating pain spreading through their hearts right now. Maggie had just heard the worst news of her life and was too stunned to move or think or speak.

The ravaging words spun in her head, dizzying, engulfing. *Jordan's gone, Jordan's gone, Jordan's gone.* Her stomach revolted. She jumped up and ran to the bathroom and was sick with dry heaves. She hadn't felt so bad since the flu two years ago. Afterward, a sour taste lingered at the back of her throat. She rinsed her mouth out in the sink and rubbed some toothpaste on her teeth.

She stared at her reflection in the medicine cabinet mirror. Her face looked chalky, her eyes wide and stunned, her pupils large and black as bullets. She looked like someone else, a stranger, someone she didn't want to know. What was she going to do now? How was she going to get through the night? And the next night? And the next? How was she going to endure the rest of her life without Jordan?

"God, help me," she whispered as she smoothed her damp, mussed hair back from her face. "Help me through the next minute, the next hour. I can't do this alone." She reeled, her ankles weak, her legs like mush, and gripped the sides of the smooth, cold, porcelain sink. She leaned forward and held on for dear life. "Lord, take care of Jordan, . . . if he's still alive."

Dear God, was she already saying *if?* As if her mind were already accepting the inevitable? "Be with Jordan," she said aloud, forcefully. "Watch over him. Protect him." She touched the gold locket that lay in the hollow of her throat. It was a part of Jordan. Represented his love. Love that would never die, no matter what. A sob tore at her throat, and hot tears scalded her eyes as she choked out the words, "Wherever he is, Lord, please let Jordan know how much I love him."

6

With the news that Jordan was missing in action and presumed dead, Maggie's safe, predictable world came tumbling down, crashing in on her, nearly suffocating her. Unwittingly, paradoxically, she had been swept up into the war's horrifying madness, sent reeling by the madness. Somehow she muddled through the next few days.

Every sun-washed spring morning she awoke, her pain momentarily blunted by the sweet amnesia of sleep, only to face her bitter loss all over again. Every day she prayed Jordan's family would learn that he had been found, that he was safe, that he was coming home.

Compulsively, day and night, she played other scenarios over in her mind. It was another plane, not Jordan's, that had gone down. The authorities had notified his parents by mistake. Or if Jordan's plane had gone down, he had somehow escaped and made it to a friendly village where he was recuperating. The Red Cross would find him and send him home safe and sound. There was no limit to the stories Maggie's imagination concocted, the gamut of possibilities she entertained. But inevitably the stark, excruciating truth struck home with shattering reality: Jordan was gone, lost to her forever.

Every day in her prayers she bargained with God. She would do anything He asked if He would bring Jordan home to her. She would go anywhere He sent her. She would even give Jordan up entirely if God would just let him be alive. But God remained painfully silent in her grief.

In the midst of her prayers and at the zenith of her torment, Maggie received two letters from Jordan. The first arrived one week after she learned his plane had gone down. The familiar writing on the envelope shocked her. How could it be? Had he written her from beyond the grave? Was this proof he hadn't really been shot down? *He's okay or he wouldn't be writing,* she told herself. But her heart sank when she saw the date. He had written the letter several days before his plane went down.

A second letter came three days later. She was less shocked, but for a full minute she was convinced he had written to tell her he had survived the crash, or the navy had made a mistake and it wasn't his plane after all. But again, her eyes flew to the date and she realized he had written the letter the very morning of his fateful flight. As she scanned the tissue-thin sheets, her tears flowed so hard she could barely read the words, especially Jordan's final paragraphs.

Maggie, my darling girl, I dreamed of you last night. Not so strange, of course, since you're always in my dreams. But this dream was extraordinary. We were in church and I saw you walking down the aisle toward me in a beautiful satin and lace wedding gown. You looked like an angel, your eyes bright as diamonds, your hair cascading over your shoulders like a summer waterfall. At the altar we said our vows and then I took you in my arms. We kissed for a very long time and I knew you were mine, all mine.

The dream was so real, Maggie, I know I'll be walking on air for a week. That kiss and the image of you in your wedding gown may see me through till my tour of duty is done and I can come home and make the dream come true. God willing, we'll soon be together again, and we can begin making all our dreams come true, sweetheart. Till then, remember how much I adore you. Wear my locket

*until I return and I'll carry your picture next to my heart until I
hold you in my arms once more.*

All my love, Jordan

Two weeks after Jordan's plane went down, Maggie and Chad
graduated with honors from Willowbrook University. But, for
Maggie, walking across the stage to receive her diploma was a hollow accomplishment without Jordan to share her joy. After the cere-
monies, she and Chad had no party, no celebration, except for a
quiet dinner at Maggie's home with Chad's parents.

In a way, Maggie felt cheated. Not only had she lost the love of her
life, but she couldn't even take pleasure in her own hard-won
accomplishments. She sensed that Chad felt the same way. He had
never measured up to Jordan in his parents' eyes. And since earning
a college degree couldn't compare with sacrificing one's life for
one's country, Chad would always remain a distant second to his
brother.

For dinner Grandmother Anna served lamb chops with mint
sauce, boiled red potatoes, creamed peas, and fresh biscuits with
homemade strawberry preserves. It was a delicious dinner, but
Maggie had little appetite. The two families ate in silence, except to
praise Grandmother Anna for the dinner or to comment politely
about the graduation ceremony. "It was very nice, don't you think?
Dignified but not tiresome, and thank goodness, the speeches
weren't overlong. With so many graduating, it could have gone on all
night."

Maggie and Chad said little; they responded to halfhearted
inquiries with perfunctory monosyllables.

Her mother asked Chad, "So what will you be doing now that
you've graduated?"

"Be a photojournalist. If I can land a job."

"Have you applied anywhere?"

"The *Willowbrook News*."

"That would be wonderful, to work for our local paper. Knowl was editor of the newspaper before he went into book publishing."

"Maggie told me."

"So have you heard anything yet from the paper?" asked her father.

"No, sir. They're still considering my application."

"I'd be glad to put in a good word for you, Chad."

"I'd appreciate that, sir."

"What about you, Maggie?" inquired Daniel Barrett. "What are your plans? Going to write that great American novel like your mother?"

"Maybe someday. I'd love to be a writer. But right now I'm hoping to work as an editorial assistant for Herrick House Publishers."

"I see. Is it all set then? You have a job lined up?"

Maggie smiled shyly at her father. "I think so. I've got a pretty good connection with the publisher."

"Yes, she's got the job, Daniel," said her father, "but she'll have to prove herself just like anyone else."

Barrett gave her an approving smile. "Well, I'm sure she'll do a wonderful job for you."

"Thank you, Mr. Barrett," Maggie said dutifully. She knew, in spite of all of this desultory chitchat, that everyone's thoughts were on the one person who wasn't present. Her beloved Jordan. How could she endure this languishing celebration without him beside her? How could she face the rest of her life without him?

Grandmother Anna seemed determined to squeeze some merriment out of this forlorn affair. "I hope you all still have some room for dessert!" she declared as she brought out a towering three-layer chocolate cake with mounds of white icing. Bright red frosting spelled out the words CONGRATULATIONS, MARGARET AND CHAD!

"Oh, it's beautiful!" Maggie exclaimed. But secretly she wished her grandmother hadn't bothered. The more everyone tried to pretend it was an evening for celebration, the more miserable she felt.

When her grandmother bustled off to the kitchen for the ice cream, Jon Knowl blurted the words they had been dancing around all evening. "Jordan should be here. It's no party without Jordan!"

Clara Barrett looked as if her expression would shatter like a broken china teacup. Her thin fingers flew to her pale lips, then she excused herself and jumped up and fled the room. With a low guttural exclamation, Daniel Barrett pushed back his chair and went after her.

Maggie's father glared at Jon Knowl as if he'd struck their guests with a baseball bat.

"What are you giving me that look for, Dad?" Jon Knowl demanded. "You know Jordan's the only thing on our minds. We're just going through the motions here. This isn't a party, it's a wake. Why should we even bother pretending?"

"For Chad's sake and your sister's sake, young man. They've worked hard to earn their diplomas, and they deserve to be honored. Life has to go on."

Chad tossed his linen napkin on the table. "Jon Knowl's right, Mr. Herrick. Why should we pretend? No one feels like celebrating, least of all me. Nothing's going to be the same without my brother Jordan." He slipped out of his chair and squeezed Maggie's shoulder. "I'd better go check on my parents. We should probably call it a night."

After he'd gone out, Jon Knowl rapped his dinner knife on the tablecloth and gazed stonily at their father. "I suppose you figure this is all my fault, huh, Dad? I should have kept my big mouth shut about Jordan."

"Well, Son, you do have a way of—"

"Knowl, don't," said their mother. "Don't cast blame."

Maggie reached across the table and touched her brother's hand.

He stopped the tapping. "It's nobody's fault, Jon-Jon." She hadn't called him that since he was a toddler. "We're all hurting, and we can't make it go away. We just have to keep loving one another, no matter what."

Jon Knowl started the tapping again, more vigorously, the serrated blade striking the linen tablecloth. "It's this blasted war! Jordan wouldn't be missing if the president had gotten us out of Vietnam."

"It's not that simple, Son, and you know it."

"It is to me, Dad. You know what the guys are saying at school? 'Hey, hey, LBJ, how many kids did you kill today?'"

"That's not fair, Son," said their mother. "Johnson wants the war over. Peace talks are going on right now in Paris."

"And they're already deadlocked," said Jon Knowl. "Besides, all the talks in the world won't bring Jordan back."

"We don't know that," said Maggie sharply. "Jordan's still alive. He has to be."

Jon Knowl's mouth twisted in a sneer. "Then where is he? Why haven't we heard something?"

Maggie shook her head gloomily. How could she argue with her brother when she couldn't even convince herself Jordan was still alive?

Grandmother Anna returned from the kitchen with a huge tub of homemade vanilla ice cream. "Who wants some?" she asked. She looked around, puzzled. "Where did the Barretts go?"

"It's okay, Mother Reed," said Knowl. "They'll be right back. You cut the cake and I'll dish out the ice cream."

But Jon Knowl wasn't ready to let their conversation end. "I'll tell you one thing, Dad, if I get drafted, I'm out of here. Heading straight to Canada. I won't let them do to me what they did to Jordan."

Her father's expression hardened. "Being a coward is no answer, Son."

"You calling *me* a coward? The real cowards are the ones who won't stop the war."

"Your uncle, Chilton Reed, wasn't afraid to fight for his country."

"And he died too. Is that what you want me to do, Dad? You won't be happy until I die like Jordan and Uncle Chip?"

Knowl's face turned scarlet. "Of course not, Son! But if men like Jordan and your uncle didn't fight for our freedom, we'd all be sitting under Hitler's thumb right now."

"I would have fought Hitler. World War II was a just war. Vietnam isn't."

"Who decides that, Son? You? Your friends? We'd have anarchy if every man decided for himself whether to fight or not."

Jon Knowl let his silverware clatter on his plate. "The way I see it, Dad, our own government doesn't know whether it wants to fight or not. If we'd wanted to, we could have bombed the VC right off the map, and it would all be over now. And maybe Jordan would be coming home to us."

Knowl was silent for a moment, a muscle working along his jawline. "All right, you have a point, Son. I wouldn't want you going to war if you had to fight with one hand behind your back. I'd want you to be the best soldier you could be. Throw yourself wholeheartedly into the fight."

Jon Knowl folded his napkin into a triangle and set it up like a little tent beside his plate. "I'm going to fight, Dad, but not in Vietnam."

"What do you mean by that, Jon Knowl?" asked his mother.

"I'm going to fight against the war. I'll do whatever I have to do to make the president listen. I'm going to do it for Jordan. In his memory. You watch and see."

Knowl's tone turned brusque. "What do you think you're going to do, Son? Protest in the streets like those hippies in California? Or like those student rabble-rousers at the universities?"

Jon Knowl shrugged, his hazel eyes flashing a cheeky insolence that would surely ignite their father's wrath and indignation. "I don't know, Dad. Maybe I'll join a protest movement. Or maybe I'll join up with Bobby Kennedy's election campaign. At least he's got the guts to straighten out this country."

Before Knowl could launch a heated reply, Chad returned to the dining room with his parents. They sat down, still grim-faced and mumbling apologies. "You're just in time," said Grandmother Anna brightly. She handed Clara a serving of cake and ice cream. As she passed heaping servings around the table, Maggie's father and brother glared at each other, Chad's mother dabbed at her tearful eyes . . . and Maggie prayed that the whole intolerable evening would soon be over.

The last week of May, Jon Knowl finished his sophomore year of high school. He came home, tossed his books on the sofa, greeted Maggie with a distracted nod, and went straight to his room. Later, he ate dinner with the same preoccupied demeanor, refusing to engage in conversation or make eye contact with anyone. Maggie's parents pretended not to notice his remoteness, so Maggie let it go too. No sense in stirring up trouble. At least for a change, Jon Knowl wasn't arguing with their dad.

Maggie didn't give her brother's odd behavior another thought until the next morning when she heard her mother cry out in alarm. Both Maggie and her father hurried to Jon Knowl's room, where her mother stood holding her hands up in bewilderment.

"What's wrong, Mama?" asked Maggie.

"Jon Knowl's gone!" she blurted.

"Gone?" echoed her father, glancing around. "What do you mean, gone?"

"His things. Clothes. Shoes. His duffle bag. All gone. His bed hasn't been slept in. Oh, Knowl, what are we going to do? Our son has run away."

"Impossible." Knowl looked in the closet and inspected several dresser drawers. "You're right, Annie. Some of his things are missing. But where would he go?"

Maggie riffled through the papers on Jon Knowl's desk. Under his geometry book she found a spiral notebook open with Jon Knowl's familiar scrawl across one page. "Mom, Dad, look. A note."

Knowl seized the notebook and scanned the message. "It's a note, Annie. Listen. 'Dear Mom, Dad, and Maggie, by the time you read this, I will be far away. I'm leaving with several buddies who feel the same way I do about things. We believe we can make a difference in our country. I know our convictions aren't the same as yours, but we've got to follow them anyway. We've got to fight for what we believe in, and we'll do whatever it takes to make things right. Please don't try to find me. I'll be home when I've fought my own battles and made our government see the truth. I know you won't understand, Dad, but I've got to be true to myself just as you are true to your beliefs. I'll be in touch one of these days. Give Mom a kiss for me . . . and Maggie too. I love you all. Please don't hate me for doing what I have to do. Love, your son, Jon Knowl.'"

Maggie's mother made a sobbing sound and covered her face with her hands. "Oh, Knowl, I was afraid of this. We should have known. We should have done something."

Her parents embraced. "What could we do, Annie? Keep our son under lock and key?"

"Yes, if that's what it took. Now, who knows when we'll see him again? Anything could happen to him."

Maggie foraged through the papers on her brother's desk. "He must have left a clue, something that will tell us where he's gone."

They all began to look, rummaging through Jon Knowl's possessions—his books, drawers, closet. In one desk drawer Maggie found a folder filled with newspaper clippings. "Look, Mom, Dad. A bunch of newspaper articles."

"Articles?" said her father.

"Yes, look at them, Dad. They're all about Robert Kennedy's campaign. Why would Jon Knowl save all these articles?"

Her father scanned several of the clippings. "You heard him talk about Kennedy, Maggie. How much he admires him. It's hero worship, plain and simple."

"Maybe not so simple," said her mother, fingering one article. "This tells about the primary elections. Which ones Kennedy's in. Where he's traveling across the country. What stops he's making."

"Annie, you think our son's trying to join up with Kennedy? He wouldn't. He's a fifteen-year-old kid, for heaven's sake!"

"He doesn't see it that way, Knowl. Like so many young people his age, he's out to change the world."

"Change it . . . or destroy it?" countered Knowl hotly.

"I don't know, Knowl, but I'm scared. The world has become such a turbulent place. Protests. Violence. Riots. Drugs. If we don't find him right away and bring him home, he could destroy his own life. We might never see our son again."

Maggie's heart pounded furiously as the truth of her mother's words hit home. Jon Knowl was gone, and she might never see him again. Wherever he was, he was in peril. Anything could happen to him. Maggie had just lost her precious Jordan. Would God snatch her only brother away from her too?

7

For two days Maggie and her parents watched and waited for Jon Knowl to return home. Every time the phone rang, her mother rushed to answer it, expecting to hear her son's voice. But each time she sagged in disappointment when someone else greeted her. They took turns telephoning every friend and acquaintance of Jon Knowl's since grade school. No one had seen him. No one knew where he had gone.

Three days after his disappearance, on Saturday, the first of June, Chad came to the house with news. "Where are your folks?" he asked Maggie at the door, excitement animating his sturdy face. "I've got some news about Jon Knowl."

Maggie quickly led him to the parlor where her parents were going through Jon Knowl's personal papers and schoolwork, looking for clues to his whereabouts. They looked up curiously when Chad burst into the room.

"I think I know where Jon Knowl went," he said breathlessly.

Maggie's father stood up, dropping a thumb-worn spiral notebook onto the coffee table. "Where, Chad?"

Chad sat down in the overstuffed chair across from Maggie's parents, his fingertips drumming the tufted arms. "I'm not sure now, but I've got this feeling. It rings true."

"Tell us," urged Annie, sitting forward eagerly. "Where is my son?"

"California," said Chad. "I think he headed for California."

"But how? He has no car, no money."

"I know, but I talked to this guy—"

"Who?" demanded Knowl.

"Just a guy I used to know in school. He moved to Fort Wayne a year or so ago. I ran into him today, and he said his brother just took off for California in his old Chevy with a couple of other guys—one from Fort Wayne, the other from Willowbrook. He was pretty sure the guy's name was Jon Herrick."

"Where in California were they going?" asked Knowl urgently, adjusting his spectacles with an unsteady hand.

"Los Angeles, I guess. His brother said that's where everything's happening. He said they want to be there when Bobby Kennedy wins the primary."

"The California primary is next Tuesday," said Annie. "Do you really think he'd go all the way across the country just to see Robert Kennedy?"

"I think he would," said Maggie. "He thinks Kennedy is going to save our country and end the war in Vietnam."

"What does your friend's brother plan to do after the primary?" asked Knowl. "Are they coming home?"

Chad rubbed his chin thoughtfully. "I got the impression they were planning to stay there and work for the party. I don't think they'll be coming home right away."

Knowl strode across the room and picked up the phone. "Then I'll go get him."

"Who are you calling, Knowl?" asked Annie.

"The airlines, Annie. I'll book a flight for Monday morning and, if Chad's right, I'll have that boy back here in a few days."

"How will you find him, Dad?" asked Maggie. "And, even if you find him, what if he won't come home with you?"

"He'll come home with me or I'll tan his hide."

Maggie's mother put out a restraining hand. "No, Knowl. It won't work that way. You'll only alienate him. There has to be a better way."

"There is," said Maggie. "Let me go. I can talk to Jon Knowl and make him see why he has to come home."

Knowl shook his head. "Do you think I'd let you go alone to California? It's a hotbed of radicals and hippies out there. They're all taking drugs and demonstrating against everything decent in our country."

"But if we don't go after him, Dad, he could get lost in that whole counterculture thing. You know how angry he's been since Jordan's plane went down. He could be talked into anything."

"That's why I'm taking the next plane out there, Maggie."

"Listen, Mr. Herrick," said Chad. "I'd be glad to go with Maggie to California."

She looked up at him. "Really, Chad? You'd go with me?"

"Sure. Isn't that what Jordan would have done? No sitting around waiting, twiddling his thumbs. He would have gone after Jon Knowl without a second thought."

Maggie nodded, a sudden lump in her throat. "You're right. That's exactly what Jordan would have done."

"Okay, so he's not here. But I am. And Jon Knowl just might listen to me. I'm not family; I'm his friend. So how about it, Mr. Herrick?"

"It's very generous of you to offer, Chad, but—"

"Please, Dad," urged Maggie. "Chad's right. He could reach Jon Knowl better than anyone. Let us go. Please!"

"I don't know, honey. I just don't like the idea."

"Dad, Chad and I have the whole summer before we start our jobs. It would be a . . . I don't know . . . an adventure. And think what it would mean if we brought Jon Knowl home, safe and sound."

"That would be wonderful, of course . . ."

"And a trip to California would keep my mind off Jordan for a while."

Her father gave her a solemn, cryptic glance, then removed his glasses and rubbed the bridge of his nose. His eyes looked weary, almost colorless, his lids heavy. "All right, Maggie. If you really want to go. I'll see if I can get you and Chad out on a flight Monday afternoon." He looked at Chad. "You take good care of my daughter, you hear? And bring my son home. Please, God willing, bring him home."

Chad straightened and looked as if he were about to salute. "I'll do my best, sir."

Maggie spent Sunday evening packing, or trying to pack, scouring her closet and drawers, in a quandary as to what to take for such a bizarre and unpredictable journey. When her suitcase was full, brimming with clothes, shoes, Bible, camera, journal, and toiletries, she forced the heavy lid shut and snapped the lock. If she had forgotten anything important, it was too late now. She slipped into bed shortly after eleven, but her heart was pounding too hard to allow slumber. She tossed and turned for nearly an hour before she drifted into a fitful sleep.

Sometime in the middle of the night, she awoke with a start, wide awake, a sense of foreboding tying knots in her stomach. She got up, pulled on her chenille robe, and slipped downstairs for a cup of hot cocoa. To her surprise, the kitchen light was already on, casting a soft golden glow on her mother, who sat at the table in her robe sipping a cup of hot tea. "Mom, you okay?"

She looked up at Maggie, her eyes red-rimmed. Without makeup and with her chestnut hair hanging loose on her shoulders, she looked like a pale, vulnerable child. "Hi, sweetie. I'm fine. Just sitting here praying for your brother. And for you too."

Maggie poured milk into a saucepan. "You couldn't sleep either?"

"No, honey. Too much on my mind, I guess."

"Same here."

"You don't have to go to California, Maggie. If you've changed your mind, we can cancel the . . ."

"No, Mom. I want to go. I've got to be doing something. I can't help Jordan in Vietnam. I can't reach out to him or save him, but maybe I can save Jon Knowl. It's just . . . I don't know what to expect or where to start looking. I don't know what we'll find in Los Angeles. I guess it's really a wild goose chase, isn't it?"

"God will be with you, Margaret, dear. I have peace about that. He'll show you the way."

Maggie stirred a spoonful of cocoa into the steaming milk. "I wish I had your faith, Mom."

"You do, dear. Just give God a chance to show you what He can do."

Maggie sat down across from her mother and sipped her hot chocolate. It was too hot and burned her tongue. She blew into the cup, watching the creamy chocolate make little ripples.

"You need marshmallows," said her mother gently. "Remember when you were little? You'd beg for more marshmallows and you'd wait until they melted before you'd drink your cocoa. Then you'd have a great sugary-white mustache on your upper lip."

Maggie smiled, remembering. "I still love marshmallows in my cocoa, but the mustache wouldn't look so cute anymore."

"It would to me. No matter how old and sophisticated you get, honey, you'll always be my little girl. And I'll always want to protect you and make sure you're happy."

Maggie stirred her cocoa. "You can't do that anymore, Mama."

"I know." Her mother pushed a wisp of soft brown hair behind her ear, a tentative, anxious gesture. "When you were little I could bandage your knees and give you parties and dolls to make you happy. But now you're a woman, and I can't ease your heartaches anymore. I can't make sure you'll always be safe."

"I know, Mama," Maggie said quietly. "I used to think you and Daddy could do anything you set your mind to. I thought you could fix anything. Everything. But now I know you can't. Neither can I. I can't bring Jordan home, just as you can't take away the hurt I feel. But your love helps. It does help, Mama."

Her mother reached across the table and clasped her hand.

"Then I'm sending you off with bushels of love, honey. I'll be with you every moment on the road, in all my thoughts and prayers. Remember that, Margaret."

Maggie pressed her mother's warm, smooth hand against her cheek. "I will, Mama. And I'll be stronger because of your love. I promise."

Early the next morning, Monday, June 3, as a faint orange glow dusted the horizon, Maggie got up and slipped quietly downstairs while her parents slumbered. She needed some time alone, to think and prepare her heart and mind for this day.

Only Grandmother Anna was up, bustling about in the kitchen. She always rose at dawn to fix breakfast for her brood. Maggie could hear the clink of china plates and the clatter of metal utensils against an iron skillet. Grams was probably fixing a ham and cheese omelet or potato pancakes.

Maggie moved soundlessly through the living room and parlor, careful not to make a sound. No sense in disturbing Grams. She walked on velvet feet through the familiar rooms and breathed in the familiar smells—the tang of cedar and mahogany and lemon oil, faint, comforting smells that all of her life had defined this house. She detected a lilac sachet in the cherry wood buffet, the aromas of baked apples and maple syrup drifting from the kitchen, and a fragrant potpourri of dried roses wafting from the dining room.

She looked at everything as if she might never see it again, as if she were looking at her home for the last time. Or maybe the first time.

She had lived in this house for over twenty years. When had she stopped looking at things—lamps, tables, chairs—seeing them without really seeing? The rooms of her house were so commonplace, she looked past them, saw through them. These rooms were like the veiled rooms of her own life, her very soul, so familiar she took them for granted, so predictable she never questioned them.

She was a person who had coasted through life in a cloud, taking everything for granted. She had suffered no great ills, endured no overwhelming trials. She was soft, compliant, nearly apathetic. Like her house, she never changed.

But change was all around her now. Jordan was missing in action. Her beloved Jordan. Lost to her. Perhaps wounded. Even dead. And her brother. Where was Jon Knowl? Far away, a rebel wandering the streets of some distant city, pushing the limits, living a nightmare, his anger bursting at the seams.

The world was not a nice place anymore, no longer dependable, predictable, sane. Wars swept shatteringly close to home, snatching up ordinary people, even someone she loved. Famous men like Martin Luther King Jr. chatted on their hotel balconies and were gunned down in cold blood. Every day, normal, happy teenagers like Jon Knowl were being transformed into drugged hippies or raging protesters. Or they were being sent across the ocean to a foreign land to fight and kill or be killed. Maggie wasn't ready for this, wasn't prepared to insinuate herself into a world that was going crazy. Why then had she insisted on going to Los Angeles to look for Jon Knowl? She wasn't brave and impulsive like Jordan.

"You don't have to go," said her grandmother, her light, crystal voice breaking the stillness.

Maggie looked up, startled. Grandmother Anna stood in the kitchen doorway watching her, a spatula in one hand. She looked fresh and bright-eyed in a maroon housedress accented by a frilly pink bib apron. Her cheeks glowed with the warmth of the kitchen and her silky gray hair formed a diaphanous wreath of angel hair around her head.

"Yes, I do," said Maggie.

"There has to be a better way, child. Maybe your father should go after all."

"No, I'm going," said Maggie, more firmly. "Chad will be with me. We'll be okay."

Her grandmother tapped her spatula against her open palm. "Jon Knowl was a fool to run away, a fool to think he can change the world."

"And maybe I'm a fool to think I can stop him. Is that what you think, Grams?"

"Maybe so, Margaret."

"I've got to try," she said, as if that settled the matter. No matter what anyone thought, she had to go. She didn't know why, just knew something inside was driving her to do it. An impulse she couldn't quell. Maybe she felt she had to prove herself brave like Jordan. If he could be courageous enough to risk dying for his country—and maybe he was dead somewhere already, in some dark, steamy jungle—she should be brave enough to go look for Jon Knowl and bring him back home.

Grandmother Anna shuffled over and clasped Maggie's cheeks in one bony, arthritic hand. "Well, child, you come eat a good breakfast before you go. No sense in striking out on your own on an empty stomach."

"I'd love to, Grams." With a light, pleased chuckle, Maggie wrapped her arms around her frail grandmother and held her tight for a long, sweet, extraordinary moment.

After breakfast, Maggie's father drove her and Chad to the Willowbrook depot and waved a wistful good-bye as they boarded the passenger train for Chicago. After a noisy, grinding, jouncing ride, they arrived at Chicago's sweltering Union Station, where they caught a cab to O'Hare Airport for their late afternoon plane to Los Angeles.

Each step of the way, it was a whirlwind journey, everything happening at once, everything in motion, their senses bombarded with a hodgepodge of sights, sounds, and smells. The sooty rumble of the train. The huge, echoing expanse of Union Station. The harried bustle of O'Hare Airport. Boarding the great, silver-winged bird that would transport them across the continent in a few short hours. The heart-pounding exhilaration of liftoff. The vast patchwork quilts of landscape below—deep greens, golden yellows, warm browns in neat, perfectly matched squares. Towns and cities and neighborhoods laid out like miniature play sets. And Maggie's first glimpse of Los Angeles at night—a boundless, black velvet field bejeweled with endless strings of dazzling lights.

At the airport Chad rented a car—a year-old forest-green sedan. Maggie pored over the map as Chad wended his way through the confusing labyrinth of southern California freeways. "How does anybody find their way around here?" he wondered aloud. "This place is a jumbled maze of steel and concrete."

Maggie gazed out the side window. "But look at all the palm trees, Chad. You never saw anything like that in Indiana."

After driving around downtown Los Angeles for a half hour, Chad finally pulled up beside a nondescript two-story, Spanish-style motel surrounded by tall, spiky palm trees. "Is this okay, Magpie?" he asked.

She stifled her doubts and said, "I suppose so."

"It's just a couple of blocks from the Ambassador Hotel. That's where the newspapers say the Kennedy entourage will be waiting out the election returns tomorrow night. Chances are Jon Knowl will be somewhere close by."

Chad went inside the motel office and secured two rooms, side by side, on the ground floor. He and Maggie unloaded their luggage, then drove to a nearby Kentucky Fried Chicken fast-food restaurant. They ordered two dinners to go and took them back to their motel rooms.

The rooms were small, the carpets and furniture shopworn, the air smoky and stale. Already Maggie was homesick. She and Chad ate in her room at a small pine table crowded in beside the double bed. Chad turned on the TV to the late evening news. The color was too yellow, the picture fuzzy, but when the newscaster started talking about Senator Kennedy's campaign, both Maggie and Chad listened attentively.

"Presidential candidate Robert Kennedy has had a jam-packed day on the campaign trail," intoned the announcer. "Kennedy knows the stakes are high. With Hubert Humphrey and Eugene McCarthy breathing down his neck, Kennedy must have a major win in the California primary if he's to be a serious contender at the Democratic convention in Chicago this August.

"Senator Kennedy gave it his best shot today, traveling from Los Angeles to San Francisco, then back to Long Beach and Watts, and finally to San Diego before heading back to Los Angeles. That's a total of 1,200 miles in thirteen hours—a grueling schedule for any man. And an awful lot of hands to shake and babies to kiss.

"Kennedy's hectic, last-minute campaign marathon was not without incident, however. This morning, as his motorcade passed through San Francisco's Chinatown, the entourage was shaken by a series of loud popping sounds, frighteningly reminiscent of Dallas. To everyone's relief, the explosions proved to be nothing more than firecrackers.

"During his last rally at the El Cortez Hotel in downtown San Diego, an exhausted Kennedy appeared near collapse. He left the stage for about fifteen minutes, assisted by Olympic decathlon champion Rafer Johnson. But when he returned to finish his speech, he was perhaps at his most eloquent. He closed, as he often does, by quoting playwright George Bernard Shaw: 'You see things; and you say, "Why?" But I dream things that never were; and I say, "Why not?"'

"Tomorrow, Kennedy will await the election returns in his suite at the Ambassador Hotel in Los Angeles. And, tomorrow evening, the nation will know whether the senator, who has lingered for years in his brother John Kennedy's lengthy shadow, is one step closer to his dream of becoming president of the United States."

As newsreel footage flashed on the TV screen, showing eager crowds greeting Senator Kennedy in Los Angeles and Long Beach, Maggie pushed her half-eaten dinner aside and sat forward, her eyes searching the milling, cheering throngs. Jon Knowl could be in one of those crowds; the camera could zoom in on him as it scanned the eager, upturned faces. He could be there. He could be just a matter of miles away.

"Do you see him?" asked Chad, clearing up the clutter from their meal.

"No." She knew it was foolish to even think she might spot Jon Knowl on TV. She sat back in her chair and let her shoulders slump. She was suddenly weary beyond words. The bumpy train ride, the long flight from Chicago, and the winding freeway drive from the airport had sapped all her energy. She wanted nothing more than to crawl into bed and sleep.

Chad tossed the remnants of their dinners into the wastebasket and ambled to the door. "You look tired, Maggie. I'd better let you get some shut-eye."

"You too." She pulled herself out of the chair and shuffled to the door. Chad stepped outside and looked back with a faint smile. "Sleep well, Magpie. Tomorrow will be another big day."

"Maybe we'll find Jon Knowl," she ventured.

"Maybe so. If you need anything tonight, I'm right next door, okay?" She nodded.

"Lock the door. The deadbolt too."

With another drowsy nod, she shut the door and locked it. Alone in the small motel room, she felt suddenly giddy and unsettled at once.

She had never been on her own before, alone in a motel room in a strange city. It seemed impossible that she was thousands of miles from the safe haven of her home on Honeysuckle Lane. Imagine, nearly a continent away from her family.

What was she doing here? she wondered for a fleeting, heart-pounding moment.

I'm here on a mission, she told herself. *And I won't give up until I've found my brother.*

She opened her suitcase and removed a silk nightgown, then quickly shed her clothes and headed for the shower. The warm, pelting water relaxed the tension in her shoulders and back, even though the shower stall was small and grimy. When she climbed into bed a few minutes later, she hardly cared that the mattress was too firm and the pillow too lumpy.

She stretched out languorously and stared up into the darkness. She could hear traffic from the busy streets and horns honking and doors slamming and muffled voices from other rooms and the ticking of the bedside clock. At home she knew the sounds of the night—crickets, clocks, the gentle creaks and groans of the old house; they were familiar sounds, comfortable, predictable. These noises were different, jarring; they had no rhythm, no warmth. They would take some getting used to.

Maggie closed her eyes and shut out the distant clatter. In the flickering shadows she whispered, "Dear God, help us find Jon Knowl tomorrow. Maybe even at the Ambassador Hotel with Senator Kennedy. And be with my dear Jordan, wherever he is on the other side of the world. Please let him be alive. And bring him home to me someday."

Maggie intended to say more, much more, but the murky waves of slumber washed over her, pulling her under, muffling her words and gently silencing her prayer.

8

Maggie woke up the next morning to the sound of insistent pounding on her motel door. Bleary-eyed, her body still sluggish from sleep, she stumbled out of bed and made her way to the door. Through the peephole she saw Chad standing on the walkway wearing a tee shirt and Bermuda shorts and holding two Styrofoam cups of coffee. "Get up, sleepyhead!" he called cheerily. "It's a gorgeous day out here! Come out and enjoy the sun."

She pulled on her robe and opened the door. Chad shuffled inside and handed her a coffee. "Thought you might need this. Jet lag, you know."

"What time is it?" she asked, gingerly sipping the coffee.

"Nearly ten. I thought maybe we could hit the beach and soak up some sun before canvassing the area for Jon Knowl."

Maggie sat down on the bed and took another swallow of coffee. She could feel the liquid heat spiraling down through her chest to her stomach. "Shouldn't we start looking for my brother right away?"

Chad sat down beside her, already smelling of fresh, delicious sunshine. "Tell you what, Magpie. If you feel as lousy as I felt when I got up, you'll want a little rejuvenation. And, let's face it. With the ocean a few short miles away, how can we resist? There's nothing like it back in Indiana."

Maggie stood up, put her cup on the table, walked over to the window, and cranked it open. The sun was shining with a welcoming shimmer, the air already warm, balmy, and inviting; a perfect day. "Maybe the beach would be a good place to start looking for Jon Knowl. He would love it."

Chad grinned. "Sounds like a plan to me. I'll go and let you get dressed. Wear shorts or a bathing suit under your clothes, something comfortable. We might take a swim. Meanwhile, maybe I can find some doughnuts to go with our coffee."

"And some fruit," suggested Maggie. "Bananas, oranges. California should have delicious fruit."

"Will do."

A half hour later they piled into their rental car and headed down the freeway toward the ocean. They made their way along several narrow streets flanked by rustic cottages until they found a parking spot near Santa Monica Beach. Chad grabbed his camera from the backseat and slipped the strap around his neck. "Gotta take pictures," he said. "Otherwise nobody back home will believe this incredible view."

They trekked over warm, packed wet sand swept by incoming tides and mottled by seaweed and broken shells. At the water's edge they kicked off their tennis shoes and waded into the lapping waves, holding hands to keep from falling.

"Hold it, Maggie." Chad stepped back and held the camera to his eye.

"No, take the scenery, not me," she said, pushing her straight brown hair back from her face with both hands.

"You make a better picture than the ocean," he said, snapping the photo.

Impulsively she bent her knees and splashed water at him. He jumped back, laughing, holding his camera in the air. "Cut it out, Maggie. You'll get my camera wet."

"Then don't be a shutterbug."

He snapped another picture, catching her in a gesture of protest, making an ugly face. "No fair!" she cried, slapping the water with her palm, spraying him again.

"I'll get you for that, Magpie." Chad combed the water with his large hand and sent a gusher her way, soaking her clothes. She splashed back with both hands, drenching him.

Chad slung his camera behind his back, the strap flying, and lunged for her. He grabbed her and held her tight, pinning her arms to her side, her face against his damp tee shirt. They clung to each other, both laughing, gulping for air, the warm sun beating down on their heads, the salt spray tickling their noses.

Suddenly Chad buried his face in her hair, and she felt his chest convulse. She strained to look up at him, but he turned his face away. "What's wrong?" she asked, her wet skin prickling with anxiety.

He released her and let his hands fall limp at his sides. His square jaw trembled slightly. "Nothing, Mag. Don't worry about it."

"It's something. Everything changed just now. We were laughing, and now . . . now you're crying."

He wiped the wetness from his bronzed face. "It's your fault, Magpie. The salty water. It stings my eyes."

She crossed her arms and stared him down. "No. It's Jordan. You're thinking of Jordan."

Chad kicked at a sprig of seaweed floating on the water. It washed against his calf. "Let's go, Mag. We've got a lot to do." They trudged out of the water back onto the wet sand, picked up their tennis shoes, and headed back to their vehicle.

"I think of him, too, you know," Maggie said in a small voice. "Jordan's always in my thoughts."

"I know." Chad opened the car door for her and waited while she brushed the gritty sand from her bare legs and feet. "It's just . . . for a minute there, Maggie, we were laughing and having fun."

She looked up at him. "What's wrong with that?"

He shrugged. "Maybe nothing. It just felt wrong. It should have been Jordan laughing with you on the beach. I feel, I don't know, guilty, I guess."

She reached up and touched his strong chin. "You never have to feel guilty, Chad. If it weren't for you, I don't know how I would have survived these past few weeks. Sometimes I feel dead inside, but then I think of you and feel warm and alive again."

"I wish I could feel that way."

"You can, Chad. You're part of Jordan, part of all the wonderful memories we shared. You make Jordan seem closer. You make me believe he could still be alive."

Chad's lips tightened. "He is alive, Mag. Don't you doubt it for a minute. He'll be home someday, and we'll be waiting for him, the two of us, no matter how long it takes."

She slipped into the car and he shut the door. In minutes they were back on the road again, heading toward Los Angeles. "What now?" she asked. Her hair and clothes were wet and a fine layer of sand still clung to her limbs. "We'd better go back to the motel and change."

"Okay. Then we'll grab a couple of burgers and drive around and scout out the area."

"Do you really think we can find Jon Knowl?"

Chad kept his eyes on the road. "Don't know, Mag. It's like looking for one certain pebble on the beach. There's a whole lot of beach and a whole lot of pebbles."

"All we know is that he came to California to see Bobby Kennedy win the primary. What if Kennedy doesn't win? Would Jon Knowl still try to see him?"

"Beats me. Maybe we should go back to the motel and turn on the television and listen to the election returns. If Kennedy wins, we'll head over to the Ambassador Hotel where he'll be having his victory party."

"It'll be a private party. Surely Jon Knowl wouldn't be able to get in."

"No, but that doesn't mean he won't try. It's the only thing we have to go on, Maggie."

They drove back to the motel, changed, went out for cheeseburgers and shakes, drove around for a while looking for anyone who looked remotely like Jon Knowl, then returned to the motel and watched the returns. "It's looking strong for Kennedy," said Chad, popping the lid off a Coke bottle. He took a swig and handed it to her. She drank a swallow; it was warm and the fizz tingled in her throat.

It was after 8:00 P.M. when the newscaster projected that Robert Kennedy had won the Democratic primary. The screen flashed an earlier clip of the senator, looking lean and boyish with his crinkly eyes, toothy smile, and unruly thatch of wheat-brown hair fanning over his forehead. He was saying, "We need to start working together—blacks, whites, Indians, and Mexican-Americans—to replace the hatred and distrust that now exists in the United States with compassion and understanding."

The newscaster's voice came back on as the scene switched to a sprawling hotel ballroom where an immense crystal chandelier illuminated a noisy, joyous, wall-to-wall crowd below. "The mood at the Ambassador ballroom this evening is electric and ecstatic," said the newsman. "Senator Kennedy's loyal supporters are celebrating, making toasts, and cheering his victory. Kennedy has surrounded himself with some of America's favorite celebrities. Singers Andy Williams and Rosemary Clooney. Comedian Milton Berle. Astronaut John Glenn, and many more. The crowd is eagerly awaiting the senator's victory speech."

Maggie turned down the volume and looked at Chad. "Jon Knowl should be happy now. I just hope he meant it when he said he wanted to be here when Kennedy won."

"We'll find out soon enough," said Chad, standing and stretching. "Listen, Mag, I'm going back to my room and changing into a dress shirt and tie. Then we'd better head over to the Ambassador."

She walked him to the door and flashed a smile. "I'll change too. After all, we want to blend in with the Los Angeles elite."

"Sure, why not? And if you don't mind, we'll walk to the hotel. It's only a couple of blocks, and I have a feeling with all the people crowded into the ballroom, there won't be a parking space for blocks."

"Walking is fine. It's a warm, beautiful night."

After Chad left, Maggie freshened her makeup, brushed her long, mahogany hair until it gleamed, and changed into a sleeveless baby-blue shift and stacked pumps.

When she met Chad outside the door, he looked at her and gave a long, low whistle. "You look out of this world, Mag."

"You look rather spiffy yourself," she said, noting his starched white shirt and striped red tie.

As they started walking, he clasped her hand firmly in his. "So you won't stumble in the dark," he explained with a sly little smile. They broke into an easy stride. The fresh air was invigorating after the close warmth of the motel room, and Maggie felt oddly reassured by Chad's firm handclasp. She could have strolled like this in the moonlight all night, but the walk two blocks east of Normandie Avenue to Wilshire Boulevard took less than ten minutes. Silhouetted against the darkness, the celebrated Ambassador Hotel with its blazing lights and classic beauty sat far back from the street—a palatial, semicircular building ensconced with timeless grandeur on spacious, luxuriant grounds. The famous Coconut Grove restaurant stood at the front of the hotel, and rows of tall, stately palm trees flanked its sides like lofty imperial guards. But Wilshire Boulevard itself was teeming with traffic—horns honking, lights flashing, luxury vehicles at a standstill, bumper to bumper.

"You were right, Chad. The hotel is jam-packed. Not a parking space in sight. We would have spent hours stuck in traffic."

"Told you."

As they crossed Wilshire, Maggie gazed at the crowds milling around, mainly young people chanting victory slogans and carrying makeshift signs that read, KENNEDY FOR PRESIDENT, VIVA BOBBY, and RFK IN '68. In the hazy blue rays of streetlights and the white glare of automobile headlights, Maggie studied the faces of the moving, surging throng, desperate for a glimpse of Jon Knowl. Her heart sank as she saw only strangers. "I don't see him," she told Chad, who still clutched her hand lest they be separated by the jostling humanity.

"Give it time, Maggie. There are still a lot of faces to see."

With sheer willpower, Maggie and Chad wended their way through the crowds, trekking over the vast grassy expanse, working their way closer to the hotel entrance. From inside the hotel Maggie heard muffled applause. "Kennedy's giving his victory speech," said a man closer to the door, a rangy man in a gray business suit. People quieted, their shouts shrinking to whispers, as if they actually expected to hear the speech being delivered inside the ballroom.

In that moment, as the crowd slowed and grew hushed, Maggie spotted someone, and for a moment she was sure she had stepped inside the pastel filigrees of a dream. It couldn't be her brother, but the young man's features rang true. Everything about him struck a responsive chord.

She seized Chad's arm. "Look! Is that him? It is, isn't it?"

"Who? Jon Knowl?"

The youth turned his back to them, talking animatedly with several other young men. He was wearing a fringed rawhide jacket and jeans. Now Maggie wasn't sure. Jon Knowl had no such jacket. Maybe she was wishing so hard to find her brother she saw his face in someone who only resembled him.

But then the youth turned her way again and there was no doubt. "It's him," she told Chad, her heart pounding with excitement. "Come on. We've got to get to him before he disappears again."

"He may not want to see us," said Chad as they nudged their way toward him.

"Of course he will," she protested. "We're family." She called his name, and the youth pivoted and stared straight into her eyes. For an instant she thought he would bolt. His eyes widened with disbelief, and his mouth opened in undisguised amazement. He looked around as if seeking a place to hide, then met her gaze with a scowl.

The crowd cleared enough that she could reach him now. She stretched out her hand, seizing his arm. "Jon Knowl!"

"Maggie."

"I never thought we'd find you," she said with relief.

He stared darkly at Chad, then back at her as the crowd jostled around them. "What are you doing here?"

She kept her hand firmly on his arm, afraid she would lose him again. "We came to find you."

His eyes flashed fire. "You shouldn't have."

"We had to," she said weakly. This wasn't the kind of response she had expected. He was treating her like a stranger. "What did you expect? That we'd just forget you? You left without a word. Mom and Dad are worried sick."

"I had to go, Maggie. Don't you understand? I'm doing what I've got to do."

"We understand you wanted to be here to see Kennedy win the primary," said Chad. "Now that he's won, we hope you'll come home with us."

Jon Knowl's expression hardened, his hazel eyes narrowing, his wide mouth tightening. "I can't. I'm staying here. Kennedy's victory is just the first step. I'm going to work for the party and make sure he wins the nomination in Chicago in August."

"You don't have to do this," argued Maggie. "Senator Kennedy has lots of people working for him."

"So?"

"So he doesn't need a fifteen-year-old kid following him around the country," said Chad.

Jon Knowl's jaw jutted out defiantly. "I'll be sixteen next month, and I'll follow him to the ends of the earth if I want."

Maggie ran her fingers over her brother's cheek. "Please come home. Come to our motel. We'll talk there."

He pushed her hand away. "There's nothing to talk about. You don't care how I feel."

"But I do," said Maggie. The crowd was surging around them again. She clasped his arm to keep from being separated. "I love you, Jon Knowl."

His voice rose over the surrounding commotion. "But you don't see the truth, Maggie. Even with Jordan missing in Vietnam, you don't see it."

"See what?" challenged Chad. His arm circled her shoulder to keep her from being shoved back into the throng. "What truth are you talking about?"

"That Kennedy is the last hope for our country." Jon Knowl's voice was ragged now, coming out breathless, edged with a shrill fervency. His friends—several bearded young men with bandannas around their heads—had turned their way and were warily observing the conversation. "Don't you see, Maggie? Kennedy's the only one who can end the war and save our country. He's the only one who can help the blacks and stop the riots. He's going to be our next president, and I'm going to help make it happen."

"I know that's what you . . ." Maggie stopped, her words falling away as a chill of apprehension prickled her skin. She felt more than heard a clamor coming from the hotel, an odd burst of noise, dissonant voices, a sudden agitation rippling through the crowd. The disturbance swelled, turning the warm night air electric. Maggie looked at Chad, but he was looking over her head toward the hotel.

"What in the world?" he began, but his voice was cut off by several piercing shrieks erupting from inside the hotel. Then a man broke through the hotel doors and shouted breathlessly, "They shot Kennedy!" A woman's scream cut through the darkness. A rush of dazed, shaken people spilled out of the hotel, wailing, weeping. As more screams pierced the night, the ripple of alarm sweeping the crowd exploded into a flash flood of panic and pandemonium.

"Kennedy's been shot!" someone else shouted. "Dear God, it happened again!"

Maggie shook her head, stunned. It had to be a joke. A terrible sick joke. Chad's hand tightened on her shoulder as the avalanche of hot, stifling humanity pressed around them, pushing, shoving, crushing, sweeping them off their feet. A cacophony of voices broke around her. "Kennedy shot . . . oh, God, not again . . . lying in a pool of blood . . . dear God, they killed him . . . not again, not again!"

Chad's hand fell away and Maggie felt herself propelled along with the warm, hysterical horde. She couldn't breathe, couldn't see. The world spun. "Chad!" she shrilled.

"I'm here, Maggie! Hold on!"

He broke through and caught up with her and held her tight as he pushed his way through the mob to the street. She stood on the curb, her arms wrapped around herself, trembling. "Where's Jon Knowl?"

"Stay here. I'll find him." Chad disappeared into the crowd for several long, anxious moments, then emerged with her brother at his side, looking ashen-faced, stricken.

"It can't be," Jon Knowl said numbly. "Not Bobby. It can't be!"

"Please, God, no," Maggie whispered as she sank weak-kneed into Chad's strong arms. He held her close against his chest as an eerie symphony of sirens sounded in the distance.

9

In a bewildered daze Maggie, Chad, and Jon Knowl returned to the motel and sat huddled in Maggie's room around the TV. They listened in stomach-churning silence as the newscaster revealed the chilling details of the shooting. "Moments after Senator Kennedy had finished his victory speech, as he was leaving the ballroom and going through a passageway into the hotel kitchen, a lone gunman stepped forward and fired shots that left the senator lying in a pool of his own blood. According to witnesses, the assailant fired at close range, striking the senator, then spraying the kitchen with bullets. He was apprehended minutes after the shooting and taken, under heavy guard, to the police administration building downtown. The suspect has not been identified."

The newscaster paused for a long moment, as if he himself were struggling to grasp the enormity of his words. "Mrs. Kennedy accompanied her husband in the ambulance to Central Receiving Hospital, but we have late word that he has been transferred to Good Samaritan Hospital, where he is listed in critical condition."

"He can't die," said Jon Knowl, sitting hunched on the bed, his fists white-knuckled. "He's gotta be okay."

"All we can do is pray," said Maggie. Her words sounded clichéd, useless. She wanted to say more, but dismissed the idea. Nothing she said could help Jon Knowl now. Something in her brother's face reminded her of the trusting, innocent little boy she remembered from their childhood. A sadness, a heart-wrenching vulnerability she rarely saw. She tried slipping her arm around him, but he shrugged off her touch.

A film clip flashed on the screen showing a triumphant Kennedy in the Ambassador ballroom giving his victory speech. Amid exultant cheers from supporters waving signs and wearing white straw hats emblazoned with Kennedy emblems, the senator concluded with an infectious grin, "On to Chicago, and let's win there!"

The next scene showed the eruption of chaos and confusion as gunfire sent men and women screaming and bolting from the packed ballroom. As Kennedy aides called for a doctor and admonished everyone to remain calm, the television camera zeroed in on the fallen Kennedy, relentlessly capturing the horror for posterity.

Maggie looked away and covered her mouth, her stomach turning in revulsion. Chad went to the sink, turned on the tap, and brought her a glass of tepid water. She took a sip and handed the glass to Jon Knowl. He shook his head. His hands covered his face. She knew he was hiding his tears, trying to be brave.

They sat up all night, bleary-eyed, numb with exhaustion, watching the TV, desperate for news. Maggie stared at the flashing black and white images until she felt hypnotized, powerless to move or turn her eyes away. Toward morning a reporter announced that a young Jordanian man named Sirhan B. Sirhan had been taken into custody for the shooting. Nothing was known about him. "Senator Kennedy's condition remains grave," intoned the reporter. "At this time physicians refuse to give an official prognosis, but speculation has it that if Mr. Kennedy survives, he will likely suffer severe brain damage."

Maggie winced inwardly as she watched Jon Knowl's reaction. He stood up and paced the room, shaking his head, fidgeting, running his fingers through his thick, tousled hair. His eyes were red-rimmed, his face pale, his chiseled features wrenched with torment.

Under his breath he muttered, "It can't be. Kennedy's our last hope. He's got to be president. God, don't do this to us!"

"Maybe we should get some sleep," said Chad. "Jon Knowl, you can come to my room. There are two beds . . ."

"No, I'm watching the TV until I know Kennedy's going to be okay."

"It could be days before we know," said Maggie.

"I don't care. I'm waiting right here until I know."

But with the first rays of dawn, exhaustion caught up with the three of them. Jon Knowl kicked off his tennis shoes, stretched out on the rumpled bedspread, and was soon slumbering fitfully. Chad dozed off in the overstuffed chair, his feet propped up on the small pine table. Maggie curled up on the end of the bed and fell asleep beside her brother's stockinged feet.

It was noon when Maggie finally stirred. She sat up, her muscles aching, her mouth dry and stale, her head throbbing. The TV was still on, the newscaster's voice a muffled drone. Jon Knowl was still asleep, but Chad was gone.

A prickle of alarm raised goose bumps on Maggie's skin. Where was Chad? Had he left her? Gone home to Willowbrook? Surely not, but then, where was he? Didn't he know how much she needed him?

She scrambled off the bed, rushed to the door, and opened it wide to the hot, shimmering sunshine just as Chad came striding up the sidewalk with coffee and doughnuts. She felt a startling impulse to rush into his arms, to savor his consoling closeness. She resisted the impulse and managed a smile instead.

"I figured we could use these," he said, setting the coffee and doughnuts on the table.

"I'm famished," she conceded. They both sat down at the table and helped themselves. "Don't wake Jon Knowl," she cautioned. "He's exhausted."

"Are you going to call your mom and tell her we found him?"

"Yes. Absolutely. They'll be so relieved."

Chad sipped his coffee. "Any news on Kennedy?"

Maggie shook her head. "No change. It doesn't look good."

"Your brother's taking it pretty hard."

"I haven't seen him like this since . . . since . . ."

"Since the news about Jordan," said Chad darkly. "I know. I was thinking the same thing."

Maggie turned her coffee cup between her palms. "It's so strange, Chad. I feel bad about Kennedy, but . . ."

"But what?"

"It's weird. I feel guilty saying it."

"Tell me."

"You won't think I'm crazy?"

Chad's mouth arced in an ironic smile. "Nothing you say will ever sound weird to me, Magpie."

"Really? Good."

"So say it."

"Okay. I will. I'll just say it." She pressed her thumbnail into the rim of the Styrofoam cup, splitting it. "Everybody in the world is focused on Kennedy," she said haltingly. "My own brother is obsessed with him. Here I am, listening, watching the TV, and hearing the updates, but I'm not thinking about Kennedy." Her voice swelled with emotion. "It's Jordan who's on my mind, Chad. The hurt of it. Him missing. Maybe dead. It's like it's all hitting me again, as if I'd just heard for the first time. I'm sorry about Kennedy, but the pain I feel is for Jordan."

Chad nodded. A muscle tightened along his jaw. "It's that way for me too."

"I don't understand it," said Maggie, staring into the murky blackness of her coffee. "I thought I was getting better. For weeks now Jordan has seemed so remote, so far away. I've felt an awful sadness inside, but it was like a door had closed and I couldn't see inside anymore. The pain wasn't so raw. It was as if it had burrowed deep inside my heart. It was there, always there, but it had been covered over by a rock, a wall, something hard and impenetrable."

Chad drummed his fingers on the table. "What you're saying, Maggie, is that the hurt is too deep and profound to be experienced all at once. It's the same for me. Sometimes when I'm least expecting it the grief creeps out like a stealthy headhunter and spears my heart. The pain feels red-hot and nearly steals my breath. But at other times it recedes and lingers in the shadows, moldering like a deep, festering wound I can't reach."

Maggie brushed away unexpected tears. "I hate feeling this way. It's like I'm starting over, having to get used to losing Jordan all over again. Why am I feeling so bad again? When will it go away?"

"I don't know, Mag." Chad reached across the table and squeezed her hand. "But we'll be okay. I promise. We'll both be fine again. As soon as they find Jordan."

She searched his eyes. "But what if they never do? What if we never hear anything? How can we live without knowing where he is? Or whether he's dead or alive?"

"Oh, we'll know, Maggie. Jordan's tough. He'll turn up any day now. You wait and see."

Maggie blinked and wiped the wetness from her eyes. "I pray you're right. Please be right."

After breakfast, Maggie went to the motel office and telephoned her parents. Her voice trembled with excitement as she told them she had found Jon Knowl and would be bringing him home as soon as they could get a flight out. It was worth all the trouble she and Chad had endured just to hear the elation in her parents' voices.

When she returned to her motel room, Jon Knowl was awake and sitting in front of the TV, drinking cold coffee and devouring the last of the doughnuts. When she tried to engage him in conversation, he waved her off, his attention focused wholly on the screen. He looked disheveled, his clothes wrinkled, his hair mussed. She glanced in the mirror and realized she looked no better. They all looked like they were suffering from hangovers, and they didn't even drink!

The hours dragged by with a turgid monotony, the three of them circling listlessly around the TV, waiting for news, seemingly suspended in time, held captive by a flickering image that offered the possibility of news. At dusk Chad went out to a fast-food restaurant and brought back hamburgers and Cokes. The burger was dry and tasteless, but Maggie resisted the urge to complain.

"We should just go home," she said as she swallowed the last of her cola. "If we call the airlines, maybe we could get a flight out tonight."

"I'm not going anywhere until I know Kennedy's okay," said Jon Knowl, jutting out his lower lip.

"No matter what happens, Kennedy's out of the running," said Chad. "Face it, Jon Knowl. He's not going to be president. Not this time, anyway."

"You don't know that!" Jon Knowl pitched his empty Coke bottle against the wall. It ricocheted against the bedside table, nearly toppling the bell jar lamp. For an instant he looked startled by his own sudden, violent show of emotion. Maggie and Chad looked at him, Maggie wondering if this was just the first explosion of his anger and frustration, wondering what she could do to calm him, to ease his pain. There was nothing, she was helpless to reach him, nothing she could do except sit here with him and wait out this awful night. He sank down on the bed, his back against the heavy pine headboard, and crossed his arms, his chin lowered to his chest, his brooding gaze still focused on the eerie, glowing screen.

For the rest of the evening no one spoke, except for brief, perfunctory bits of conversation, mostly from Chad. "Anyone want another Coke? It's warm. I'm opening a window. Mind if I catch a few winks? Anybody need anything from the store? I'm going for a walk. Anyone want to join me?"

Maggie considered going with Chad; she needed a walk, yearned to escape the close, stifling warmth of this motel room. She was weary of watching TV day and night waiting for news that might not come for ages, news that would surely not be good anyway; how could it be good when doctors were already hinting that Kennedy was brain dead? But what choice did she have but to wait here with her brother and listen, hope, and pray?

"You coming with me, Maggie?" Chad wanted to know. He was standing in the open doorway, the warm night air sweeping in with a slight ocean smell, pungent, salty.

"No, you go ahead," she said. "I'll stay here with Jon Knowl." What else could she do? How could she step out for a leisurely walk with Chad when her brother was beside himself with anxiety, nearly desperate, out of control? She could not risk coming back and finding him gone. And he would go, he would run, disappear without a word; no, she couldn't risk that possibility.

"Go ahead," Jon Knowl told her, still slumped on the bed. "I'm okay. Don't stay on my account."

She stayed anyway. Chad left and returned an hour later with frosty orange drinks and a bag of chips. They ate and sometime around midnight they all dozed again, Jon Knowl and Maggie on the bed, Chad in the chair.

Sometime after 2:00 A.M. Maggie woke, sat bolt upright at the foot of her bed and stared at the glimmering TV screen. She sprang to her feet and turned up the sound. The newsman was speaking in solemn tones. Maggie shook Jon Knowl, then Chad, her heart racing. "Wake up. There's news!"

Groggy, still fuzzy with sleep, they all turned their attention to the screen. The announcer, his face pale, eyes shadowed, said in a deep, resonant voice, "We've just received word from Good

Samaritan Hospital. Senator Robert F. Kennedy died shortly after 2:00 A.M., this date, June 6, 1968." The newsman shook his head and mopped his brow, then said, "It's a bitter irony. Final votes are still coming in from remote precincts, swelling the count of Kennedy's election victory. The senator won the California primary, tasted for a moment the fruits of his labors, and then lost his life to an assassin's bullet just as his brother John did five years ago."

"No, no, no!" Jon Knowl jumped from the bed and flung himself at the TV, slamming his fist against the screen. Chad sprang to his feet, threw himself on Jon Knowl, and dragged him away from the set. He pushed him down on the bed and held him fast. Maggie embraced them both, feeling in her slim body their fierce heat and anger and pain. She held them both in her arms, her brother and Chad, her cherished friend, held them tight, as if she feared they would slip away, would leave her as Jordan had done, as Jon Knowl had tried to do. Why was life suddenly so much about partings and losses and dying? She felt Jon Knowl's hot tears on her skin, felt his convulsive sobs against her chest. She wept, too, for Kennedy, for her brother, for Jordan, and for all the nameless, pressing hurts that were inevitably unraveling her once-perfect life.

10

Somehow Chad convinced Jon Knowl to go with him to his room and get some sleep. "We'll be right next door if you need us," Chad told Maggie as he brushed a feather kiss on her forehead.

She looked over at Jon Knowl, standing slumped in the open doorway, his head down, his hands buried in the pockets of his leather jacket. He looked as if he might collapse, might simply fold in on himself and disappear. He looked like the little boy she remembered, only in a man's clothes, garments that seemed suddenly too big for him. It struck her that they had found him, his physical self, but they hadn't really found the boy she knew and loved. Where was he? How had he disappeared so quickly? And who was this brooding, raging stranger who had taken her brother's place? "Take care of him, Chad, okay?" she whispered.

"Don't worry. I'll watch out for him. And in the morning we'll see if we can get a flight home."

After they left, Maggie felt a strange sense of relief. She could relax now, unwind, attend to her own needs. First, she needed a shower. She shed the clothing she'd worn for over twenty-four hours and stepped eagerly under the warm, pelting water. She washed her hair, savoring the sweet fragrance of the shampoo, and lingered, letting the steamy spray work out the knots in her muscles.

After a long while she stepped out, toweled herself dry, and slipped into a cotton nightgown. In the warm, musky room she could still smell the familiar scents of Chad and Jon Knowl. They were just next door, probably already asleep, thank heaven!

As she combed her wet, tangled hair, she realized that the TV was still playing, a low droning sound. She snapped it off with a quick flick of the wrist. She'd had enough of the outside world intruding on her life. No more tonight. She rolled up the bag of chips Chad had left on the table, dumped the last of her orange drink down the sink, and tossed the paper cup in the trash. She turned off the lights and sat cross-legged on her bed. Oddly, she wasn't ready for sleep yet. She listened to the sounds around her—distant traffic sounds, a warm wind rustling the trees, crickets chirping. But inside her room all was silent. She could feel the silence surrounding her, hushed, moving, almost tangible.

She was sitting alone in the dark in a cheap motel room in California, a world away from Willowbrook and her family. What was she doing here? How could her life have changed so much since Christmas when she and Jordan were happily planning their future? Now here she was in this frightening city where a man had been murdered only blocks away. Not just any man, but a political leader half the country was pinning their hopes on.

And Jordan, dear Jordan, where was he? Lost somewhere in Vietnam, maybe in some prison camp, maybe wounded, maybe dead. She covered her face with her hands, pressing her fingertips against her eyeballs to block out the grisly images of her imagination. She couldn't even cry, the pain was so deep, beyond reach, untouchable.

Where was God tonight when she felt so surrounded by death?

She had always taken Him for granted, trusted He would be there for her, and would bring only good things into her life. But good things weren't happening now. How well did she really know this God of the universe, this God who could allow such tragedies? Had He forgotten His children, given up on them? These days some men were even claiming that God was dead. Was God showing everyone what the world would be like if He removed Himself from them? Had He removed Himself from her? Why did He seem so far away now when she needed Him most? Why at this moment in this dark, dreary motel room did she feel as if she were all alone in the world—and was perhaps destined to be alone forever?

"God, where are You?" she whispered into the murky silence. "I need You. We all need You tonight. Please be with us. Watch over Chad and Jon Knowl. And be with my precious Jordan, wherever he is."

But even after she had prayed, Maggie felt no comfort, no peace. It was as if she were talking with an acquaintance she hadn't visited in a very long time. Her words felt stiff, unnatural, meaningless. Was God even listening? Did He really care what was happening in this twisted, hurting, broken world?

Maggie had always assumed she had a good handle on life. She didn't claim to know all the answers, but she knew the basics, enough to get by, to feel confident in the future. But tonight she had no answers. She wasn't even sure about the questions. Everything was up for grabs—her beliefs, her suppositions, her expectations.

It was as if she had to go back to square one and examine her belief system in light of all that had happened this year—Jordan missing in action, battles raging in Vietnam, student uprisings and protests, racial strife and bloody riots, Martin Luther King Jr. being murdered, and now Bobby Kennedy. Where was it all leading? The end of the world as she knew it? Yes, in a sense, that was so. The events of this year had exploded her tranquil world. Before she could even comprehend one devastating change, another event had swept her off-balance and left her numb with shock.

Why didn't God do something about it? Yes, she was back to that. God. Where was He when the world was going crazy and people were killing one another?

Another thought came, haunting, disturbing. *What did she really know of God?* Christ was little more than a collage of flannel-graph images she remembered from her childhood Sunday school classes. Those sweet, timeworn images were enough when her life was placid and predictable, but now she needed more, needed real, flesh and blood help.

Yes, Jesus had become flesh and blood; she knew it, believed it, had even trusted Him as her Savior years ago, at age ten. But now, especially now, He seemed more a figure of history than a friend she could call on in moments of trouble.

"God, help me, please," she whispered again, her voice nearly a sob. "Help me know You better." At last Maggie felt a drowsiness overtake her. She crawled between the covers and fluffed the lumpy pillow under her head and surrendered to a restless, dream-filled sleep.

Sometime toward morning, amid her dreams, Maggie heard a heavy, desperate pounding. The noise was part of a bizarre nightmare—she was pounding her fists on a stranger's door, shouting for Jordan, but no one answered. Finally, the dream ebbed away, and she realized she was still in the motel room and the pounding was on her own door.

She scrambled out of bed, stumbled to the door, and opened it without thinking. In the dusky, predawn shadows Chad stared back at her, looking disheveled in an undershirt and rumpled jeans. "Maggie, I'm sorry to wake you." His face was pale, his hair uncombed.

"What time is it?" she mumbled, her mouth sleep-fuzzy.

"Four-thirty, five, I don't know. Early."

The alarm in his voice quickly dispelled her drowsiness. She was fully awake now, her heart pumping. "What's wrong?"

"Jon Knowl," he blurted. "He's gone."

She stared up at him. "Gone? Gone where?"

"I don't know. Just gone. I woke up—maybe I heard something, I don't know—but I looked over at his bed and it was empty. His stuff is gone. He skipped out, Maggie."

Maggie rocked back on her bare heels. "Why? He wouldn't just leave. We—we were taking him home today."

Chad stepped inside and drew her gently into his arms. "That's just it, Maggie. He didn't want to go home. I could see that. He's determined to carve out a new life for himself."

"But Kennedy's gone," she whispered against his chest. "What will Jon Knowl do now? Where will he go?"

"I don't know, Mag." Chad massaged the back of her neck. "We can go looking for him again, if you want."

She met his gaze. "Yes, we've got to. I already told Mom and Dad I was bringing him home. I won't go home without him."

He released her. "Okay. Throw some clothes on, and I'll grab a shirt and meet you back here in ten minutes."

"Make it five," she said.

It was five-fifteen when they piled into their rental car and pulled away from the motel. "He can't have gotten far," said Maggie. "Where would he go at this time of morning?"

"Anywhere, nowhere, everywhere," mumbled Chad. "You know we're looking for a needle in a haystack."

"I can't help it. I've got to look." She blinked away tears of frustration. "I can't believe this is happening. We just had him. It was a miracle we found him in the first place. We had him, and now he's gone again. What chance is there we'll find him again?"

"Say a prayer, Maggie."

"I am." She didn't add that she doubted it would do any good.

For two hours they drove up and down every street within a five-mile radius. Maggie began to feel she knew every coffee shop, grill, pawn shop, theater, bar, and market in the area. The neighborhoods all began to look alike—old stucco, single-story houses tucked among eucalyptus trees; brick apartment buildings with awnings, outside fire escapes, and ornate facades; and newer glass and concrete office buildings surrounded by lofty palms. They drove down Wilshire past the Ambassador Hotel where they had first encountered Jon Knowl, but there was no sign of him now. In the first rays of dawn the luxurious hotel no longer looked inviting. It looked to Maggie more like a mausoleum, its manicured grounds still cordoned off by police barricades.

"Stay on Wilshire," Maggie suggested.

Doggedly they took Wilshire all the way to the beach, passing through Beverly Hills to Westwood, to Santa Monica, to Marina Del Ray. As Chad drove along Ocean Boulevard, Maggie watched the morning sunlight glint like sparkling rhinestones on the surging, white-capped waves. "I'd love this view," she murmured, "if I weren't so worried about Jon Knowl."

Chad arched his shoulders and inhaled deeply. "It's no use, Maggie. We can't cover every square mile of Los Angeles. Even if we could, we're not going to find your brother if he doesn't want to be found."

Tears welled again. "So what should we do?"

"Go home."

"To Willowbrook?"

He looked at her, exhaustion lining his handsome face. "What else, Maggie? We have nothing to go on. Let's go back to the motel, get our stuff, and get on the first plane home."

She stared out the window. "You go."

"What about you?"

"I'm staying. I won't go home without my brother."

Frustration edged Chad's voice. "You may be here for the rest of your life, Mag."

She swallowed a sob. "That's the chance I'll have to take."

Chad let out a relenting sigh. "Okay, Magpie, you win. I'll stay too. Why not? We've got the whole summer."

She clasped his arm excitedly. "Really, Chad? Thank you! You won't be sorry, I promise!"

He smiled grimly. "I'm sorry already, but what can I do? I never could say no to you."

They stopped at a pancake house for a late breakfast, then were on the road again, circling the neighborhoods, stopping every passerby and flashing a snapshot of Jon Knowl. "Have you seen this boy?" Maggie asked over and over. No one had.

It was dark when they returned to the motel. Chad had stopped at a nearby fast-food restaurant and picked up tacos and burritos, an unexpected treat for Maggie, who had never eaten Mexican food before. They ate in Chad's room, watching the local television newscast. Maggie figured if anything had happened to Jon Knowl, it might appear on the evening news. But this was Los Angeles, not Willowbrook. The vast, impersonal city wouldn't notice the whereabouts of one lone out-of-town boy.

Maggie was about to head back to her own room, was at the door reaching for the knob, when Chad stooped down and retrieved a slip of paper from the floor. "Did you drop this, Maggie?"

"No. What is it?"

He examined the crumpled paper. "Looks like a phone number." He handed it to her. "Look familiar?"

As she gazed at the scrawled numbers, her breath caught in her throat. "This is Jon Knowl's handwriting."

"It could be a place he's staying. A friend, contact, anything."

Maggie's skin prickled. "Our first real clue. This could lead us right to him, Chad."

"Or it could be a false alarm."

"Let's go use the office phone and find out."

The office was empty except for a lone attendant, a frail, grayhaired man who scowled when they asked to use the phone. "No long-distance calls," he warned.

Chad dialed the number and handed the receiver to Maggie. She listened with a mixture of anxiety and anticipation as it rang once, twice, three times. It kept ringing. Six, seven, eight times. Her spirits flagged. No one home. Maybe Chad was right. A false alarm.

"We'll try again tomorrow," he said, slipping a protective arm around her sagging shoulders. "Don't give up hope yet."

"I won't," she promised, steadying her chin to keep from crying. She wouldn't let Chad see how disappointed she was. She had convinced him to stay in Los Angeles; now she had to show him she wasn't a quitter. "Tomorrow," she said, too brightly. "We'll find Jon Knowl tomorrow for sure."

11

One of the hardest things Maggie ever had to do was to phone home and tell her parents they had lost Jon Knowl, or more accurately, that he had deliberately slipped away from them. "We're staying until we find him," Maggie promised her mother. "Chad and I are staying here at the motel. Jon Knowl knows where we are, so maybe he'll come back to us when he's had time to clear his head." Maggie tried to sound hopeful, for her parents' sake, but she knew it was unlikely Jon Knowl wanted to be found. "We have a phone number too," she said, too cheerfully. "A local number. It may be where he's staying. So don't worry, Mom. We won't come home without him."

After hanging up the phone, she let her smile fade. "I hate pretending," she told Chad as he gave her hand a sympathetic squeeze. "They think this is just a minor glitch in our plans. I couldn't tell them I'm afraid we'll never see Jon Knowl again."

"Don't even think that, Maggie. We'll find him, whatever it takes." He cupped her chin in his hand. "But for now we need a break. Go put on your swimsuit and let's head for the beach."

She looked up at him, stricken. "You want to loll around at the beach when we should be looking for my brother?"

"Why not? The beach is exactly the place he would head on a day like this."

"You're right. And, even if he's not there, it'll be nice to have a little break after all the heavy stuff we've been through."

An hour later, after a brief stop at a Kmart for some beach supplies—blanket, towels, suntan lotion, and a picnic basket—plus another stop for a bucket of crispy fried chicken, they drove to Santa Monica Beach, parked, and strolled over the wet, warm sand past clusters of bikini-clad sunbathers to a smooth, pristine spot close to the water.

"How's this?" asked Chad, setting down their supplies and studiously pretending not to ogle the girls.

"It's perfect. Almost," Maggie said dryly, following his gaze to a nearby coterie of shapely coeds. Already she felt overdressed in the tee shirt and shorts she wore over her one-piece swimsuit.

Chad peeled off his tee shirt and stripped down to his bathing trunks. He had an athlete's solid, well-toned physique combined with a lean, limber grace in his legs and a mischievous little-boy glint in his eyes. If Maggie hadn't loved Jordan first, surely she would have loved Chad. "Come on, Magpie," he urged with a capacious grin. "We might as well look like healthy Californians instead of eggshell-white Hoosiers."

Fighting a sudden twinge of bashfulness, Maggie slipped out of her shirt and shorts. She felt as awkward and vulnerable as a newborn colt. Her suit was modest compared to the neighboring bikinis, and yet she felt somehow exposed, especially in light of Chad's approving gaze. "You look gorgeous, Mag," he said with a low whistle.

She mumbled "thank you" and quickly turned her gaze to the swelling ocean. Several brawny young men in wetsuits were riding the surging waves on surfboards, doing an amazing balancing act, skimming the heaving breakers with a riveting grace, until the foamy whitecaps pitched them into the briny, deep green waters like rag dolls. Clutching their surfboards, they burst up through the bubbling surface, sputtering, laughing, ready to go again.

"Amazing," said Maggie. "Maybe we should try it."

"Surfboarding? Ha! Not for this Indiana boy."

Maggie gazed around the beach, trying to feel at home in this luscious land of sun and surf, squinting her eyes against the hazy brightness. "Not as crowded as I thought it would be."

"The sun's overcast and the wind's a bit brisk," noted Chad. "Maybe that's enough to keep California swimmers home."

He spread out the blanket while Maggie opened the picnic basket and removed paper plates and plastic utensils. She pulled the lid off the cardboard bucket, the hot, spicy aroma mingling with the fresh ocean air. "Ready for some chicken with just a touch of sea salt?" she asked, offering him the bucket.

He helped himself to a plump drumstick and grinned. "Suddenly I'm famished." They settled back on the blanket and leisurely consumed the chicken, potato salad, and soft rolls.

"You know, Magpie, I think I could get used to a life like this," he said when they had finished eating. "You know. Lazing around on the beach, catching a few rays, eating take-out food, spending the day with my favorite girl."

Maggie glanced over at him, a tickle of surprise playing under her ribs. What did Chad mean, *my favorite girl*? It sounded almost as if they were a couple, as if he considered her . . . but no, she must have been mistaken. Surely it was just an innocent remark. She and Chad were friends, always had been, always would be. Friends, nothing more.

Chad broke into her thoughts. "Hey, you're burning, Maggie. Your shoulders and back. You're cooking, red as a beet. Better use the lotion."

He handed her the bottle, but as she struggled to smear the lotion over the back of her neck, he took the bottle from her and poured some out in his palm. "Here, let me do that. I can reach where you can't."

She sat stiffly, hardly breathing, as his large hands spread the cool, smooth liquid over her shoulders and back. She felt an impulse to let herself relax in his strong, protective arms, but immediately she dismissed the idea, silently chastising herself for such a compromising thought. She belonged with Jordan, wherever Jordan was . . . if he was still alive.

Of course he's still alive, she told herself sharply. *He'll be home again before I know it, and everything will be the way it was.*

"Maggie, you okay?" Chad's hands relaxed on her bare shoulders. "You're tight as a drum."

She looked around at him, her face warming. "I'm fine. Just . . . worried."

"About Jon Knowl?"

"Yeah." It wasn't exactly true, but somehow she felt guilty mentioning Jordan at such an intimate moment as this. Not intimate— that was the wrong word. She and Chad were doing nothing wrong sitting together on the beach like this, him rubbing lotion on her sunburned shoulders. It was innocent; it meant nothing. They were only friends, the best of friends. They both loved Jordan with all their hearts, and that love drew them close together, made them soul mates, kindred spirits. But Jordan would always be the love of her life.

Then why was it she couldn't seem to trace his face in her mind anymore, couldn't summon the sound of his voice in her memory? She had lost him to the war. Was time insidiously snatching away his face, his voice, all the precious memories of him she carried in her heart?

She pulled away from Chad, bristling suddenly at his touch, and stretched out on her stomach on the blanket, her cheek resting on her crossed arms. From the corner of her eye she could see Chad smearing suntan lotion over his muscular torso and legs. She closed her eyes, lest he ask her to return the favor and rub lotion on his back. She didn't want Chad's physical closeness to compete with the fragile images of Jordan in her mind. Her memories of Jordan were already growing flimsy as gossamer, elusive as the wind. The harder she tried to resurrect his features in her mind, the more his face slipped into the shadows. A tear streaked her cheek; she bit her lower lip, refusing to let Chad see her cry.

He lay down beside her on the blanket, his face mere inches from hers, his breath warm on her face, and rubbed her tear away with his thumb. "What's up, Mag? Are you crying?"

"No," she said, promptly rolling over on her back and turning her face away.

"Looks like it to me."

"It's just, you know . . ."

"Your brother."

She looked back at him. "I felt weepy, but I'm fine now."

They lay side by side under the baking sun. They dozed for a while until someone ran by, spraying sand over them. Maggie sat up, rubbed the grit from her eyes, and realized she was getting too much sun. She pulled on her tee shirt and shorts and slipped on her sandals. "Chad!" She shook him until he roused.

He squinted up at her, covering his eyes with his hand. "What's wrong?"

"We'd better go, or we'll both look like lobsters."

He got up and dressed and gathered their basket, blanket, and towels. "I'll put these in the car. Then why don't we walk around among the shops and see if we spot Jon Knowl."

She grimaced at him. "You're just doing it to humor me, aren't you?"

He scowled. "Of course not. I just thought—"

"That we'll run into Jon Knowl at some surf shop as easily as we did at the Ambassador Hotel? It won't happen, Chad. We knew my brother wanted to be near Kennedy's campaign celebration. But now we don't have a clue where he might be."

He shrugged. "So what do you want to do, Maggie? Go home?"

"No. Let's head for the shops." They trudged across the rolling sand to the parking area, sidestepping seaweed, broken shells, and debris. Chad put their belongings in the trunk while Maggie ran a brush through her long hair. Her gaze moved laconically over a group of teenage boys crossing the street. Several had long hair and wore headbands. One young man looked familiar. It wasn't Jon Knowl, but someone who reminded her of him. Who? Then she remembered. He was one of the boys with her brother at the Ambassador Hotel.

"Chad, hurry! That boy! See him? He knows Jon Knowl."

Chad slammed down the trunk lid, came up beside her, and followed her gaze. "Who? Where?"

She grabbed his hand and darted into the street, her gaze fixed on the distant youth. The sudden squeal of tires turned her attention to a black, late-model sedan roaring toward them. Chad yanked her backward onto the curb as the vehicle veered around them, nearly sideswiping them. Breathing hard, Maggie leaned weakly against Chad.

He held her up, his strong arm circling her waist. "Close call, Maggie girl. Be careful. I don't want to lose you!"

She inhaled sharply, her heart pounding. "I'm okay. Please, let's go." In their near collision with the sedan, she had lost track of the boy. The street was clear now, so they broke into a run. Safely on the sidewalk, she spotted the boy again—a tall, lanky, long-haired youth in a tie-dyed shirt and jeans—mingling with a cluster of scruffy-looking young people beside a surfboard shop.

She strode up to him and touched his arm. He turned sharply from his companions, flashing a look of surprise that flip-flopped into a leering grin. "Yeah, babe? What's happening?"

"You were with my brother," she blurted. "At the Ambassador Hotel. The night Kennedy was shot."

He flicked ashes from his cigarette. "Don't know what you're talking about, lady."

"You were with my brother," she repeated, knowing she wasn't handling this right. "At the Ambassador, remember?"

The scraggly youth ran his hand through his long, greasy hair and his eyes narrowed. "Maybe I was there and maybe I wasn't. What's it to you?"

Maggie's frustration was growing. "My brother. Jon Knowl Herrick. You're a friend of his, right?"

The youth dropped his cigarette on the cement and ground it out with the heel of his scuffed work boot. "Sorry, lady. Never heard of him."

"But I'm sure you were—"

Chad came up and grasped her arm. "Maggie, he's not the one. You're looking for someone else."

She looked up, baffled. "But—"

"Come on, Maggie. Let's go."

Reluctantly she let Chad escort her back across the street to their car. She could feel the insolent eyes of the youth and his friends following her. "You're wrong," she told Chad. "He *was* with my brother. I'm sure of it."

Chad lowered his head confidentially. "Listen, Mag, I know you're right, but that guy wasn't going to give you the time of day. I figure we'll just keep our distance and keep our eye on him. See where he goes. Maybe he'll lead us to Jon Knowl."

Maggie gave Chad a spontaneous hug. "You always know what to do. Thanks."

"Let's just see if it works."

They strolled along the beach for a few minutes, pretending to watch the lowering sun. When the motley band of young people ambled on down the street, Maggie and Chad followed. They trailed the group for two blocks to a sprawling, tumbledown building that could have doubled for an unpainted Indiana barn. A sign over the door said, NEW MOON COFFEE HOUSE.

They waited until the youths were inside, then slipped in too. The place was crowded, the lights dim, the sweet, noxious smell of marijuana cigarettes heavy in the close, warm air. Couples were gyrating to a Simon and Garfunkel tune—willowy, long-haired girls in miniskirts or peasant dresses and young men in psychedelic shirts and bell-bottom trousers or rawhide leather jackets, beads, and bandannas. Astrological posters celebrating "The Age of Aquarius" and signs proclaiming "Make Love, Not War" covered the pine walls. Mingled among the posters, theater handbills promoted the Broadway musical *Hair*, and black-and-white photographs showed Indian gurus and potbellied Buddhas.

"Well, Maggie, this isn't Indiana," said Chad with a bemused smile.

"I'm not even sure it's planet Earth," Maggie returned.

They made their way to the back corner and sat down at a small table where incense wafted from an earthenware cruet. They ordered two mocha coffees from a girl in a floral dress with daisies in her straight, waist-length hair. After a while, three young men in leather vests and jeans, their dark hair tied back in ponytails, mounted a makeshift stage and sang a Beatles song. One youth strummed a guitar, another played a sitar, giving the piece a haunting, East Indian sound.

As the crowd applauded and the trio began another tune, a gaunt, bearded, fiery-eyed man sat down beside Chad and held out a closed hand. "You looking for something to make you feel good, mister?" he whispered in a slow, drawling voice. "Listen, man, I got plenty of Mexican weed. Or maybe you wanna drop acid. How about some orange sunshine? Pure, good quality, I swear. No bad trips. Good price. Real good price. Come on, man. You won't find no better stuff than this."

"No thanks," said Chad. "We're not into that."

The rangy man stood up, his footing unsteady, and leaned over close to Maggie. She caught his ripe, pungent smell and turned her head away. "Next time the price goes up, missy. Tell your boyfriend the next time you wanna get stoned, it'll cost you plenty. Don't say I didn't warn you."

"I said, we're not interested," said Chad firmly.

The unkempt man gave Chad the peace sign, then stumbled over to the next table and began his pitch again. Maggie clasped Chad's arm. "I'm ready to go."

Chad glanced around the darkened room. "Looks like our friends have already split."

Maggie looked over at their empty table and sighed her disappointment. "That druggie distracted us, and now our only chance of finding my brother is gone."

"Not necessarily," said Chad. "We know this guy knows Jon Knowl, and this part of town looks like his turf, so I'm betting your brother isn't far away. We'll just come back tomorrow and keep looking."

"You make it sound so easy," said Maggie as they left the coffee house and headed back down the street toward the beach.

"Not easy, but possible. If we look long enough and hard enough, we've got to find him."

Maggie wound her arm around Chad's. "You don't know what it means to me, having your help like this, having you to lean on."

He patted her hand. "I wouldn't be anywhere else, Maggie." His voice grew solemn. "There's nothing I can do to help my brother in Vietnam—he's missing, maybe dead, maybe we'll never know what happened to him—but I promise I won't give up until we've found *your* brother, if it takes the rest of the summer!"

12

The days melted into one another—Maggie and Chad driving to the beach, this beach, that beach, wandering among beachfront shops, around old, settled neighborhoods, drifting here and there, growing dazed and lethargic under the shimmering summer sun, looking, always looking for that one clue that would lead them to Jon Knowl.

One afternoon they browsed through a tumbledown thrift shop on Ocean Boulevard and traded their conventional Indiana duds for a mishmash of psychedelic hippie garb so they wouldn't stand out like the cultural foreigners they were. Chad was letting his hair grow longer and took to wearing Levi's and leather; Maggie donned peasant dresses and plaited her flowing hair with daisy chains. Now they looked the part of the hippie milieu, blended in with student protesters and activists, and mingled comfortably with the southern California subculture that celebrated the credo, "Drop out, tune in, turn on."

But their efforts proved futile, for after a week they had still found no sign of Jon Knowl or his friend. The only clue they had was the telephone number scrawled on a crumpled piece of paper. Every day Maggie dialed the number, praying someone would answer. Finally someone did. When Maggie asked if Jon Knowl was there, the young man on the other end of the line paused for a long moment before asking suspiciously, "Who wants to know?"

"A friend," said Maggie, her hopes rising. "May I speak to him, please?"

"He ain't here," came the abrupt response.

"When will he be there?" Maggie persisted.

"Don't know, don't care."

"Then I'll try again later."

"Suit yourself."

After hanging up, Maggie gave Chad a bear hug. "He's there, I know he is."

"How do you know?"

"I just know. We're getting close, Chad. Maybe a few more days . . ."

He playfully knuckled her chin. "I hope you're right, Magpie. Summer's going by."

On Sunday afternoon they returned to Santa Monica Beach and walked hand in hand along the water's edge, soaking up the sun, sizing up every passerby. Toward evening they moseyed over to a small cove where a large crowd of young people had gathered. The lilting refrains of a gospel chorus filled the warm, salt-scented air.

"Another hippie enclave," mused Chad.

They joined the periphery of the gathering, where young women in peasant dresses swayed and clapped their hands, and young men in tee shirts and cutoff jeans raised their arms to the music—a robust rhythm with a vigorous beat; a moving, spirited blend of guitar, harmonica, and drum. *Jesus, my Jesus, I bow down my knees to the One who died for me. Jesus, my Jesus, I lift up my voice to the One who rose for me! Hallelujah! Hallelujah!*

Another group of young people stood clustered together in the ocean as a bronzed, long-haired man lowered a woman into the water, said something Maggie couldn't hear—a prayer, a blessing, then lifted her back out. Her companions hugged her and helped her back to shore while the man lowered the next in line into the sparkling green waters.

Maggie nudged Chad. "It's a baptism. Right here in the ocean. Can you believe it?"

Chad grinned. "What better place? Plenty of water and God's heavens overhead."

"I've never seen anything like it. All we had back home was a cramped little baptistry on a snowy winter morning."

Chad feigned a shiver. "I remember."

"Do you suppose it's a cult?" she whispered.

"Probably. Remember, this is southern California."

A tall young man on the fringe of the crowd turned and looked at Maggie with a warm, riveting gaze. He ambled over, his long flaxen hair rippling in the breeze; Maggie tried to look away but couldn't. He was wearing a tank top, frayed jeans, sandals, and a leather headband. His eyes crinkled with merriment. "Hi, I'm Jeff. Have you come to be baptized?"

Maggie cast a sidelong glance at Chad and mumbled, "No. We've been."

"Baptized, she means," finished Chad. "In our church back home."

"Then you know Jesus?"

"Yes, we're Christians," said Maggie, feeling a sliver of defensiveness. She wasn't sure how to take this young hippie with his breezy, confrontational demeanor.

"Well, praise the Lord!" boomed Jeff. "You walk with Jesus. Then you are one of us." He offered Maggie his hand and she clasped it reluctantly. "Welcome, sister." Her hand seemed swallowed up in his. He wasn't a huge man—he was lean and muscular, but not quite as tall as Chad—and yet his presence seemed somehow bigger than life. He would have been unacceptably intimidating were it not for his expansive smile.

He shook Chad's hand too. "Glad to have you join us, brother."

"We didn't exactly . . . we just sort of stumbled onto your group," said Chad. "Are you from some church around here?"

Jeff's smile widened as he held out his arms, palms up. "We are the church. And we meet anywhere, everywhere. Here, between the earth and the sky, surrounded by God's creations."

"But surely you have a church building somewhere?" prompted Maggie.

Jeff's eyes crinkled merrily. "I meant it when I said we meet anywhere, everywhere. Some of us meet in a tent. Others in an old bowling alley. Some in homes, some in abandoned stores or schools or old movie theaters. We go wherever the Spirit of God takes us." He paused and looked toward the ocean as another convert was baptized, then swiveled back to Maggie. "Some people call us Jesus freaks. If that means being sold out to Jesus, that's what we are." He turned to Chad. "If you want to see what we're about, come to our Bible study on Wednesday night. We pray, look into the Word, and share our personal stories. And do we have some stories to tell!"

"We'll think about it," said Chad. "Where are you meeting?"

Jeff pulled a crumpled piece of paper from his jeans pocket and scribbled out an address. "We meet around seven. See you there."

As Chad and Maggie walked back to their car, he said, "What do you think? Are they for real?"

She shrugged. "He sounded kind of far out, but I could see the love of Jesus in his eyes. There's something compelling about him. I say let's go and see what they have to say."

Chad nodded. "Maybe I'll take my camera. It should be an interesting diversion after all these days of combing the streets for your brother without a modicum of success."

Maggie smiled. "Who knows? Maybe these Jesus people will give us something to write home about."

On Wednesday evening, after another discouraging day of false leads and no sign of Jon Knowl, Chad and Maggie debated whether to bother going to the Bible study. But they had nothing else to do and hadn't been to church in weeks, and Maggie was feeling a gnawing in her spirit, a yearning for a touch of God, reassurance that He was still there for her. So, on a lark, they piled into the car and drove to the address the young hippie had given them.

But as Maggie gazed at the menagerie of humanity streaming into a sprawling army surplus tent that occupied a vacant lot in a run-down neighborhood, she almost gave in to her misgivings and asked Chad to drive on. But something in her spirit told her to go inside.

"Well, this should be quite an experience," said Chad as he pulled over to the curb and turned off the engine.

They followed the others into the huge tent and tramped through thick sawdust to a row of rough-hewn benches. There was no stage or pulpit, no organ or choir, just a scruffy group of musicians in tee shirts and jeans playing guitars, harmonicas, and drums. Maggie didn't recognize the tune, a chorus perhaps, surely not a conventional hymn, but everyone sang with remarkable energy, their bodies swaying as they clapped with the beat.

Maggie noticed that she and Chad were the only ones not clapping. "What have we gotten ourselves into?" she whispered. "This isn't like any church service I've ever attended."

Chad grinned. "Come on, Maggie. Let's just go with the flow and have fun with it."

She stole a glance around. Most of the audience were her age or younger—a colorful, motley collection of beach bums and hippies, bikers and flower children, the misfits and mavericks of society. Some wore beads and flowers and leather headbands; others wore no shoes. But there was something in their faces, a glow, a passion, a sense of wonder and excitement that held Maggie spellbound.

When the musicians had finished playing, a bearded man stepped forward from the audience and said, "God spoke to me last night and gave me the words to a song. I'd like to sing it now."

"Go ahead, brother," said one of the guitar players.

Without accompaniment, the man began to sing a simple chorus about Jesus putting him on the right road and turning the darkness to light. He had a smooth, pleasant tenor voice and he sang earnestly, without affectation. Afterward, as he sat back down, everyone applauded and said amen.

Then Jeff, the man they had met at the baptism on the beach, came forward, a large Bible in his hand. He raised the Book high over his head. "Brothers, sisters, for years our generation has wandered around looking for the truth. We've turned on to drugs and tripped out on LSD. We've tried free love and dabbled with Eastern religions, and we've ended up stoned, disillusioned, and suicidal."

He lowered the Bible and pushed his shoulder-length blond hair back with his free hand. His tone softened. "Okay, maybe that wasn't you, but it was me. I spent two years in a hippie commune in San Francisco's Haight Ashbury district. Man, I tried everything—drugs, sex, yoga, higher consciousness-raising stuff. I was looking for some meaning in my life, a reason to keep living. I was looking for truth, whatever truth was.

"One night I went out on a bluff overlooking the ocean. It was a clear, starry night, and I was about to drop enough acid to kill myself. I figured dying was the only way I was ever gonna see the face of God. While I stood there listening to the wind, I started sobbing like a baby. The wind howled, drowning out my cries. And it came to me—these words from somewhere, I don't know where—like a voice in my head, 'The truth shall set you free.' And I thought, *That's what I want. To be free.* Because I wasn't free. I was trapped by my habits. I was going down for the count. The devil had me hooked.

"And I thought, that's what it's all about. Freedom. That's what all of us are striving for. We're yearning to feel free inside. At peace. So all I had to do to be free was to know the truth. But what was this truth that could set me free?"

Jeff held up the Bible again. His hazel eyes flashed fire, and his tanned, sculpted face glistened with perspiration. "I knew those words were from the Bible, so I got myself this Book and started reading it. Started reading about Jesus and what He said and what He did. And I read how He loved us enough to go to the cross and die. And what I saw in this Book wasn't some lofty God just going through the motions. What I saw was this flesh-and-blood Man who was also God Himself, but who let Himself feel all it means to be a man, to be a dying, broken, bleeding, hurting, weeping man. A man who could be so distressed He could sweat great drops of blood. Who could beg God to let this cup pass from Him because He knew the agony it would bring. But he drank it anyway because He loved us so much. He felt the weight of our sins so heavy on Him He cried out to God and said, 'Why have You forsaken Me?' And just when it looked like everything was lost, like the devil had won, Jesus rose from the dead and proved He was God. Fully God. Fully man. And because He loved us so much, He paid the price for our sins, got us out of debt with God, and made us free. You and me."

Jeff paused and with the back of his hand wiped the sweat from his brow. His voice broke with raw, heartfelt emotion. "Who could turn away from love like that?" he asked, looking around from face to face. "Can you? Are you gonna spit in the face of God after what He did for you? Or are you gonna throw yourself at His feet and beg Him to save you?

"That's what I did. He picked me up and put me on the right track, and I tell you, it's a trip, it's a mind-blowing trip. God saved me, the wreck that I was; I was broken and wasted; I didn't need a makeover. I needed to start over, from scratch. And that's what He did. He made me a new person. I was born again with His Spirit inside me, making everything new. And that's what He'll do for you if you just open your heart to Him.

"Brothers, sisters, you can go from one end of the earth to the other, from the pit of hell to the highest heaven, and you won't find greater love than this—the love Jesus gives. It's better than a mother's love. Better than a father's love. It'll clean you up, turn you inside out, make you someone you never dreamed you could be. His love. You're hungering for it. Well, He's the Bread of Life. You're thirsting for it like a man lost in the desert. Well, He's the living water; you'll never thirst again. He's what you've been looking for your whole life long. He's waiting to fill that cold, aching, empty place inside you. He's waiting to gather you into His arms and cradle you like a little lost child. How long are you gonna turn away from love like that? How can you turn away?"

The tent rang with a ponderous, breath-catching silence, the night suddenly so hushed that time might have stood still, the moment frozen in place, time held suspended, no clocks ticking, no chimes pealing, no bells tolling, the world waiting, everyone quiet and waiting. Maggie felt an ache deep in her chest and realized she was on the verge of tears. It seemed the impassioned young man was speaking directly to her, challenging her very faith, her personal commitment to God.

I've been a Christian all my life, she wanted to tell him. *I know these things; I've always known them; I've lived them. You're not telling me anything new.*

Then why didn't she feel a passion for Christ like this man felt? Why didn't she love Jesus with the same sort of fervor and zeal these Christians exhibited? Had she ever felt that way? What had they discovered that she had somehow missed?

In the close, suffocating warmth of the darkened tent, it seemed to Maggie that Jesus Himself stood before her, asking these questions, inquiring in a voice soft as the rustle of leaves, a loving, sorrowful voice that pierced to the very core of her emotions.

Do you love Me, Maggie, as these, my wayward children love Me? How long since such love has flamed in your heart? How long since you opened your heart and let Me shower My love on you?

Maggie closed her eyes, closed out the voice—it wasn't Christ, surely it wasn't. It was only her own imagination. This group, these people were manipulating her emotions, making her feel as if . . . making her feel, stirring up feelings; they had no right! She loved God, knew Him as well as they did, better; she had been trained from childhood, could recite Scripture verses, entire passages, had been raised in the church, said her prayers every day . . . almost every day, whenever she thought of it, even if they didn't get through, even when she wondered who was listening; was anyone there? Did God really care? Even then, she prayed, dutifully, even when she felt no connection, no intimate sharing, but that didn't mean He wasn't there.

God, I've always known You, always loved You. Haven't I?

After nearly three hours of Bible study, prayer, and testimonies, each more horrific and amazing than the one before—tales of God's deliverance from drugs, sex, and every sort of debauchery imaginable—the meeting ended with a string of rousing praise choruses—voices rising, the music swelling with an eager fervency, hands clapping, bodies swaying, bare feet stomping.

Afterward, as Maggie and Chad wended their way through the surging crowd, many people greeted them, offering smiles and handclasps and words of encouragement. "Welcome, brother." "God loves you, sister." "Come worship with us again." "The peace of God go with you."

In the car, on their way back to the motel, Chad looked over at Maggie and said, "So what do you think? Was it what you expected?"

She weighed her words, her opinions mixed, her thoughts still not crystalized, and finally conceded, "It was one of the most memorable evenings of my life."

"Same here," said Chad. "Know what I'd like to do?"

She was afraid to ask.

He rushed on, not waiting for her reply. "I'd like to do a photo story of the Jesus people. The rest of the world needs to know what's happening here. I have a feeling this is going to be big, Maggie. It could be a whole new movement. It could be the answer to all the violence and disenchantment of the whole youth counterculture. Look at what we've seen tonight. Drug addicts and hippies and prostitutes and lawbreakers who've fallen in love with Jesus. He's transformed their lives, Maggie. Do you see what a miracle that is?"

Maggie folded her arms and stared out the window at the road. "It makes being saved in Bible school at age five seem rather tame, like, what can we do to top them spiritually?"

Chad looked over at her. "What God has done for them doesn't negate what He's done for us, Maggie. We're as saved as they are. But I realized tonight I could learn something from them about having a close, personal walk with Christ. I'd like to learn to love Him the way they do."

Maggie lowered her gaze and confessed, "So would I."

"Then why don't we do it, Maggie?"

"Do what?"

"Make it a project. We could do it together. Immerse ourselves in this new Jesus movement. I could take pictures, you could write a story. We could put together an article, maybe even a book. Who knows? Maybe we could even get it published. And while we're at it, maybe we can discover how they've turned on to Jesus with such passion and power."

13

For the next three weeks Maggie and Chad divided their time between looking for Jon Knowl and researching the Jesus people. With camera and notepad in hand, Chad and Maggie followed the so-called "Jesus freaks" around, became part of their group, sang their choruses, attended their services in homes and tents and old roller skating rinks, and joined them as they witnessed of their faith at the beach and throughout the coastal towns of southern California.

At first Maggie considered herself merely an outside observer, an objective reporter, a writer with a fascinating project she had assigned herself. Chad, too, at first viewed the project as a professional opportunity, a chance to let the public know about an intriguing social and religious phenomenon taking place in southern California.

But then something happened, imperceptibly, unexpectedly, not just in their outward circumstances, but in their attitudes, their perspective; it was something that struck at the very core of their emotions. As they participated in the praise services, as they joined hands and sang the choruses, as they shared their faith with strangers on the street, as they prayed together in intimate groups far into the night, Chad and Maggie began to change.

One Sunday night late in July, a warm, sultry summer night, following a lengthy prayer service in a tumbledown, turn-of-the-century theater, Chad and Maggie joined Jeff and half a dozen others on the beach, passing out gospel tracts Jeff himself had written. They roamed the beach in pairs—Chad and Maggie together as always—and thrust the tracts into the hand of anyone who wandered by. "Do you know where you'll spend eternity?" they asked each person they met.

Maggie was amazed at how bold she had become—how at first she had been terrified, had cringed at the thought of challenging anyone with the claims of Christ, had nearly retched the first few times—but now the words flowed quickly and easily from her lips. What spurred her on was the responses she had received from several who actually took time to listen, who reacted with surprise and amazement and then excitement, who accepted her invitation to pray to receive Christ into their lives.

The first time she prayed with someone—a teenage girl named Theresa just a few years younger than Maggie—Maggie found herself trembling as fiercely as the girl. Would she be able to continue, to say the right words, pray the right prayer without stumbling and making a fool of herself? Somehow she managed, spoke the appropriate words, prayed with the girl, and handed her a New Testament (Jeff always gave converts a New Testament). Bursting with appreciation, the girl hugged her and wept. Maggie nearly collapsed, marveling at what she had just done. Saved a soul for heaven—she, the timid, conservative, impassive Maggie Herrick. What a marvelous, astonishing thing to lead someone gently into the arms of Christ, to see the change in their expression, the sudden vitality in their demeanor, the light of understanding bright in their eyes.

Since praying with that first convert, Maggie found herself thriving on the impassioned, revolutionary lifestyle of the Jesus people. Chad, too, was caught up in their bold, vigorous, passionate approach to Christianity. These new Christians had the same fire and assertiveness that Jordan possessed, the same voracious appetite for life, except that their hunger was for God. Now it seemed at last that she and Chad were breaking out of their self-imposed inhibitions and becoming brave and confident like Jordan, like Jeff. But one question nagged at Maggie. Was it possible that her growing involvement with Jeff and his group had overshadowed her compulsion to find her brother?

But on this starry July night, as Chad and Maggie sat with Jeff on a grassy bluff overlooking the ocean, even that question didn't seem important. She was too caught up in the fragile beauty of the moment and the close camaraderie the three of them shared. Everyone else had drifted off to their homes for the night, but for Maggie this night and all it offered was too perfect to relinquish to a stuffy motel room.

As she sat in the moist grass, Chad on one side, Jeff on the other, making small talk as they watched the moonlight glitter over the surging tide, Maggie felt the moment take on a heady transcendence. With the smell of the sea pungent in her nostrils, she felt a wave of exhilaration ripple through her, energizing her. It struck her that she could do anything, be anything God called her to be. She did not have to be weak and helpless, tossed to and fro by the uncertain tides of life. She had power. In Christ. She could accomplish great things for Him.

"I don't want this night to end," she murmured, plucking a blade of grass. "I feel so good, so on top of things. What's the word? Euphoric. That's it. I feel this wonderful euphoria, as if God is so close, as if He's mapping out everything for us, every hour, every task, just waiting to surprise us tomorrow with more wonderful things."

"He is," said Jeff, sitting back and inhaling deeply. "That's the beauty of walking with Christ. You never know what He's going to do next. But you know He's going to give you His best."

"That's a hard attitude to keep sometimes," said Chad. "I still find it hard to understand why God let my brother be shot down in Vietnam, left him missing in action, maybe dead."

"And why did He let my brother run away from home?" said Maggie.

Jeff gave her a knowing glance. "If you and Chad hadn't come to California looking for your brother, we never would have met."

"You're right," she admitted. "And I wouldn't want to miss this time with you and your friends for anything in the world."

"It's been good," said Chad. "It's going to be hard to leave and go home."

Maggie felt a catch in her throat. "Oh, Chad, I'm almost afraid to go back to Indiana. What if all of this is just a dream? What if we get back home and we're the same people we were before? I don't want to give all this up."

"You'll be going back with the same Savior you came with," said Jeff. "He's just given you a fresh glimpse of Himself."

"Maybe we can stir people up at home," said Chad. "Tell them what's happening out here and get them excited about their faith."

Jeff sat forward, his long hair brushing his shoulders. "Most of us Jesus freaks were druggies stoned out of our minds or hippies playing in the devil's backyard. We needed a powerful touch from God to turn our lives around. Not everyone's going to have such a dramatic encounter with Christ."

"I know," said Maggie, "but until this summer my feelings for God bordered on apathy. Now I feel excited, invigorated. I want to love God the way He commanded—with all my heart, mind, soul, and strength. I've seen His love at work in your praise services, Jeff. I want the people back home to worship God that way."

"They may balk at the long hair, blue jeans, and bare feet," said Jeff with a chuckle.

She smiled. "I may not tell them everything."

"It's a little premature to talk about going home, Maggie," said Chad. "We still have to find Jon Knowl. And right now the trail is stone cold."

"But there's always tomorrow," said Jeff. "I'll be praying for a miracle."

The miracle came the very next afternoon. Maggie and Chad were paying a return visit to the New Moon Coffee House where they had last seen Jon Knowl's friend. Maggie's breath stopped for an instant when she spotted the youth sitting at a table with two other boys who looked vaguely familiar. They, too, could have been with her brother at the Ambassador that night.

Chad and Maggie took a table on the opposite side of the room and watched the youth until he and his friends got up and left. Quietly they followed, keeping their distance. When the boys climbed into an old, dented Chevy and drove off down Ocean Boulevard, Chad and Maggie stayed several car lengths behind. They tailed the vehicle to a small, dilapidated bungalow about four blocks from the ocean.

"What do you think?" said Chad as they watched the youths enter the house. "Should we go knock on the door and ask them if they know Jon Knowl?"

"But what if we're wrong?" asked Maggie. "What if that's not the right house?"

"I have an idea," said Chad. "There's a phone booth at a service station about a block from here. You go call the number your brother left behind and I'll sneak up close to the house and listen for the phone to ring. Call and hang up, then call again, twice, so I'll know it's you. If the phone doesn't ring, we'll know we have the wrong house."

Maggie looked doubtfully at him. "Are you sure? What if they catch you? I don't want you getting hurt."

"I'll be fine," he said, slipping out of the vehicle.

"Be careful, Chad. I'll be back as soon as I can." She slid over to the driver's side as he shut the door. She watched him dash across the street and crouch down as he passed under a window. Fighting a wave of anxiety, she drove directly to the station, made the two calls, hanging up each time someone answered, then drove back to the bungalow, her heart pounding. She prayed Chad was there and everything was okay. Thank God, he was waiting there by the curb. Relief washed over her. She slid over as he climbed in.

"It's the right place, Mag. I heard the phone ring twice. That means Jon Knowl is connected with those guys in there. He was carrying their phone number. I wouldn't be surprised if he's stayed in that very house sometime this summer."

"Oh, Chad, he could be there right now!"

"Could be. There's one way to find out."

"You're not going in!"

"Why not? I say let's both of us march up to that door and ask to see Jon Knowl. Catch them off guard. If we wait, he could slip away again."

With misgivings, Maggie followed Chad out of the car and across the street. "My knees are shaking and I've got a knot in my throat, so you do the talking."

"Will do. Come on," he said as he led her up the sagging steps and rang the bell. "Say a prayer, Magpie!"

"I am," she whispered. "I won't stop until I see my brother."

The door opened, and the young man from the coffee house stared out at them. He was wearing a faded tank top and jeans, his straggly hair hanging past his shoulders. He removed a cigarette from his lips and growled, "Yeah?"

Maggie smelled the pungent stench of marijuana.

"We're here to see Jon Knowl Herrick," said Chad.

"You got the wrong house." He started to shut the door, but Chad held it fast.

"Would you tell Jon Knowl he has company?" said Chad.

The youth's jaw hardened. "I said there ain't nobody here by that name."

"I think there is," countered Chad. "We're not leaving until you tell him we're here."

"He's my brother," said Maggie. "He'll want to see us." She

reached into her handbag and produced a snapshot of Jon Knowl. "Please tell us. Have you seen him?"

The youth tried forcing the door shut again. "I don't want to see no pictures. You two scram before I call the cops."

Chad held the door firm. "Go ahead, buddy. Call the police. They'd like to know you're smoking pot. Last I heard it was still against the law."

With a sneer the youth flicked his cigarette into the grass and glanced at the picture, his expression sullen, inscrutable.

"Have you seen him?" persisted Chad.

"Maybe I have and maybe I haven't."

Chad leaned into the doorway. "So which is it, man? It's not too late for me to call the cops myself."

"Okay, man, so I know the dude. He was a groovy kid, young, wet behind the ears, but a real crusader, out to change the world. I let him stay here for a while, but now he's gone."

"Gone where?" asked Maggie urgently.

"Who knows? Guys come and go all the time. He could be anywhere by now. Santa Barbara . . . San Francisco . . . Seattle."

"What's your best guess?" said Chad. "You help us out and we won't bother you again."

The youth pushed his hair back from his face and leaned against the door jamb, his smoky eyes narrowing. "Okay, man, you got a deal. Here's my best guess. This kid you're looking for—I don't know where he is right now, but in a few weeks he'll be on his way to Chicago, hitchhiking, I'd guess."

"Chicago? Why Chicago?" asked Maggie.

"Everybody's heading for Chicago the end of August. Going to the Democratic National Convention. It's gonna be big, man."

"The convention?" echoed Chad, puzzled.

"Yeah, man. The SDS [Students for a Democratic Society] is planning to protest the war and stir things up good. The whole world will be watching the convention on TV. Every antiwar activist I know is gonna be there to make sure the world hears what we got to say. There'll be riots in the street, you wait and see."

"I don't believe you," said Maggie. "My brother wouldn't be part of a demonstration like that."

The youth's thin lips curled in a sneer. "No? Well, then you don't know your brother, lady. Since Bobby Kennedy took that bullet, your brother knows there's only one way to change this country. We gotta protest, make a whole lot of noise. Stand up to the pigs in Washington."

"You really think Jon Knowl will be at the convention in Chicago?" said Chad.

"He won't wanna be nowhere else." The youth stepped back inside and shoved at the door. "Now scram, you two. I told you what you wanna hear. So get out of here."

Chad and Maggie stepped back as the door slammed in their faces. They retreated from the bungalow and crossed the street to their car. As they drove back to the motel, Maggie said, "Do you believe him, Chad? About Jon Knowl going to Chicago?"

Chad sighed. "I don't see where we have any choice but to believe him. We have no other leads."

"So what now?" she asked in a small, discouraged voice.

"We'll watch the bungalow for a few days on the sly to see if we catch a glimpse of Jon Knowl coming or going. If we don't see any sign of him, we might as well head home to Indiana."

Maggie's muscles tensed. A protest rose in her throat. "Go home? We can't, Chad. How can we leave now?"

"Why not now? What else can we do here?"

She scoured her mind, feeling a wave of desperation. "What about . . . what about our story about Jeff and the Jesus movement?"

"We have enough material. More than we'll ever use. I've taken tons of photos and you've taken tons of notes."

"But it's more than that," she argued, tears starting. "We're not just doing a story, Chad. The story's not what's important anymore. It's what's happened to us. The way our faith has grown because of Jeff and the others. We've become part of them. I don't want to leave what we've found here."

Chad looked at her with a mixture of sympathy and pragmatism. "I agree these past few weeks have been extraordinary, Maggie, but it's time to head back to our real lives. We both have jobs waiting for us . . . and our families."

She brushed at a tear. "I know you're right, but these weeks have been like a dream, a fantasy. I don't want them to end." She didn't add that going home would bring back the bitter reality of her beloved Jordan missing in action. Presumed dead. In her search for Jon Knowl and their involvement with the Jesus people, she had been able to forget her heartache for a few blissful weeks. But going home would bring back all the heart-wrenching pain.

"What about Chicago?" she asked at last.

"The convention?"

"What if Jon Knowl is there?"

"You want to go to Chicago? Is that what you're saying? We could go, Mag. It's just a few hours' drive from Willowbrook."

"Would you take me? The last of August, when the convention starts?"

"Sure, I'll take you, but Chicago's a big city. You think we can just go and find your brother, just like that?"

"We'll go where the convention is. Stay as long as it takes."

Chad heaved a disgruntled sigh. "We can't chase your brother all over the country, Mag."

"Just Chicago. If we don't find him there, we'll give up. I promise."

"I'll hold you to that, Magpie. Meanwhile, I'd better make us some plane reservations home."

"Give us just a few more days, Chad," she begged. "Time to say good-bye to Jeff and the others. And to this city and the ocean and . . ."

"You win, Mag. A few more days in sunny California. Make the best of them. They may have to last you for the rest of your life."

14

During their last day in Los Angeles, Maggie and Chad drove around the city, taking in the sights and tourist attractions they hadn't seen before. He wore a dark blue suit; she wore a pastel green chemise with a long overblouse over a pleated skirt. They drove through Chinatown and bought souvenirs at the Mexican marketplace on Olvera Street. At the La Brea Tar Pits on Wilshire Boulevard, they observed the sticky asphalt beds where prehistoric animals had been trapped and preserved. Toward evening they drove along Hollywood and Sunset Boulevards, noticing amid the bright lights the colorful hippies, stoned potheads, blank-faced homeless, and woebegone vagrants who congregated on street corners and in darkened storefronts.

Maggie's heart went out to them, but there was nothing she could do to alleviate their suffering. In a few hours she would be winging her way home to a world vastly different from this crowded, astonishing metropolis by the sea. She would be going home to Willowbrook without her little brother, making her mission in one sense a failure. But so much had happened, so many good things, that she would never regret making the trip. And she still had hopes—slim at best, of course—of finding Jon Knowl in Chicago.

That evening Maggie and Chad had dinner by candlelight at a cozy, rustic steak house in North Hollywood. Afterward they drove along Mulholland Drive, parking long enough to gaze at the vast panorama of city lights, glittering like a million jewels on black velvet. Then they followed Topanga Canyon Boulevard south to the beach and sat in their rental car for over an hour talking and listening to the radio—to the mellow sounds of the Beatles and the Beach Boys—and savoring the warm, starry night.

Chad slipped his arm loosely around Maggie's shoulder and put his head back on the seat. His voice was soft, lilting. "It's been a great day, hasn't it, Maggie?"

"Wonderful," she said, her voice hardly more than a whisper. She was afraid to move, afraid almost to breathe. She was too aware of Chad's closeness, the warmth of his solid arm around her, the tangy fragrance of his aftershave filling her nostrils. Suddenly what she was feeling, what she sensed he was feeling didn't feel like mere friendship; it felt like something more, much more. Frightening. Unexpected. Something she wasn't sure she could handle.

He shifted and looked at her, his handsome face sculpted by lights and shadows. "Being here like this, Maggie," he said softly, "it seems like we're the only two people in the world. Do you feel that way too?"

She forced her voice to remain calm. "It must be this place, Chad. This city. The ocean. It's like magic. It has us both spellbound, caught up in the romance of it all."

"I don't know, Maggie. I think it's you. You've got me bewitched."

She was trembling now, but not from the cold. "Chad, you shouldn't say . . ."

"Shouldn't say what, Maggie?" He drew closer and moved his fingertips lightly over her chin to her mouth. "Are you saying I shouldn't say I've wanted to do this nearly forever?" Before she could utter a word of protest, his lips came down firmly on hers, warm, tender, insistent. For several moments she resisted, but then something happened. She found herself returning his kiss with a sweet, passionate abandon that astonished her.

Chad was the first to break off the kiss, leaving her weak, breathless, her head spinning. "I'm sorry, Maggie," he said huskily. "I shouldn't have done that."

"It's okay," she murmured, still trying to process what it meant and how she truly felt. Was she disappointed that he had stopped? Surely not, and yet . . .

"I know you belong to my brother," Chad went on solemnly. "I never should have stepped over the line. Will you forgive me?"

"There's nothing to forgive." How could she forgive what she had wanted as much as he? Had she ever felt such delicious enchantment in Jordan's arms? She honestly couldn't remember.

Chad released her and moved over. He gripped the steering wheel with both hands and kept his gaze focused outside the window. He spoke over a heavy knot of emotion. "Listen, Maggie, we've got to forget this happened, okay? I . . . I would never betray my brother . . . and I know you wouldn't either."

"No, I wouldn't," she managed.

He rushed on, the words coming pell-mell. "So no matter how we feel, Maggie—and I'm not even asking how you feel about me; I don't want to know. And I won't burden you with how I feel about you, how I've always felt. It wouldn't be fair. We're friends, and that's all it is, all it can ever be. So, if you're willing, we won't mention this again." He looked miserably at her. "That is what you want, right, Magpie?"

She twisted her hands in her lap, her gaze lowered, her heart pounding with indecision. What could she say? She honestly didn't know what she wanted. She loved Jordan, surely she did, but he had disappeared from her life and might never return. And Chad, whom she'd always adored, was here beside her, his kisses so warm and inviting. Was she being fickle, selfishly wanting the boy who was near because his brother was too far away . . . and might never come home?

"It's okay, Maggie. You don't have to answer. I wouldn't blame you if you never spoke to me again." Chad started the car and pulled back onto the street. "Tomorrow we'll be on an airplane heading home, and we'll both forget this night ever happened."

But would they? How could they forget when everything had changed between them? How could they ever go back to being merely friends when Chad had stirred emotions she had never expected to feel for him? Did he love her, or was he simply expressing the remnants of a childhood crush? Did she love him, or was she in her grief transferring her yearnings for Jordan to the person most like him?

These questions nagged Maggie's mind and were still simmering at the back of her consciousness the next morning as they boarded their plane in Los Angeles, and as they flew to Chicago and boarded a train for Willowbrook.

The questions ebbed away into the shadows of her mind only after they pulled into the rustic Willowbrook depot and she spotted her parents and Chad's waiting on the platform. The next few hours were a pastel blur of hugs and tearful greetings, of excited conversations and nostalgic reflections as the two families gathered at Maggie's home for a huge roast beef dinner with browned potatoes, creamed cauliflower, hot biscuits, and fresh strawberry shortcake with mountains of whipped cream for dessert.

"We would have come home a long time ago if we'd known a feast like this was waiting for us," quipped Chad as he took a second helping of everything.

"Well, young man," said his mother, "now that we've got you home, we're keeping you. No more gallivanting around the country on wild-goose chases."

"Looking for Maggie's brother wasn't a wild-goose chase, Mom," said Chad between mouthfuls. "It was something we had to do. I can't do a thing to help my own brother. I'd give my own life if I could bring Jordan back, but I can't. I hate like the dickens feeling so helpless inside. It gnaws at me, drives me crazy. That's why I've got to help Maggie bring her brother back."

"And we deeply appreciate all your efforts, Chad," said Annie. Maggie's mother looked older than Maggie remembered, her hair more streaked with gray, worry lines pinching her eyes. "We know you both did your best. Jon Knowl evidently doesn't want to be found, so, as hard as it is, I suppose we're going to have to accept that fact and trust God to take care of him, wherever he is."

"Just as we must trust God to take care of Jordan, wherever he is," said Chad's father quietly. "And pray to God that he's still alive."

"We all have a lot of praying to do," said Annie. "I believe with all my heart that God will bring both Jordan and Jon Knowl home in His time."

"Chad, dear," his mother broke in with concern, "you said a moment ago you've got to help Maggie bring her brother back. It sounds like you haven't stopped looking for him. I thought you had given up and come home to stay."

Chad and Maggie exchanged furtive glances. "No, Mom," Chad replied at last, with an edge of defensiveness. "Maggie and I have another lead. Chicago. We have good reason to believe Jon Knowl will be joining protesters at the Democratic National Convention at the end of August. Maggie and I intend to be there and look for him."

Chad's father shook his head, his high, shiny forehead furrowed. "That sounds dangerous, Son. I don't think that's wise . . ."

"I agree," said Maggie's father, adjusting his wire-rim glasses on his ruddy, aquiline nose. "If there's going to be trouble in Chicago, I don't want you two getting involved. It's enough that we have to worry about Jon Knowl. We don't want to lose any more of our children."

In spite of their parents' warnings and misgivings, early on Wednesday morning, August 28, Chad and Maggie threw a lunch basket and a few belongings into his automobile and headed for Chicago, a two-hour drive when traffic was light. They arrived in time for the snail-paced noonday traffic heading north along Lake Shore Drive to the heart of the city.

Folk songs by Bob Dylan and Joan Baez played on the car radio until the noon news came on with a crackling noise and then the announcer's smooth voice. "Along with delegates to the Democratic National Convention, our city has seen a dramatic influx of young people gathering to protest the war, many of them members of the Students for a Democratic Society. Some estimate that over ten thousand young activists have flooded our city. Abbie Hoffman and Tom Hayden, the protest organizers and leaders of the antiwar movement, had promised that the demonstration would be peaceful and nonviolent, but since Mayor Daley refused to extend a park permit to allow protesters to march and hold rallies, Chicago has become virtually an armed camp."

The radio announcer paused for a moment, perhaps for effect, then went on in his resonant voice. "In a television interview, Abbie Hoffman declared, 'America is devouring its youth. We'll resist. We will not participate in America's "Children for Breakfast" program.' But Mayor Daley states that he is prepared for any eventuality. Reports have it that the mayor has called out twelve thousand police officers, six thousand Illinois National Guardsmen, and six thousand army troops. And he has ordered barbed-wire fences erected to control access to the convention hall.

"Still, protesters have gathered around Democratic headquarters at the Conrad Hilton Hotel, and several thousand demonstrators are presently holding a peaceful rally at the band shell in Grant Park. With all of the commotion and tension gripping Chicago during this convention, the question of who will be elected seems almost an afterthought."

Chad snapped off the radio. "The reporter mentioned a rally at

Grant Park. Check the map, Maggie. I think it's just a few blocks from here."

She studied the map. "You're right, Chad. Take Balbo Drive to Columbus and head south. That's just where Jon Knowl would be."

As they drove through the lush, sprawling park, Maggie spotted the shiny white band shell in the distance. But the crowds were immense. There was no way they could even get close.

"We'll park and walk," said Chad, pulling over to the curb. It was the only parking space in sight. As they struck out across the grassy park, he said, "Hope you're wearing your walking shoes."

"Don't worry. I came prepared—for hiking as well as the heat." Besides her tennis shoes, she was wearing a sleeveless tunic top and her comfortable jeans. Chad wore a casual shirt and slacks. But as they began mingling with the raucous crowd, Maggie realized that nothing could have prepared her for the hot weather or the hot tempers.

Young men in tee shirts and jeans, with stringy hair and unkempt beards, waved signs that read, END THE WAR! and STOP THE KILLING! Students in Nehru jackets and love beads waved their arms and made peace signs and chanted against the "pigs." Girls in flowered dresses, with wild, frizzy hair tied with leather headbands, swayed and sang Grateful Dead lyrics. Some girls were barefoot and braless. Others wore peacoats or jean jackets or psychedelic shirts and bell-bottoms. Some of the boys had short haircuts and were dressed in army fatigues; they looked as if they had just returned from Vietnam.

As she and Chad were jostled and pushed by these warm, sweating, agitated tides of humanity, Maggie had no choice but to move with the flow, to let them carry her where they would. Chad stayed close beside her, his hand firmly on her arm. As they were swept along, Maggie desperately scanned every face, praying that by a miracle of God she would find Jon Knowl amid this noisy mayhem and madness. But, to her growing disappointment, every face was a stranger's face.

Amid the strident chants and shouts, Chad nudged her and said, "Look. There, beside the band shell. Some jerk has shimmied up the flagpole. He's taking down the American flag."

Shouts of approval rose from the audience, their chants and screams rising to a fever pitch, their bodies gyrating with a drugged frenzy. Chad pulled Maggie against his chest and held her tight to keep her from being shoved beyond his reach.

Within minutes, a new commotion erupted near the perimeter of the crowd. Sirens screamed in the distance. "The police are breaking this thing up," said Chad. "Let's get out of here, Maggie."

She looked up urgently at him, her heart hammering. "Where can we go? We can hardly move!"

Even as she spoke, the crowd began to surge away from the band shell, panic transforming the audience into a stampede. She stumbled, but Chad caught her in his arms and steered her through the shrieking melee.

Somehow they got back to Chad's car. Maggie climbed inside, locked the door, and sank back against the seat as Chad started the engine. "The streets are teeming with protesters and police, Maggie. We may not be able to get out of here."

"Then we'll wait. At least we're safe in the car."

"The students—I heard some of them talking. They're heading for the Hilton. The Democratic campaign headquarters. There'll be more trouble over there."

She looked closely at him. "What are you saying? Do you want to give up and go home?"

"It's up to you, Mag. We can go home and thank our lucky stars we got out of this alive. Or we can just plunge right back into the craziness and pray to God we find your brother in time."

"In time?" she echoed warily. "Chad, what's going to happen?"

"Look down the street. Heading for Michigan Avenue. A whole line of jeeps filled with military police. It's going to be war around here tonight, Maggie, and I don't want you in the middle of it."

A sob rose in her throat. "But Jon Knowl could be here. In that very crowd. He could get hurt. You know how he is. He's so hot-headed, he'll get right in the middle of the fray. He could be killed, Chad. I can't leave, knowing we're this close."

"Then we've got to be careful. Let's stay on the fringes, so we can get away if we have to."

"I'll be careful, Chad. I promise. But we've got to keep looking."

"Then we'd better leave the car here and follow the crowd over to Michigan Avenue. Let's say a prayer first, okay?" They bowed their heads, and he held her hand as he asked God to give them all His protection tonight and to lead them to Jon Knowl.

"Now, whatever happens tonight is in God's hands," said Chad solemnly. "Let's go."

"Are we crazy, Chad?" she asked in a hushed voice.

"Probably."

Linking hands, they joined the protesters surging across Grant Park to Michigan Avenue where the spacious Hilton Hotel overlooked the park. As they approached the hotel, Maggie heard several youths beside her talking. "Can you believe it, man? The Democrats voted down the peace platform this afternoon! They gotta have straw for brains!"

"They don't have no brains," said another, a lanky youth in a leather vest and stovepipe pants. "They're cowards, plain and simple. How could they do it? The Vietnam plank—gone, just like that. Don't matter now who wins the election. The war's gonna go on forever."

The throng of demonstrators surrounding the hotel was so vast that Chad and Maggie couldn't get close. Several girls handed out antiwar pamphlets to the crowd, while two men in soldier garb waved an enormous banner urging, GET US OUT OF VIETNAM NOW! Television cameramen and reporters mingled with the crowd, the glare of their TV lights illuminating the throng with an eerie, bluish glow. Students linked arms and marched in front of the hotel between Michigan Avenue and Grant Park, chanting something Maggie couldn't decipher.

As the mob pressed in on her, the heat of so many bodies suffocating her, the drenching humidity oppressive as a blanket, the stench of marijuana turning her stomach, Maggie began feeling light-headed, dizzy. Every face looked like Jon Knowl's face, but why were the faces spinning, blurring, going round and round? She swooned against Chad, her ankles like jelly. He caught her, held her in his arms, gently slapped her cheek. "Maggie, you okay? Maggie!" She rallied enough to stand on her own again, but a sensation of weakness and nausea lingered in her belly.

The chanting seemed louder, more intense. "End the war . . . end the war . . . stop the killing!"

Above the chants Maggie heard something even more ominous—the roar of military jeeps and trucks. She could feel the rumble in the earth under her feet. Michigan Avenue was suddenly filled with a steady stream of army jeeps and troop trucks brimming with soldiers, their rifles poised in the air. Military police with helmets and rifles marched beside the jeeps. Behind them, national guardsmen marched shoulder to shoulder up the street. A helmeted military man in the first jeep raised a bullhorn to his lips and ordered everyone to clear the area.

The crowd ignored him and became more agitated. Voices rose, spewing slurs and profanities. Chad gripped Maggie's hand and tried to lead her out of the crowd, but they were wedged in by masses of teeming, shouting, angry humanity.

Suddenly, as the militia converged on the crowd, the entire landscape exploded with hysteria and pandemonium. Screams and shrieks pierced the night as protesters and police raged, battling one another like enemies at war. Officers burst through the horde, brandishing billy clubs, striking anyone who confronted them. As television cameras rolled, they clubbed demonstrators, reporters, and bystanders with equal ferocity.

Guardsmen advanced, wearing gas masks and looking as if they had just stepped down from Mars. A noxious, blue-gray haze clouded the air, bringing with it the choking stench of tear gas. Maggie gagged and clutched Chad for dear life. Her eyes searing with pain, she gazed around in blind terror and confusion as the wounded fell in blood-spattered heaps on the pavement, in the grass.

One helmeted officer in a short-sleeve blue shirt shoved past Maggie, knocking her to the ground. The crowd crushed in on her, several sidestepping her, others kicking her inadvertently with their boots and sandals, until Chad managed to pull her to her feet. She was trembling, bleeding, weeping, abrasions crisscrossing her forehead, elbows, and legs.

"You're hurt," said Chad, coughing, gagging, thrusting his handkerchief at her to cover her mouth and eyes. "Come on, Mag. Let's get you out of here."

Somehow Chad delivered her to the edge of the frenzied mob, away from the effects of the tear gas. Her eyes still burned and were watering heavily, but she could see and, thank God, she could breathe again.

Parked by the curb was a string of blue and white paddy wagons with CHICAGO POLICE DEPARTMENT printed on their sides. Police officers were arresting bloody, disheveled protesters and herding them into the back of the vehicles, twisting their arms behind their backs as they pushed them through the double doors. A cluster of young people stood off to one side, under police guard, waiting to be marched into the wagons and taken to jail.

Chad gripped Maggie's arm. "Look! Isn't that Jon Knowl?"

She squinted as she scanned the doleful figures, her heart lurching as she spotted the dear, familiar face of her brother. "Dear God in heaven, it's him!" She broke free from Chad and rushed over to the scruffy youth, seizing him by the shoulders, touching his cheeks and chin. "Jon Knowl!" she cried. "It's me, Maggie!"

He stared at her with glazed, unfocused eyes, his expression blank, oblivious to the world around him.

"Jon Knowl," she cried, "what's wrong?"

"Death to the pigs," he muttered vaguely, gazing past her.

"No, it can't be! He's on drugs," Maggie told Chad. "LSD or something. He doesn't recognize me. He doesn't even know where he is."

A police officer in a blue shirt and white helmet lumbered over and grasped Jon Knowl's shoulder with a beefy hand. "Come on, kid. You're next."

"Wait," cried Maggie, clinging to her brother's arm. "Where are you taking him?"

"Jail, lady. Booking him for disturbing the peace, like the rest of these rascals."

She held firm to Jon Knowl's arm. He was wearing a shabby denim jacket, jeans, and combat boots, a red bandanna tied around his thick, uncombed hair. He stood unmoving, impassive, expressionless. "He's only a boy," she pleaded. "Just sixteen. He's my brother. Please let me take him home."

The officer stared sullenly at her for a long moment, his heavy jaw grinding as if he were chewing something. Finally his steel gray eyes narrowed, and he made a snorting sound. "All right, lady, you win. But get him out of here now, or I'll arrest you both!"

Chad put his arm around Jon Knowl's shoulder. "Come on, buddy. Let's go home."

Jon Knowl held his ground, a haunted, faraway look in his hazel eyes that chilled Maggie. "Stop the killing," he mumbled in a sluggish monotone. "End the war . . ."

"Get him out of here," demanded the officer, "before I change my mind and book the lot of ya!"

Maggie and Chad each took an arm and led a reluctant Jon Knowl through the whistling, jeering, chanting crowd, wending their way past the jeeps and soldiers that lined Michigan Avenue and surrounded Grant Park. Somehow they got him to the car and urged him into the backseat where he collapsed into a drugged sleep.

All the way home, Maggie's eyes burned and she tasted the odious tear gas at the back of her throat. Her bruised arms and legs ached to her very bones. But in the rolling, humming silence of the automobile, her mind trumpeted the same terrifying questions over and over: Had they found her brother in time? Had they truly rescued him from harm? Was he still the tender, gregarious, fun-loving brother she remembered? Or was she taking home a broken, empty shell?

15

Jon Knowl's homecoming was bittersweet. Maggie's parents were overjoyed to have their son home again, but they quickly realized he was no longer the person they knew and loved. He had changed in every way. His healthy good looks had given way to a pale gauntness in his face and a wild, tormented expression in his once-clear hazel eyes. His clothes were bedraggled, his hair long and unwashed. His keen mind and gregarious personality were lost in a drugged stupor.

His first night home was pure torture for everyone. Sometime after 2:00 A.M. Maggie heard a bloodcurdling shriek followed by a crashing sound from Jon Knowl's room. She ran down the hall, meeting her frightened parents in his doorway. As her father flipped on the light switch, the room was flooded with a stark, eye-blinding light that captured Jon Knowl in a gesture so shocking Maggie thought at first she must be dreaming. Jon Knowl had pulled the drapes down from the window, and a linen panel of goldenrod yellow was twisted around his torso. The overhead light caught him climbing the maple highboy, a bare foot in one open drawer, a knee in another, as if he were scaling a mountain.

"Jon Knowl, get down from there," commanded their father in a brittle, shaken voice.

Jon Knowl, his eyes wide as saucers, his pupils mere pinpoints of black, leapt back from the dresser and tumbled noisily to the floor. He scrambled onto his knees and crawled to the corner of the room, where he crouched like a wild animal, covering his face with his arms.

Annie ran to her son and tried to embrace him, but he made a low, guttural growl and swatted her away. She rushed into her husband's arms, gasping, appalled. He held her for a moment, then said, "Go call the doctor, Annie. Call an ambulance. Our boy needs help."

Staring in bafflement at her cowering brother, Maggie felt a momentary stab of guilt. She had brought Jon Knowl home like this—a shattered, twisted shadow of the boy she loved. Now his afflictions would change her entire family. Their grief would be immeasurable. Maybe it would have been better if she had never found him.

She had to try to help, so she stepped forward cautiously and gently touched her brother's head. "It's okay, Jon Knowl. You're home now. Everything's going to be okay."

He seized her wrist and stared up at her, his face contorted, his eyes fierce and defiant. "Don't let them get me," he said in a tight, raw voice.

"Who?" she asked helplessly.

"The faces. They keep coming. Laughing at me. Snapping their jaws like wolves, their fangs like knives."

She freed her hand and ruffled his tousled hair; it was damp with perspiration. "You must have been dreaming, Jon-Jon."

"No, they're real," he whimpered, his eyes glazing with tears. He rushed on, his voice urgent, breathy, like an excited child's. "Real faces, Maggie. They're real. They laugh and growl and snap at me. Then they melt. They fall away in clumps, like ice melting in the sun; they slide down, the skin running like warm ice cream, the eyes tumbling out like grapes. Then they come back and it starts all over again."

Maggie got down on her knees and wrapped her arms around her brother and held his head against her chest. "It'll be okay, Jon-Jon," she whispered. "I won't let the faces hurt you."

The next morning an ambulance came and took Jon Knowl away and delivered him to the psychiatric ward at Willowbrook Hospital. Half a dozen doctors examined him, and they all agreed that Jon Knowl was suffering the results of a bad batch of LSD. They had no idea how long his hallucinations would last or if he would ever return to his normal self. It was possible, they conceded, that he had lost his mind forever.

Chad and Maggie and her parents visited him every day at the hospital, taking him books and playing his favorite records. Maggie and Chad took turns reading to him—the Bible, the newspaper, even the textbooks he would have been studying, had he returned to his junior year of high school.

But Jon Knowl remained impassive, lethargic, remote, refusing to speak, refusing even to acknowledge their presence. He lay staring at the wall, refusing to eat, accepting only sips of water from a straw, so within a couple of days his physician inserted an IV to provide nourishment.

Just when Maggie began to think her family would spend the rest of their lives visiting her comatose brother in the psychiatric ward, an amazing thing happened. One day when she entered his hospital room, she found him sitting up in bed drawing cartoons with a black crayon on a paper napkin. "Get me some paper, will you, Maggie? Sketch paper? And pencils? I feel like drawing."

After that Jon Knowl seemed nearly his old self. Every day he became stronger, his mind clearer, his personality reflecting the winsome boy they feared they had lost. After two weeks he was released from the hospital and returned to school, studying on weekends with Chad to make up the work he had missed. He made weekly visits to the doctor for treatment of his addiction; he wasn't out of the woods yet. Twice after being released from the hospital, he suffered flashbacks from the LSD, but they were short-lived and relatively mild compared with the episode that had landed him in the hospital.

The second week of September, Chad began his official position as a photojournalist for the *Willowbrook News*. At about the same time, Maggie started working as an editorial assistant for Herrick House, her father's publishing company. It seemed strange that after the closeness they had shared all summer, she and Chad were now heading off in different directions, both professionally and personally.

Sometimes days passed before they saw each other, and even then it was likely that Chad had come to tutor Jon Knowl rather than to see Maggie. She was amazed to realize how empty her life seemed now without Chad, how often she found herself wondering what he was doing or when she would see him again. But more likely it was really Jordan she missed. Somehow in her grief, she had allowed Chad to fill that empty place in her heart for a few magical weeks over the summer.

As the vibrant, colorful autumn of 1968 drifted toward a dreary, bone-chilling winter, Maggie found her life settling into a predictable, if not unpleasant, sameness. Her life was divided between work, home, and church, and each day seemed somehow a repetition of the day before. She liked her work at the publishing house and found satisfaction teaching a children's Sunday school class and singing in the choir. She felt safe and secure being back in her beloved house on Honeysuckle Lane with those she adored, especially after her curious, precarious summer.

On November 5, Richard M. Nixon was elected president of the United States, with Spiro T. Agnew as his vice president, thus defeating his Democratic opponent, Vice President Hubert H. Humphrey and Humphrey's running mate, Senator Edmund S. Muskie. The election seemed almost anticlimactic after the turbulent days that had preceded it.

Most folks Maggie knew showed little excitement or enthusiasm over the election results. Maybe after all the divisiveness across the land, they were afraid to be overly optimistic. Still, they hoped against hope that the country would somehow regain its moral and political moorings and be at peace. But that looked unlikely. The day after the election, dissident students at San Francisco State College initiated a strike, calling for campus reform. The mood of protest and alienation was still strong across the country.

Maggie knew that best of anyone. At times her brother embodied that spirit of seething, inward anger and disenchantment. Jon Knowl, who had championed Robert Kennedy so fervently, said nothing about the candidates or the election; in fact, he said little about anything these days. Although he had seemed like his old self after his release from the hospital, after the election he ebbed into a morass of depression.

Had the election brought home the horrifying reality of what he had experienced that night outside the Ambassador Hotel? He had been virtually just outside the door when his hero was slain and his dreams shattered. Even an older, more stalwart person would have been shaken. Maggie herself still had nightmares about it.

So it wasn't surprising that Jon Knowl had moments of normalcy followed by periods during which he drifted aimlessly through the day like a sleepwalker, a zombie. During those times he seemed to curl in on himself; he showed no emotion, no interest in anything or anyone, no enthusiasm for life or the future.

The only glimmer of hope Maggie saw for Jon Knowl was Chad. The only times Maggie saw a light of anticipation in her brother's eyes was when Chad came over to tutor him. Their sessions always turned out to be half work, half play. After they had cracked the books and Chad was assured Jon Knowl knew his stuff, their hours together metamorphosed into fun and games. The two would rough-house together in Jon Knowl's room like a couple of mischievous youngsters, wrestling and shadowboxing and making such a racket that eventually Grandmother Anna would bustle up the stairs and demand to know what was going on.

Minutes later, she would descend the stairs shaking her head and would tell Maggie, "I don't know what gets into those two boys. That Chad Barrett is a grown man. He should know better than to be so rambunctious in the house."

"It's good for Jon Knowl," Maggie always reminded her. "It's the only time Jon Knowl acts like a normal kid again."

"I suppose you're right, Margaret," her grandmother would say with a sly smile that showed she secretly agreed. "But I just wish they would take it outside if they want to behave like little monkeys. They have the whole outdoors to tussle around in."

One snowy Saturday in mid-December, after Chad had tutored Jon Knowl and the two had finished their session with a snowball fight in the backyard, Maggie invited a wet and weary Chad to stay for dinner. He refused at first, displaying his wet flannel shirt, but he accepted eagerly after Maggie took him to Jon Knowl's room and gave him one of her brother's shirts to wear. "Does it fit?" she asked, noticing that the sleeves were a little short.

"No, this is great, Mag," he said, working with the buttons. "I'm warm as toast. So after dinner you and I will have to go outside and have our own snowball fight."

She sat down on Jon Knowl's bed and smiled tolerantly. "No, thanks. I'll leave the clowning and cavorting to you boys."

Unexpectedly he grabbed her hands, pulled her up, and swung her around playfully. "Come on, Magpie. You're too serious. Have a little fun. Remember our good times last summer in California?"

She felt breathless as she sank back on the bed. Was it from being swung around suddenly or because Chad was still holding her hand as he sat down beside her? "California seems like another lifetime," she murmured. "Did it really happen? Was that us?"

He moved closer to her. "You bet. It changed our lives, Maggie. Changed mine anyway. Jeff, the Jesus people, their passion and zeal. Sometimes when I sit down and look at all the photographs I took of them, I wish I were back there, passing out gospel tracts at the beach, worshiping in their sawdust tents."

"So do I, Chad," she admitted. "It hasn't been the same since I got home. I remember how I felt then, but it's like it was all a dream and now I'm back to the person I used to be. I don't want what we found there to slip away."

"Neither do I, Maggie." Tightening his hold on her hand, he gazed deep into her eyes, his face so close, too close, and for a moment she wasn't sure whether he was talking about the Jesus people or the two of them. She gently pulled her hand away. "We'd better go to dinner, Chad, before it gets cold."

"Relax, Magpie. Your grandmother hasn't even called us yet. Besides, it's been ages since we've talked. We pass each other here and there like strangers. We're always surrounded by other people. I miss you, Maggie. I miss the closeness we shared in California."

"I miss it, too, Chad," she said, trying to sound reasonable and detached. "But we're both so busy these days with our work and church and everything. And when you do come over, it's to tutor Jon Knowl . . . which I don't begrudge for a moment. It's wonderful the way you've taken him under your wing and helped him. You're making a difference in his life. He really looks up to you."

Chad sat back on the bed, giving her space. "Well, your brother's coming along, Maggie, but he still has a long way to go. He's still holding on to some of those demons in his life—anger, resentment, bitterness. He hasn't been able to let go and let God have his life."

"But at least he listens to you. He opens up to you. He still won't talk to Mom and Dad, or even me. You're the only one. You've really been a brother to him."

Chad stared down at his hands, rubbing his thumb over his knuckles as if he were trying to rub something away. His voice took on a new resonance. "Jon Knowl is my brother now, Maggie. The only brother I've got. With Jordan gone, I don't have anyone to be a brother to."

"But you'll have Jordan again—" She let her words drop away as she realized she couldn't promise that.

Chad's voice tightened with emotion. "Jordan was my big brother, Mag. He watched out for me, took care of me, kept me honest, kept me straight. Gave me someone to look up to and try to be just like, even though I could never match him in anything we ever did. He always came out the winner. But that was okay, because I expected Jordan to always come out on top. He was the best and everybody knew it, and it made me love him all the more because he still had time for me; he still treated me like he thought I was the best. I knew he loved me with everything he had. So I could be happy for him, you know? Even when he beat me at something, even when he won you, Maggie. I was happy for him, because I loved him that much."

Maggie moved over closer to Chad and rested her hand on his arm. "I know, Chad. We both loved him."

Chad's voice deepened. "So now he's not here for me anymore, he's gone, and I still have all these feelings I've got to give a brother. So who better to give them to than Jon Knowl? If anyone ever needed an older brother, it's him. And I'll be there for him, Maggie, no matter what, I promise."

Maggie moved her palm lightly over his arm, feeling the warmth of his skin coming through the nubby fabric. "I love you for that, Chad. Thank you."

"I love you, too, Maggie," he said softly. The moment hung between them for an eternity, as if time itself had paused and taken notice of his words. Then his face reddened as if he realized what he had said, and he chuckled, a false, mirthless sound. "I mean, if Jon Knowl's my brother, that makes you my sister, right, Magpie?"

She smiled back, a brief, forced smile. During that timeless moment her heart had soared at his words, *I love you, Maggie,* but he had just as quickly snatched them back with his farcical explanation. His sister? She didn't want to be his sister. But then, what did she want?

The answer was simple. She wanted what they both wanted. Jordan back.

"You talk about Jon Knowl being like a brother to you," she began, her words faltering, "and that's fine. I'm glad he has you. But it's as if . . . as if you don't think Jordan is ever coming home. Chad, is that right? Is that how you feel?"

He cupped her slim hand between his palms. They felt warm, sturdy, safe. He met her searching gaze with his own glistening, blue eyes. "Maggie, dear Maggie, I don't want to say anything to destroy your hope . . ."

Her pulse quickened with dread. "You aren't. You won't. Just tell me what you think."

A tear—an actual tear—slipped from the corner of Chad's eye and rolled down his cheek. He ignored it, letting it fall on their cupped hands. "He's dead, Maggie," he said with wrenching anguish. "Jordan's dead."

A shock wave zigzagged through her body. "You don't know that," she shot back defensively. "You haven't heard . . . oh, dear God, have you heard something? Have you got word?"

He squeezed her hand tightly. "No, Maggie, nothing like that. I wish to God we had some word. Knowing anything would be better than knowing nothing at all. My folks are on the phone all the time, calling Washington, the Department of the Navy, the War Department, the Chief of the Armed Forces, the Pentagon. Man, they're calling anybody who might have a clue what's happening over in 'Nam. And writing letters to everybody on God's green earth. But they can't find out a thing. It's like Jordan disappeared off the face of the earth."

Maggie choked back a sob. But she couldn't keep the words, or her emotions, locked away any longer. They poured out of her like a torrent, urgent, unstoppable. "I try not to think about Jordan, I really do. Sometimes I go for hours without thinking of him. Most of the time I pretend he's off somewhere and he'll be back soon. Sometimes I feel like I'm just holding my breath, waiting for news of him."

She fingered the locket, Jordan's locket, that hung under her shirt, against her breast. She rarely wore it out anymore, visible to others; it was too painful a reminder of what she'd lost. "Chad, it's like I haven't been able to breathe since I learned Jordan was missing. I'm in this state of suspended animation or something, my emotions on hold, my whole life on hold, waiting, waiting for things to get back to normal, for someone to come and tell me Jordan is alive and coming home."

"I know, Maggie, I know. We're both waiting, holding our breath, our lives on hold."

"I haven't been able to grieve, Chad," she rushed on, "or cry, because I've been holding it all in, waiting to know for sure." She clutched his hands, the dam of tears finally crumbling, breaking. "But he's not coming home, is he, Chad? He's dead. He's really dead!"

Chad gathered her into his arms and let her sobs heave noisily against his chest. He ran his fingers through her long, flowing hair, damp with her own tears, and massaged the back of her neck. "It'll be okay, Maggie. Don't cry. It'll be okay."

He held her for a long time. She allowed herself to relax in the curve of his arms as her tears subsided. She felt safe in his embrace, his warmth tender and consoling, the way her father's arms had felt when she was a little girl.

Then, shattering the fragile mood, she broke into a spasm of hiccups. They both started laughing; the laughter had a tight, hysterical edge. She gave him a playful push and he pushed her back. She pushed again and he grabbed her wrists and started tickling her. "This will make the hiccups stop, Mag."

"No, don't!" she cried, the hiccups coming louder than ever. He tickled her neck, her ribs, under her arms, the way they had played as children. Her laughter was nearly convulsive. "Stop, Chad! I mean it!"

He stopped tickling her, but he didn't let her go. He was holding her in his arms, bending over her, his face mere inches from hers. "Oh, Maggie," he moaned, his eyes glistening with pain and love. He brought his mouth down hard on her lips. She couldn't breathe. Couldn't move. Couldn't think.

Suddenly, before she quite realized what she was doing, she pushed him away with both hands and sprang off the bed, trembling, breathless. "What are you doing?" she demanded.

He gazed up at her, looking wounded, puzzled. "Kissing you."

"How could you? How could we? What about Jordan?"

"What about him, Maggie? What if he never comes home?"

She couldn't stop shaking, couldn't catch her breath. "He will! He will come home, Chad. I'll wait for him forever, if I have to."

Chad's voice sounded pinched, small. "What about us?"

"There is no us," she cried. "We're friends, Chad, that's all. That's all we can ever be. Don't you know that?"

He stood up and faced her squarely, holding her arms firmly just above the elbow. "I hear what you say, Maggie, but that's not what I felt when I was kissing you. And I know you felt the same thing I was feeling. We love each other, Maggie, whether you admit it or not."

"I never—!"

"When you were with Jordan, I kept my feelings to myself, Maggie, because Jordan always won, always got what he wanted.

All these years since we were kids, I held back, because I knew you belonged to him. And that was okay, because I loved you both, and I wanted you to be happy. But now, Maggie, it's just us. It's been almost a year since Jordan was home. It's time to face the truth and pick up the pieces of our lives."

"No, Chad, I won't give up on Jordan. I can't. You're his brother. How can you give up on him? It's like we're sealing his fate, proclaiming him dead. Don't you see, Chad? It's like we're killing him ourselves!"

Tears shone in Chad's eyes. "Maggie, darling, if there was one chance in heaven Jordan was still alive, I wouldn't be saying these things to you. But he's gone. It's been nearly a year and not a word. Not a single word. We've got to accept it, or we'll both be miserable for the rest of our lives."

"I can't, Chad. Don't ask me—"

The door opened suddenly. Jon Knowl burst in and stared at the two of them in surprise. "What are you guys doing in my room?"

Maggie brushed away her tears and tried to find her voice. "I was getting Chad a shirt. His got wet in the snowball fight."

"Yeah, buddy, you beat me good. Got me drenched." Looking a bit sheepish, Chad ran his fingers through his hair and straightened the collar on his borrowed shirt. "Thanks for the shirt. I'll get it back to you real soon."

"Don't bother," said Jon Knowl. "I got more shirts than I know what to do with." He looked back at Maggie. "Hey, Sis, Grams has been calling you two for about ten minutes. Dinner is ready."

"Are Mom and Dad here?" she asked, trying to force some normalcy into her voice.

"Yeah, they just got home. Mom had a book signing in Fort Wayne. Dad drove her. The way they're laughing, they must have sold a ton of books."

Maggie glanced in the bureau mirror to see if her mascara had smeared. It had. She grabbed a tissue and wiped the smudge marks from under her eyes. "Tell everyone we'll be right down."

After Jon Knowl left, Chad caught Maggie's elbow as she headed for the door. "Maggie, wait. Listen."

She gave him a guarded look. "What is it, Chad?"

"I'm sorry."

"For what?"

"For everything. For what I said. For what just happened between us. I'm not sorry about the kiss, but I apologize if I was out of line. I promise never to push myself on you again."

She shook her head. "I'm not angry with you, Chad. It's just . . . I don't know . . . I can't explain how I feel."

He managed an uneven grin. "Well, I'm glad you're not mad. I wouldn't jeopardize our friendship for the world." He gently lifted her chin. "We're still friends, aren't we?"

She relaxed a little and allowed a smile to escape. "Of course we're friends, Chad. Nothing will ever change that." But even as she said the words, a nagging doubt crept in. Things *had* changed between them. Tonight they had said too much and felt too much to go back to being just friends. She couldn't deny the spark of yearning Chad had stirred in her. And yet she had pledged her love to Jordan. Could she ever resolve the conflicting emotions these two brothers kindled in her heart?

16

Everyone was already seated around the linen-draped table when Maggie and Chad entered the dining room. Grandmother Anna was serving her delicious Waldorf salad and chicken and dumplings while Maggie's parents chatted eagerly about the success of the autograph party in Fort Wayne. When everybody was seated, Maggie's father waited for everyone to join hands; then he asked the blessing on the food in his warm, sonorous voice.

While they ate, the topic returned to Annie's book signing. "It was one of the most successful I've had," she said, beaming. Maggie loved the way her mother's face lit up when she talked about her books. "Autograph sessions can be very painful," Annie went on as she spooned up a dumpling. "Sometimes no one comes near and you sit there praying someone will come over and buy your book. But this session was an author's dream. People were lined up from one end of the bookstore to the other."

"It helped that the local newspaper did a wonderful story on your mother," said Knowl. "Front page. Acclaimed author in town. Great copy."

"Is that really what it said?" asked Maggie, pleased. "Acclaimed author?"

"The very words, Margaret, dear," said her mother, chuckling. "I told your dad I'd get a swelled head if I believed all those press releases."

"But it's true, Mrs. Herrick," said Chad, passing Maggie the salad. "You are a famous author. Lots of people think so."

Annie smiled warmly at Maggie and Jon Knowl. "Thank you, Chad, but I'm content just to be well-received in my own home."

"You know, Mrs. Herrick," Chad went on brightly, "your daughter's going to be a famous writer someday too."

Maggie nudged Chad's arm. "Oh, Chad, I am not."

"Sure you are, Maggie. What about the book we're going to do together? I bet you it'll be on the best-seller list someday."

Her father's brows arched quizzically. "You two are going to write a book together? What about?"

"Tell them, Maggie," urged Chad, his mirthful eyes challenging her.

She hesitated. She wasn't ready yet to share her ideas and excitement about the Jesus movement. What if her parents thought she was crazy? Would it dampen her enthusiasm if they didn't approve?

"We're waiting, Margaret," said her mother with a bemused smile. "It must be a wonderful idea for you and Chad to want to do a book together."

"Actually, Maggie will do the writing," said Chad. "I'll provide the photographs."

"Now we are curious," said her father. "Tell us, honey."

To her dismay, she had a hard time getting the words out about why she believed the world needed to hear about the Jesus people. Falteringly she told them how she and Chad had become involved with the group and what a difference their worship style had made in her own life. "I know they sound radical and strange," she concluded, feeling as if she herself were somehow on trial, "but I believe the Jesus people are going to revolutionize the way a lot of people worship God."

Maggie could see by her parents' dubious expressions that they weren't pleased with her idea. In fact, they were obviously displeased.

"Margaret, darling," said her mother with a hint of disapproval, "this Jesus movement, it's not a church, is it? Isn't it some sort of cult?"

"No, Mom. They believe the same gospel we believe."

"Well, this Jesus movement might be fine for hippies and reformed drug addicts in California," said her mother, "but I can't see how you can think their approach to worship would benefit churches like ours here in the Midwest."

"If you brought drums and guitars into our churches," said her father soberly, "you'd have half the congregation walking out, convinced you had sold out to the devil."

"But it's not like that," protested Maggie, on the verge of tears. "Mom, Dad, you'd have to be there to understand."

Her mother blotted her lips with her napkin. "I think it would be a mistake, Margaret, for you to write a book encouraging churches to embrace such a group."

"I think these Jesus people sound cool," said Jon Knowl, who until now had remained silent. "They sound far out. I'd go hear them."

"So would I," said Grandmother Anna. "The church could use a little shaking up once in a while to get folks out of their rut."

"The church doesn't need to be infiltrated by a bunch of barefoot, guitar-strumming hippies," said Knowl. "Next thing you know, they'll get rid of the pipe organ and the choir."

"Mr. Herrick, even though they're different from us," said Chad, "Maggie and I think these people have a lot to offer the Christian community. We think they could be the wave of the future. Sure, they'll stir up some controversy, and they're going to need older, more experienced Christians to teach them correct doctrine and theology, but they sure know how to love and worship God."

"Chad's right, Dad," said Maggie. "I never knew what it felt like to fall in love with Jesus until I worshiped with these people. In our church here at home, sometimes I feel like I'm just going through the motions, doing things just because that's the way we've always done them. But it's as if my emotions are dead or in a deep sleep."

"Whose fault is that, Margaret?"

"Nobody's fault, Dad." A painful lump swelled in Maggie's throat. She would never be able to make them understand. "Wait until you read Maggie's book," said Chad. "Then you'll get the idea."

"No one will publish a book like that," said her father.

She stared at him, her heart aching with disappointment. "Oh, Daddy, I was hoping Herrick House might consider—"

"Publishing a book promoting these hippie Christians?" challenged her mother. "Oh, Maggie, no. We couldn't possibly."

Chad spoke up, his voice unexpectedly forceful. "Shouldn't you wait until you read the book to make that decision, Mrs. Herrick?"

Annie's expression softened. "You're right, Chad. I'm sorry, Margaret. Your father and I shouldn't criticize your book before it's even written. We . . . we look forward to reading the final manuscript, don't we, dear?"

Her father nodded, tight-lipped, his brown eyes showing resistance. "We'll give you a fair and impartial reading just as we try to do with all our authors, sweetheart."

Maggie managed a smile. "Thanks, Daddy. That's all I ask."

After dinner, as Maggie walked Chad to the door, he squeezed her hand and said, "Don't be discouraged, little Magpie. You write that book just the way you imagined it. Think of your parents as the readers you're targeting. If you can win them over, you'll win the rest of the world as well."

The very next day, after church, Maggie began working on her manuscript in earnest, determined to communicate in words the ardor, inspiration, and excitement of those fledgling Christians in the Jesus movement. She would write the book whether or not she had a publisher; it was something she was called to do, had promised herself and God, and she wouldn't rest until the project was finished.

After work on Monday she phoned Chad and asked him to bring

over the photographs he'd taken in California. He arrived with a heaping shoe box full, and together they browsed through the snapshots, some stunning and poignant, others grainy and blurred, but all stirring a bittersweet nostalgia. As they sorted through stacks of glossy black-and-white photos of Jeff and the others, of their sawdust services and their baptisms on the beach, they laughed, reminisced, and talked about how the pictures would fit in with the text Maggie was composing.

"Sometimes I wish we were still back there," she said softly as they examined a picture of Jeff baptizing a convert in the ocean. "I miss what we found there. Why can't we feel the same way here?"

Chad gently squeezed her shoulder. "Maybe we can. Maybe we just haven't tried."

Over the next few weeks Chad and Maggie spent every free moment together working on the book. As Maggie sat at the typewriter composing each new chapter, Chad sat at her desk editing the previous chapter. Then they went through the photographs, determining where each one would go.

They took a break only during the Christmas holidays, since Maggie had rehearsals for the church cantata and the newspaper sent Chad on extra holiday photo shoots. On Christmas Day, after a simple church service, Maggie's family and Chad's gathered at her home for Christmas dinner just as they had the year before. Snow was wafting gently outside as Anna served a sizzling brown turkey and all the trimmings. But this year there was no Jordan, no excitement over his plans to win the war single-handedly, no send-off parties, no welcome-home celebrations. Just a lonely, empty place at the table.

Jordan was still a huge question mark in everyone's mind. As hard as the Barretts had worked to glean even a shred of information about their missing son, they had come up empty-handed. No one had a clue as to his disappearance. His plane had not been found nor his body recovered. He was still out there somewhere, maybe dead, or alive, or wounded. It was anybody's guess. Someone Mr. Barrett talked with in the State Department suggested he hold a memorial service for his son and consider him dead and buried so their family could get on with their lives. "I'll never believe my son is dead," Mr. Barrett fired back. "Not until I see his body with my own eyes!"

But for Maggie Christmas Day was a turning point. Until now she had held out every hope that Jordan would come home someday; she had refused to consider any other option. Surely she would never seriously entertain the thought that he was dead. But now, as she gazed around the festive table and remembered how it felt last year to have Jordan by her side, all the heartbreak rose in her chest in a geyser of anguish. She was about to say something about Jordan, about trusting God that he was okay and would come home again, but she couldn't get the words out. Her voice broke with a sob and the tears flowed. Ashamed of her sudden outburst, she jumped up from the table and ran to her room and flung herself on her bed and wept convulsively.

Within moments there was a knock on her door, and Chad slipped inside and sat down beside her on her bed. He placed a consoling hand on her back and rubbed her shoulders gently. "It'll be okay, Maggie. Cry it out, honey. You'll feel better."

She sat up and allowed him to gather her into his arms. They rocked slightly, her tears wetting his cheek, his neck, his shirt front. "He can't be dead, Chad. I can't let myself believe Jordan's dead."

"Me neither, little Magpie. I'm holding out hope just like you. Jordan's tough. Tougher than either of us. If anybody can survive incredible odds, it's him."

She looked up at him and searched his eyes. "Are we just believing what we want to believe, Chad? Are we fooling ourselves? You've as much as hinted at it before. What if Jordan's already dead?"

With his thumb Chad gently wiped away the tears from under her eyes. "Listen, Maggie, my girl, I know I've had my doubts. I've said things, wondered aloud if my brother was still alive. But, the truth is, if Jordan was dead, don't you think we'd know it? We'd feel it right here in our hearts. Somehow we'd know, right?"

She nodded, fingering the locket that still hung in the hollow of her throat. "You're right, Chad. If he wasn't alive, we'd feel it. We'd know."

"Right, girl. You know the old saying. One for all and all for one. The Three Musketeers, right? I believe our love and our prayers are keeping my brother alive. So we've just got to keep praying and keep him alive in our hearts. And we've got to believe that Jordan will be home with us by next Christmas. Can you believe that, Maggie?"

She managed a faint smile. "If you say so, Chad."

"Say it. Make me believe it," he urged, his eyes twinkling. "Jordan will be home this coming year."

Her smile deepened. "Jordan will be home . . . in 1969, in time to share Christmas with us. I won't stop believing. I promise."

True to their promise, Chad and Maggie, along with their families, the Herricks and the Barretts, ushered in the new year, 1969, with high hopes and deep faith. At the Paris peace talks on January 16, no one missed the bitter irony when United States and North Vietnamese delegates finally agreed on the shape of the table they would be using when the South Vietnamese and the National Liberation Front joined the negotiations. The four parties began their talks two days later, with a multitude of more formidable issues to settle than the shape of a table.

At breakfast one morning in April, Maggie's father read aloud a disquieting statistic. United States combat deaths in Vietnam since January 1, 1961, had reached 33,641, toppling the death count of 33,629 in the Korean War.

In the months that followed, the Vietnam War took more perilous twists and turns in a series of momentous events. On April 24, in the heaviest bombing raid to date, U.S. B-52s dropped three thousand tons of bombs on enemy forces northwest of Saigon near the Cambodian border. On May 14, President Nixon proposed an eight-point Vietnam peace plan that would include the withdrawal of most foreign troops within a year and the establishment of an international body to supervise elections.

On May 20, after a bloody, ten-day battle, Hamburger Hill was captured by American and South Vietnamese troops, but on May 27, the hill was abandoned to the North Vietnamese.

On June 8, President Nixon met on Midway Island with President Nguyen Van Thieu of South Vietnam, and they agreed that by August 31, U.S. troops in Vietnam would be reduced by 25,000. On July 8, the first wave of returnees, 814 men in the Ninth Infantry Division, were brought home. Every day Maggie watched the television newscasts, scanning newsreel footage of soldiers coming home, desperate for a glimpse of Jordan. But while thousands of battle-weary young men were winging their way back to the States, Jordan wasn't one of them.

Maggie tried not to think about Jordan. She threw herself into her work and her writing. By the middle of July, she had finished writing her book. With fear and trepidation she gave it to her parents to read. They, in turn, shared it with Robert Wayne, Maggie's uncle and copublisher of Herrick House.

Two weeks later, Maggie's father rang the editorial department where she was working and invited her to come by his office. He was sitting at his immense mahogany desk, looking solemn and imposing as he riffled through some papers. He was her father, yet she still felt nervous as a cat on a high-tension wire. Her mother was there, too, standing by the window talking with Robert Wayne, a big bear of a man who walked with a limp from an old war injury.

"Sit down, Margaret," said her father with a warm smile.

She took the nearest chair, relieved to be off her wobbly ankles. Her mouth was dry, her heart thundering in her chest. In a few moments she would know whether she was wasting her time trying to be a writer or whether her dream of being published was about to come true.

Her father was still smiling. "Well, Margaret, your manuscript has stirred a great deal of debate here at Herrick House. You realize that from the beginning your mother and I felt this was not a project we would be comfortable with. We know our readership, and we felt this was a subject they would not readily embrace."

Her heart sank. "Then you're saying you're not going to publish it?"

"That's not what I'm saying, Margaret. I want you to appreciate our dilemma—your mother and I, faced with rejecting our own daughter's pet project. And yet we certainly couldn't play favorites. Your book had to stand on its own merits. It had to win the favor of our marketing people as well as our editorial staff."

"Daddy, please, just tell me what you've decided!"

Her mother stepped forward and clasped Maggie's arm. "What your dad is taking his long-winded time to tell you, honey, is that we're going to publish your book!"

Maggie stared in astonishment at her mother, then her father, then Uncle Robert. "You—you are?"

Robert ambled over and shook her hand. "It's a fine piece of literature, Maggie. Beautifully written. Sensitive, poetic, and painfully honest. And you have something extremely important to say, something our readers need to hear." Robert chuckled. "I admit we may be testing their comfort level, but all of us need to be reminded that God entreats us to love Him with all our heart, mind, soul, and strength. And it seems to me that's the essential message of your book. And in spite of our different approaches to worship, I believe that's what this Jesus movement is all about."

"I must confess," said her father, "that Robert cast the deciding vote. Your mother and I felt we couldn't be objective, but, honey, we're very pleased that you're going to be one of our authors."

"We tried to call Chad," said her mother. "We wanted him to be here, too, to hear the news, but he's out on an assignment. We thought you might want to invite him over tonight and tell him the good news yourself."

Maggie beamed. She couldn't stop smiling. "I would. I will. Yes, that would be perfect."

"Chad's photos are exceptional," said Uncle Robert. "They add a wonderful dimension to the work. You two make quite a team."

"Yes, we do," she agreed breathlessly. "We really do!" Maggie had had enough of trying to be properly restrained and professional. With a little exclamation of triumph, she leaped out of her chair, hugged her mother and uncle, then rushed around the desk and threw her arms around her startled father. "Daddy, this is the best day of my life! Thank you! Thank you!"

"Don't thank us, sweetheart. You're the one who convinced us with your fine writing and your worthy message. And, to show you the priority we're giving your book, we're going to do our best to have it on the bookstore shelves by the holidays."

Her father was true to his word. On December 15, 1969, Maggie's hardcover book was shipped to stores across the nation. It was titled, *Inside the Jesus Movement: One Woman's Spiritual Journey,* by Margaret Kate Herrick, with photographs by Chad Barrett. On the cover was Chad's picture of Jeff baptizing a new convert in the Pacific Ocean, surrounded by a group of eager young hippies with their arms raised in praise to God.

On the same day that Maggie's book was released, President Nixon announced that the number of U.S. troops in Vietnam would be cut to 434,000 by April 12, 1970. That would mean 110,000 soldiers returning home since Nixon took office.

Maggie closed her ears to the report. Other girls would be

welcoming home the men they loved, but not Maggie. No matter how many soldiers came home, she still hadn't heard one word about her beloved Jordan. Her heart ached with loneliness. Every day she wondered, *Was she destined to spend her entire life waiting for a man who might never return?*

17

By mid-January of 1970, Maggie's book was number ten on the *New York Times* best-seller list. Sterling reviews appeared in the *New Yorker* and *Atlantic Monthly*. To Maggie's amazement, invitations poured in for guest appearances on local and regional radio and TV shows, and bookstores across the country wanted Chad and Maggie for autograph parties.

The publicist at Herrick House, taken by surprise at the book's popularity, scurried around to set up a brief publicity tour through the Midwest. For two weeks Chad and Maggie drove from town to town, showed up at the local radio or TV station in the morning for a live interview, then headed to the local bookstore for an autograph session after lunch, then appeared at a local church in the evening to relate their experiences with the Jesus people. Congregations everywhere seemed curious about this emerging group of hippie believers that were having such an impact on the Christian community.

Chad and Maggie usually spent their nights while on the road in the home of some church pastor or deacon. Occasionally they stayed at a local motel, taking adjoining rooms. After their speaking engagement they would have a late dinner in the motel coffee shop and linger over dessert, reminiscing about that summer in California that changed their lives. Then Chad would walk Maggie to her room and give her a circumspect kiss on the cheek and tell her he'd see her in the morning for breakfast, to begin their routine all over again.

It was an exhausting two weeks, driving from town to town, then running from place to place, facing the cameras, the microphones, the interviewers, the audiences, the fans. But it was a special time as well, a chance for Maggie and Chad to renew the bond of closeness they had shared in California. They both recognized that a friendship like theirs was not something to take for granted, but a gift to be nurtured and cherished.

Their last night on the road, on their way home from a book signing in Indianapolis, they stopped at a rustic steak and seafood restaurant along the Wabash River just outside of Lafayette. They were seated by a window overlooking the river; their small pine table was covered in red-checkered oilcloth, with a flickering white candle in the middle. A Simon and Garfunkel tune was playing on the jukebox. When the waitress came, Chad ordered Cokes, garden salads, medium-rare steaks, and baked potatoes for the two of them. "And a side of sauteed mushrooms," he added as he smiled at Maggie.

As they ate, Maggie gazed around at the dimly lit room with its unadorned walls and folksy atmosphere and said, "This is the perfect spot for our last evening together, Chad. It's so quaint and cozy."

He gazed at her across the candlelight, the orange flame dancing in his crinkly eyes and giving his perfectly chiseled features a soft, tangerine glow. "What do you mean 'our last evening together'? You make it sound so final, Maggie."

She laughed lightly. "I didn't mean . . . come on, you know what I mean. This is our last night on the road. After tonight we'll be back in our own homes, going to our separate jobs, with hardly a chance to see each other."

"We'll have to make sure that doesn't happen."

"We'll have so much to do, Chad. So much to catch up on. And don't forget the graduation party for Jon Knowl. It's Saturday night."

Chad forked up a juicy pink morsel of steak. "I haven't forgotten. How could I forget? My hair nearly turned gray tutoring that boy. Trying to get him through high school."

"You did a wonderful job, Chad. He wouldn't have made it without your help. And who would have thought he would be graduating a semester early!"

"The way I hear it, he's not letting any grass grow under his feet."

Maggie turned the straw in her Coke glass. "He's going right on to college. Can you imagine? My rebel of a brother, Jon Knowl, a college student?"

"I imagine your parents are happy he's not heading off to some radical university in San Francisco or some other far-off place where he'd get himself in trouble."

"Absolutely. They worried about him for so long. Now they're delighted he's going to a school so close to home. Kent, Ohio. Just a pleasant day's drive away. And everyone says Kent State is a good school. I just hope Jon Knowl settles in and gets serious about his studies. The only trouble is, Chad, he won't have you to spur him on."

"Oh, I'll spur him on all right, via the U.S. mail."

"I'm so glad. I knew you wouldn't give up on him." She paused and looked him in the eyes. "And thank you for not giving up on me, too, Chad."

He smiled. "I'd never give up on you, little Magpie."

"I mean, the way you stuck with me on the book. You wouldn't let me quit, even when my parents were less than enthusiastic, even when we thought it might never be published. You were there for me every step of the way. Without you there wouldn't have been a book, Chad."

"Sure there would have, Maggie. It just would have taken a little longer."

"No, Chad. You made it happen. Do you know what that means to me?" Her voice took on an emotional edge. "All my life I felt inferior around my parents. I felt like a little kid who could never measure up. Think about it, Chad. My mother was a famous author, my father an important publisher. When I was a child I wrote little stories, and I would run to my mother with them and beg her to publish them in a book just like hers. And she would smile and pat me on the head and tell me how cute I was to write these little stories."

Maggie paused to steady her voice. "But I hated it when she said that, because I knew she didn't take me seriously. More than anything in the world I wanted my parents to take me seriously, to believe that I could be a successful writer just like my mother. Now, at last, with this book, I feel I've written something significant and timely. I've created a literary work separate and unique from my parents' accomplishments. I can finally look them in the eye as an equal. Do you have any idea how happy that makes me, Chad?"

He grinned. "I have a pretty good idea from the light in your eyes. You make this whole room glow, Maggie."

Her face flushed with warmth. "It's not me, Chad; it's the candlelight."

"No, Maggie, it's you. Take my word for it."

Maggie lowered her gaze, unsure how to respond. They ate in silence for a few moments, savoring their charbroiled steaks. But their eyes met knowingly as a Beatles song, "Yesterday," began playing. "Reminds me of California," said Chad.

"Me too," Maggie said softly. "I'll always remember our summer of yesterdays. In some ways they were the best days of my life."

"Mine too." Chad set down his silverware and reached across the table for her hand. There was an urgency in his eyes. "Maggie, there's a way we could have those days again."

She looked curiously at him. "How? You mean go back to

California? We can't. We have our jobs. We've taken off enough time with this publicity tour."

His fingers tightened around hers. "That's not what I meant, Maggie. I've been wracking my brain for some easy way to say this, but I can't seem to get the words out."

"What words? What are you—?"

"I love you, Maggie."

She nodded. "I love you, too, Chad. We'll always be best friends."

"No, Maggie, you don't understand." He sat forward, his warm eyes glinting in the flickering candlelight. "What I'm trying to say, Maggie, is . . . I'm in love with you."

Had she heard right? "In love with me?" she stammered.

"Yes, my silly Magpie. The way a man loves a woman. I want to marry you. Say you'll be my wife, Maggie, and we can have those wonderful California summers together for the rest of our lives."

Her mind was reeling. "Chad, surely you don't mean—"

"But I do, Maggie." His voice was warm, insistent. "I've loved you all my life. You know that. And this past year, the way we've worked together on the book, our minds in sync, our hearts sharing the same dream . . . I'll never feel closer to anyone else on this whole green earth, Maggie." His lips curved in a tender smile. "And I know you love me too. I see it in your face, in your eyes. I hear it in your voice, I feel it when we're together, no matter what we're doing. There's a bond between us that nothing can break, a love God put in our hearts. I know He wants us together, Maggie."

She stared incredulously at him. "But what about Jordan?"

Chad's smile faded. "He's never coming back. We both know that."

Tears burned under her lids. "I won't believe it. I can't."

His voice hardened. "Jordan is dead, Maggie. It's time we faced it. Time we got on with our lives."

She clasped the locket at her throat. "I promised him I'd wait."

"Then you'll be a sad, bitter old lady waiting for someone who'll never come. Is that what you want, Maggie?"

"Someday he'll come home and replace this locket with a ring," she said over a rising sob. "He promised."

Chad's voice deepened with emotion. "Some promises can't be kept, Maggie."

Tears streamed down her cheeks. "I'm sorry, Chad. I care about you, I do. Maybe it's genuine love, I don't know. But I can't risk having Jordan come home and finding me married to his brother. I just can't!"

"You won't even take time to think about my proposal?"

"I won't change my mind, Chad. Please understand."

His hold on her hand relaxed as his mouth twisted in disappointment. She could feel a wall of coldness settling between them. "So that's the way it is," he said at last, with a distant, distracted air. He sat back in his chair and drummed his fingers on the tabletop. "Are you ready to go, Mag?"

"Yes, if you are." She gathered her purse while he reached for the bill. But something didn't feel right between them. There was more to be said. She searched his face. "What is it, Chad? I have the feeling you have more to say."

A muscle twitched along his jaw. "I guess I do. I've been wrestling with a decision, Maggie. But tonight you helped me make my choice."

"A decision? What decision?"

His expression remained guarded, his eyes looking past her. "I'm going away, Maggie."

"Away?"

"Yeah. I'll be leaving town."

"But . . . where?"

He met her gaze squarely. "Vietnam."

Maggie recoiled as if she'd been struck hard in the stomach. "Vietnam? No!"

"Looks like I'll be leaving next week."

She covered her mouth with her hands. "But your heart murmur . . . I thought the army turned you down."

"I'm not enlisting."

"But . . . you're going to war?"

"I'm not going as a soldier, Maggie."

"Then what? How?"

He traced a water ring on the oilcloth. "I've been offered a job with the *New York Times*. They saw your book and liked my photos. They're sending me to Vietnam as a foreign correspondent. They want me to capture the war in pictures."

Maggie felt a gag reflex at the back of her throat. "No, Chad, you can't!"

His voice took on a note of bravura. "I can and I will, my little Magpie."

"No, Chad, please!" She was crying now, tears streaming down her cheeks. "I won't let you go. I've already lost one man I love to Vietnam."

He sat forward, his arms crossed on the table, and said confidentially, "I've got to go, Mag. You had something you had to prove to your parents, and you did that when you wrote your book. Well, I've got to prove something to mine too. They see Jordan as the brave one, the hero. I'm just the laid-back guy who always takes the easy way out."

"You are not, Chad. I've never thought of you that way."

"But my dad has. He pinned all his hopes and dreams on Jordan. Now Jordan's gone, and my dad's a broken man. So that means it's up to me now. I can't fight in the war. But I can go and take pictures and write articles so the rest of the world will know what's happening over there. Maybe I can make a difference. And who knows? Maybe I'll even find Jordan while I'm at it."

"You could be killed," she said in a hushed voice.

He chuckled mirthlessly. "I'll do my best to come home in one piece."

She brushed angrily at her tears. "Why are you doing this? To punish me for not marrying you?"

"No, Maggie. I wouldn't do that."

"But you are. That's exactly what you're doing."

"Okay, I admit it would be hard being around you if we can't be together. But, the truth is, I've been wrestling with this offer for weeks now."

"You never told me."

"I didn't want to upset you until I'd made my decision."

"And if I'd said I'd marry you, we wouldn't be having this discussion now, would we? You would have turned down the offer and never told me."

He lowered his gaze. "Maybe, I don't know. You just made it easier for me to make the right decision, Maggie."

Her voice took on an edge of resentment. "And if anything happens to you, I'll carry the guilt with me for the rest of my life."

"No, Maggie. Don't feel bad. If anything, I'm indebted to you. For once I won't feel like a coward taking the easy way out. Maybe I'll even do something to make my dad proud of me."

"He *is* proud. We all are."

"Then why do I always feel like I'm running a distant second to Jordan, even when Jordan's gone? First with my parents, then with you?"

"You're wrestling with your own demons, Chad. Don't blame us."

"Maybe so. Who knows why they do what they do? But I've prayed that God would make it clear what He wants me to do. I can't help it if He showed me . . . through you."

Their conversation faltered after that. What else was there to say? Chad paid the bill, and they returned to his car and drove the rest of the way to Willowbrook in a heavy silence. Maggie felt a dreadful chill in the air, a coldness that ate at her bones and left her shivering. She had never felt so alone, so isolated, so alienated from someone she loved. The breach between them was nearly palpable, enormous; it was a rift that might never heal. One question kept thundering in her mind: *How was she going to get along without Chad, her best friend?*

18

Chad Barrett left for Vietnam on the last day of January 1970, the same day Jon Knowl left for Kent State. But Chad had left Maggie emotionally that night at the steakhouse along the Wabash, when she had refused his marriage proposal. The two had hardly spoken since that night, except in brief, stilted, superficial conversations. Now he was gone, on an evening train to New York City, where he would catch a morning plane for Vietnam.

Jon Knowl had taken a train, too, to the far side of Ohio, to begin his first semester at Kent State. He was the most excited Maggie had seen him in years. Not quite eighteen and brimming with expectations, he looked somehow older, wiser, and more settled in spirit than Maggie had seen him before. If there was one bright spot on this day of good-byes, it was that her brother was finally on track with his life.

But without Jon Knowl at home and without Chad popping in and out, the house on Honeysuckle Lane was suddenly a very lonely place to be. For weeks after Chad and her brother left, Maggie drifted through each day with a yawning emptiness in her heart. She went to work, edited manuscripts, taught her Sunday school class, sang in the choir, went to occasional TV interviews and autograph parties, and made a halfhearted start at writing a novel, but she knew she was just going through the motions.

Even her walk with God seemed different. Gone was her enthusiasm, her passion, the excitement the Jesus people had generated in her that magical summer. She still prayed and read her Bible consistently, but the God she prayed to and read about seemed somehow distant, as if He, too, had gone on a far journey from her. Had her closeness with Christ been tied somehow to Chad, to the closeness and fellowship they shared? Surely not, and yet how else could she explain this growing coldness in her heart?

She had spent so long trying not to blame God for taking Jordan from her; surely she wasn't angry at God, didn't blame Him, and yet a part of her couldn't help questioning why God would burden Chad with a need to go to Vietnam when He had already taken Jordan. It felt like a punishment; it felt wrong, as if she must have taken a wrong turn or made a terrible blunder she hadn't even recognized. Why else would God snatch Chad away from her when she was still struggling to accept losing Jordan?

Almost in self-defense, Maggie decided she had no one to depend on now except herself. No matter what it took, no matter what it cost her, she would become a strong, independent, self-reliant woman. She would steel herself to the heartaches that plagued her. In order to forget the two loves she had lost, she threw herself into her work, staying overtime every night to read through the huge "slush pile" of unsolicited manuscripts that poured into the publishing house each week. She kept herself so busy that she would fall into bed each night in a state of exhaustion and slip into a heavy slumber.

Each morning she awoke with a nameless burden on her heart, a vague sense of doom in her spirit, pressing, sapping her strength. Why did she feel so depressed? As the soothing anesthesia of sleep ebbed away, it all came back to her with a sickening jolt. Jordan was missing, presumed dead, and Chad had put himself in harm's way because she had rejected him. Once more her moorings had been shaken, the emotional underpinnings of her life knocked out from under her.

During those early months of 1970, Maggie received an occasional letter from Chad—brief and curiously impersonal, relating his impressions of Vietnam, but rarely asking about home. One letter was typical of them all.

Hi, little Magpie,

I'm traveling with the Green Berets right now; stayed in their camp a few nights along the Cambodian border. Talk about roughing it. Survival is the only thing on your mind when you're out here. Vietnam is what you see on the news, only a million times worse. Steamy jungles, lots of sandbag trenches and bamboo villages, minefields everywhere, the rat-a-tat of machine gun fire, jeeps rumbling through the marshy vegetation carrying the dead in body bags, helicopters landing and taking off, their spinning blades fanning the fields, their loud whirring hum like the drone of a thousand insects.

The other day I was close enough to one skirmish that an exploding bomb nearly knocked me off my feet. The force of it rattled my teeth and left me deaf for over an hour. The explosion sent fireworks pinwheeling across the night sky. It was the Fourth of July magnified a hundred times. Would have been beautiful if it wasn't so deadly. You should have seen it, Mag. Shrapnel falling from the air like confetti. But nobody was celebrating!

I spent my first weeks here in Cam Ranh Bay, an ugly sand bowl of a beach. Not much there. Stayed a few days at the 4th Division headquarters in Pleiku. A desolate place. Nondescript army buildings. Nothing to write home about. Joined a unit patrolling Highway 19 from Cambodia to Qui Nhon. Watching out day and night for Vietcong; they're

*everywhere, nowhere, prowling around like invisible
ghosts, skulking through the shadows like cats, silent and
undetectable as the air.*

*I'm supposed to be sending my spin on things back to my
newspaper in tidy little articles, with lots of photos capturing what's really happening here. But once you get sucked
into this crazy, jumbled milieu, you feel overwhelmed; you
lose your perspective, your sense of judgment and balance.
You get caught up in the sweep of things, the randomness,
the chaos. Nothing much makes sense; there seems to be no
rhyme or rhythm to things, no cause and effect, no strata-
gem or agenda.*

*I can see now how Jordan could be swallowed up by this
place and never seen again. This strange, beautiful, terrifying land devours you bit by bit, piece by piece, if not your
body, then your soul. Still, I keep asking everyone I see
about Jordan. He's my greatest motivation for being here.
And somehow, being here, I feel closer to him than ever
before.*

*Got to close for now, Maggie. Lots to do. Places to go.
Pictures to take. Word has it that things will soon be hop-
ping in Cambodia. Something's in the works. Big time.
Can't say more, except keep me in your prayers, as you are
ever in mine.*

Love, Chad

Maggie treasured every letter from Chad and wrote back immediately, imparting the latest news from Willowbrook—how her writing
was going, the manuscripts she was editing, how Jon Knowl was far-
ing at Kent State. But she, too, kept the tone light and impersonal, the
kind of chatty missives one would send a casual friend.

During March and April, Maggie began to see Chad's byline in national magazines and syndicated newspaper articles. Two of Chad's most memorable stories about Vietnam appeared in *Life* magazine and *Look*. Both articles were brief, but they contained several of Chad's distinctive photographs that captured the raw emotions of soldiers at war. One showed a young G.I. sitting huddled in a trench writing a letter home; another revealed a distraught soldier dragging his wounded buddy back to camp; another pictured several Vietnamese peasants fleeing their burning village, their gaunt faces ravaged by misery and grief. As disturbing as the photos were, Maggie felt a swell of pride for Chad. He was doing what he had hoped to do—putting a personal face on a vast, baffling, impersonal war.

By the end of April, Maggie knew what Chad had meant about something brewing in Vietnam. On April 29, 50,000 U.S. and South Vietnamese troops launched a military invasion into Cambodia to cut off Communist supply lines. President Nixon, in a televised address on April 30, called the operation not an invasion, but an *incursion* aimed at destroying Vietcong and North Vietnamese base camps and sanctuaries. A news reporter, quoting Defense Secretary Melvin R. Laird in Washington, announced that the full length of the Cambodian border would be attacked by the Allies.

Within a few days, American and South Vietnamese soldiers had carried out both air and ground strikes in regions of Cambodia known as the Parrot's Beak and the Fishhook and had attacked enemy strongholds from the western Mekong Delta to north of Saigon. Maggie couldn't help but worry about Chad. She knew if he had his way, he would be right there in the thick of things, snapping lots of pictures for the newspapers back home.

On the evening of May 4, 1970, after an early dinner of ham and sweet potato pie, Maggie, her parents, and Grandmother Anna sat around the TV in the parlor to watch a game show. Midway through the program, a special news bulletin flashed on the screen. A reporter appeared and announced in somber tones, "In response to President Nixon's recent invasion of Cambodia, student unrest at Kent State University in Ohio has erupted in violent protest. When the ROTC building was firebombed earlier today, the governor called in the National Guard. A thousand student demonstrators gathered on the commons at the center of the campus, jeering and throwing rocks. When they refused to disperse, guardsmen wearing gas masks and carrying M-1 semiautomatic rifles fired tear gas grenades at the mob. Believing a sniper had shot at them, several guardsmen opened fire on the students, killing four and wounding at least a dozen more, three critically, before order was restored."

Maggie and her family sat riveted to the TV screen, staring in stunned silence at the flickering images of students protesting and guardsmen advancing amid shouts and screams, the air around them filled with clouds of tear gas.

"Jon Knowl," said Annie, her voice wrenched with anguish. "He's there. He could be one of those killed!"

Maggie reached over for her mother's hand. "Don't even think that, Mother."

"I'm sure he's fine," said her father, a tremor of worry in his voice.

"How can you say that, Knowl?" challenged her mother. "He would be out there protesting with the others. You know that. He would have been on the front lines of any demonstration against the war."

"I'll call his dormitory at school," said Maggie. She went to the phone and dialed the number. There was no answer. She tried several other university numbers. Again, no answer.

Her father took the phone and dialed the police. From his days as editor for the local newspaper, he knew how to finagle information out of the authorities. He talked in low tones for a minute or two, then hung up and turned to Annie and Maggie. "There's no way to get the names of the dead or wounded tonight. At least not over the phone."

"What are you saying?" asked Annie.

"I'm driving to Ohio. To Kent. Tonight. I'll check out the hospitals myself, if I have to."

Annie covered her mouth with her hand. "Then you do think Jon Knowl was involved."

"Like you said, Annie. Whenever students start demonstrating against the war, Jon Knowl is the first in line."

"And the first in the line of fire," said Annie in a horrified whisper. "I'm going with you, Knowl."

"Me too," said Maggie.

"We'll be on the road half the night," Knowl said.

"So be it. You can't go without us. If our son is in trouble, we all need to be there for him," Annie answered.

He held up the car keys. "All right, then. Let's go."

Grandmother Anna stood up shakily, her wrinkled face pale as the moon. "I'll go fix you some sandwiches and a Thermos of coffee to take with you."

"Thanks, Mama," said Annie. "I'll go throw a change of clothes and some toiletries in a valise. We may not get home right away."

Maggie's grandmother clasped her mottled hands together. "I'll say a prayer for Jon Knowl. For all of you."

They were on the highway in less than a half hour, driving through the darkened Indiana countryside, the sweet, pungent smells of ripening wheat fields and cornfields wafting on the warm, moist air. Maggie sat in the backseat of her father's comfortable sedan, remembering her childhood days when she and Jon Knowl sat in the backseat on vacation trips playing their favorite traveling game. *The first one who spots a yellow Volkswagen wins ten points . . . the first one who spots a red tractor pulling a plow . . . the first one who spots a Dairy Queen . . . a Burma Shave sign . . . an Amish horse and buggy . . .*

Life seemed so innocent in those days, so carefree and uncomplicated, so safe and secure. Back then Jon Knowl was a darling, round-faced, happy-go-lucky child with twinkling eyes and a mischievous grin. Who would have thought he would become a sullen, angry, steely-eyed rabble-rouser? And now he could be hurt . . . even dead. No, Maggie told herself sternly, there was a handful of students killed or wounded among a thousand protestors. Jon Knowl would be okay. She had to believe he was okay.

They arrived in Kent at 3:00 A.M. and drove straight to the local hospital. Even though it was the middle of the night, the lobby was ablaze with activity—medical personnel rushing about, doctors conferring with one another, parents lined up at the information desk or huddled together in the visitors' waiting room, and media people—newspaper and television reporters and cameramen milling around, obviously seeking a story.

"It's a zoo," lamented Annie. "How will we ever find out if Jon Knowl's here?"

"Give me a minute," said Knowl. He managed to intercept a physician crossing the lobby. The two spoke briefly, then made their way over to the information desk and conferred with several medical personnel there. Finally Maggie's father came striding back toward them, alone, his brow furrowed over shadowed eyes.

Annie hurried to him. "Is our son here? Knowl? Tell me!"

"He's here, Annie."

"Is . . . is he hurt? Dear Lord, he must be hurt if he's here. How bad is it?"

"I don't know, Annie. They said to go sit down and someone will come and talk with us in a few minutes. I tried to get more information, but they weren't about to divulge a word."

"Then you don't know how badly he's hurt?" pressed Maggie as they headed across the wide expanse of gray linoleum to the visitors' waiting room. They sat down on a sagging brown vinyl couch between the coffee machine and a small laminated table stacked with dog-eared magazines and crumpled newspapers.

Ten minutes passed before a portly, graying physician in a lab coat and surgical trousers came ambling over. They stood to greet him, and as he offered his hand, a weary smile played on his corpulent face. "Mr. and Mrs. Herrick, I'm Dr. Glasgow."

"How's my son?" asked Annie, desperation in her voice.

"Let's sit down." They returned to the couch, and the surgeon took the chair across from them, pulled it over, and sat down. He leaned forward and spoke in a husky, confidential tone. "We tried phoning you earlier, but obviously you were on your way here."

"We heard about the rioting and shooting on TV," said Knowl. "We had a feeling our son was involved."

"Yes, he was in the crowd of demonstrators. He was wounded in the scuffle."

"Shot?" cried Annie.

"No," replied Dr. Glasgow solemnly. "He was struck in the head with a nightstick and sustained another injury when his head hit the concrete."

Annie covered her face. "Dear God, no!"

"How is he, doctor?" Knowl's voice was raw, urgent.

"Mr. Herrick, your son was in surgery for several hours."

"Surgery?" echoed Maggie. "What for?"

"A head injury. Swelling on the brain. We had to go in and relieve the pressure to prevent brain damage."

Maggie reeled slightly. Her mother began to weep.

"Is he okay?" demanded her father.

"Only time will tell, Mr. Herrick. We've done what we can. We won't know if the boy has sustained brain damage—or to what degree—until he awakens."

"When can we see him?" cried Annie.

Dr. Glasgow hoisted himself out of the chair. "He'll be in recovery for the next hour or so. Then he'll be taken to his assigned room. The nurse can give you the number. You can see him then. I'll keep you posted on any changes, but right now I'd better get back to my patient."

The surgeon shook their hands again and lumbered off, leaving Maggie and her parents to stare at one another, shaken, speechless.

"At least he's alive," said her father as they sat back down.

"But . . . brain damage," said her mother in a soft, stricken voice. "Not my baby. Heaven help me, not my baby!"

"We've got to trust God." Her father looked dazed, drawn, his usually ruddy face drained of color.

Maggie stood up, hugging her arms to keep from trembling, nearly biting her tongue to keep from sobbing. She couldn't let her parents see her lose control. "I'm sorry, Mom, Dad. I can't just sit here and wait. I've got to do something." She looked around desperately. "There must be a chapel here somewhere. Do you mind if I go?"

"Do you want us to come with you, honey?" asked her mother.

She shook her head, a convulsive sob gathering in her chest like a tidal wave. "No, Mom, I . . . I'd rather be alone right now." Before they could respond, she pivoted on her heel and ran down the hall, the sobs breaking, the tears gushing. She walked blindly until she spotted a door that said CHAPEL. She burst inside and exhaled a sigh of relief. It was empty. She had the quaint, cozy room to herself.

She sat down in the front pew and stared up at a carved oak cross framed by three stained-glass windows depicting Christ the Good Shepherd. Gazing down lovingly, the Shepherd cradled the lost lamb in the crook of His arm, held the lamb tucked securely against the warmth of His chest, protected from the winds and the storms of life.

Maggie wept. She was that lost lamb. Alone, frightened, drifting off course, directionless. She hadn't even realized how lost she was until now, this moment, when once too often someone she loved had been torn from her arms. First, Jordan. Then Chad. And now Jon Knowl. How many more losses must she suffer before God took pity on her?

"My Father God," she said aloud, the words breaking on a sob, "why are You doing this to me? Haven't I loved You enough? What have I done that You would punish me like this? Are you testing me to see what I can bear? Do You hate me so much that You take pleasure in seeing me grieve?"

She pulled a tissue from her handbag and blotted her eyes. "Lord, I never thought I could stand losing Jordan. I thought I'd die without him, but somehow I kept on living. I don't know how. You saw me through, I believe that. I kept going, pretending life was going to be okay after all. Maybe because of Chad. Maybe that's how I made it. Chad, my devoted friend.

"And yet You took him too. Or was it me? It's my fault, isn't it? I sent him away because I couldn't marry him. God, why did You put me in such a dilemma? And now, because of me, he risks his life every day in Vietnam. Oh, God, maybe he'll never come home again, just like Jordan."

A new wave of tears started. "And now Jon Knowl! Oh, Lord, my only brother. The war has nearly claimed him too. Not in battle, but here at home. How could this be? How could he be hurt, maybe brain-damaged, maybe dying because of a war so far away? How could my life be so ruined by things people are doing on the other side of the world?"

Maggie was silent for a few moments, letting the pain wash over her. She had no more words, no arguments, no way to understand what was happening. An enormous rock lay on her heart, cutting off her breath, the pressure so great she was sure her chest would explode. "Oh, dear God," she sobbed brokenly.

In the stillness she thought she heard a voice, then realized the voice was only in her head, her heart. It said, "Trust Me." Just those two words. *Trust Me.*

"I can't! You've taken too much. What else will You demand of me? Who else will You snatch away? I loved You, Lord. Tried to live my life for You. And what have You done? One by one You've taken everyone I love. Who's next? Grams? My parents? You won't be satisfied until You've taken them all, will You!"

Trust Me. Those words again. The voice was so soft, she couldn't be sure she'd heard it even in her head. But the words struck at the very core of her being. Did she trust God? Even now, at one of the worst moments of her life? She didn't know. Right now she couldn't be sure of anything. Her very faith seemed up for grabs. God was either there or He wasn't. He cared for her or He didn't. Either possibility seemed entirely feasible.

"I can't do this," she said with a low moan. She rocked back and forth in the pew, her arms crossed, her eyes closed. "I'm empty, God. I can't summon faith or love or trust or hope. I have nothing to give You except a broken heart. Help me. God, help me. And I beg of You, please don't take Jon Knowl from us!"

19

As Maggie returned to the hospital waiting room, she knew she was experiencing a crisis of faith. Was God whom she believed Him to be, or was He a mere invention of her own imagination? Either He was real and could be trusted for every detail of her life, or He was a flimsy illusion that would burst like a bubble during the genuine crises of her life.

But if He wasn't real, then with whom had she communed during her quiet times each day? Who had sustained her during the hard times—when she lost Jordan, when she searched for Jon Knowl, when Chad went away? Someone was there for her, ministering to her heart a dozen times a day. Someone was with her now, even as she argued with herself over His existence, His compassion, His solicitude. This was by no means a one-sided relationship. To deny the reality of her Savior was to deny her own existence, all that she knew herself to be. She was turning herself inside out trying to rationalize this thing, trying to pin God down, trying to squeeze Him into a bottle. But He refused to be contained or suppressed.

Perhaps the question wasn't whether or not He existed—for she knew the answer to that already. He existed as surely as she did; to doubt His existence would be to doubt her own sanity. Perhaps the real question was whether God deserved her displeasure. Did she have a right to be angry with Him? For indeed she was angry, angry over her losses, angry over the war, angrier than she had ever felt in her entire life.

God was God; He could have made things turn out so differently. He could have ended the war long ago. He could have protected Jordan and brought Him home safely. What whim prompted Him to take Jordan and Chad from her, and now Jon Knowl? What satisfaction did He receive from wounding her so deeply?

As Maggie took her seat beside her parents in the waiting room, the questions swirled in her mind, each one stirring greater indignation. But amid the questions came the answers she already knew, the answers she didn't want to hear: Indeed, God could have manipulated everything; He could have made a perfect world where everything ran smoothly, peacefully, like clockwork. No wars, no strife, no struggles.

But at what cost?

At the cost of freedom. He could have made people mindless robots to do His bidding; yes, she knew this. Instead, He honored mankind with the gift of self-determination and free will, so they could choose to love Him or choose not to. She knew this, too, had learned this truth as a child in Sunday school. She knew it was sin that ushered in the very things she was blaming God for now—wars, riots, discord, death.

But knowing sin was to blame didn't dispel the darkness of her acrimony against God or the heavy gloom of despair nearly suffocating her now. If she couldn't blame God for her losses, then what was she to do with all this pent-up fury? How could she sit still in this whitewashed hospital waiting room that smelled of disinfectant and death? How could she remain in her chair, her hands folded in polite silence, her face a demure mask, when her emotions were raging inside?

"Margaret, are you all right?"

Startled, she looked over at her mother. "Yes, Mama, why?"

"I was talking to you, and you seemed a million miles away."

She stared down at her folded hands. "I've just got a lot on my mind, Mama."

"Did spending time in the chapel make you feel better?"

Maggie hesitated. How could she confide to her mother, who surely never had a crisis of faith, that praying hadn't helped, had in fact stirred up deeply buried emotions that left her feeling devastated? "I'm fine, Mama. Yes, I . . . I feel better."

Her mother patted her hand. "Good. I knew you would. I don't know how I could have survived all these years without the Lord's help."

Guilt stabbed Maggie's heart. She had felt that way for most of her life, too, but now . . . she wasn't sure how she felt, or how God felt about her. Would He stop loving her because she was angry with Him? Would He turn His back on her because she was such an ungrateful child? Even as the questions raged, her anger was losing steam, giving way to a void in her spirit, a hollow, nameless yearning. A strange irony. She was angry at God, yet she realized the truth of her mother's words. Even in her anger, she longed for the comforting arms of Christ around her, His Spirit ministering to her hurting heart. How could she be furious at God, yet hungry for His closeness, His sweet consolation?

Her questions were left hanging when a nurse's voice broke into her reverie. "Mr. and Mrs. Herrick, your son is out of recovery. He's been taken to Room 186. You may see him now."

"Is he awake?" asked Annie.

"He woke up briefly in recovery, but he's very drowsy. He'll probably be asleep when you see him."

"Is he okay? His mind?" asked Knowl. "He has a head wound. Has his brain sustained any permanent injury?"

The young, dark-haired nurse shrugged. "I'm sorry, Mr. Herrick. You'll have to discuss that with Dr. Glasgow."

"Please tell him I want to see him as soon as possible."

"I will, Mr. Herrick."

Within minutes Maggie and her parents found their way to Jon Knowl's room. They entered slowly, quietly, wary of what they might find. With the curtains drawn, the room lay in murky shadows, so that Maggie couldn't be sure the pale figure in the bed was actually her brother. The room felt stuffy, closed in, heavy with the reek of illness.

A gag reflex tightened in Maggie's throat as she drew close to the large hospital bed. Jon Knowl, his eyes closed, his ashen lips partly open, looked so fragile and still, she wondered if he was still alive. Yes, thank God, she could see the slight rise and fall of his chest under the sheet. With his head bandaged and his skin so white, he looked ghostly. And yet there was a sad, vulnerable, little-boy quality to his sleeping face.

Annie began to weep softly. "Oh, my son, my sweet baby."

Knowl circled Annie's waist with his arm. "It'll be okay, Annie. We've got to trust God that he'll come back to us."

Maggie blinked back bitter tears. Oh, God, how she wanted to believe, but she wasn't the same naive, trusting girl who had gone to California looking for her brother two years ago. Too much had happened since then. Too many losses. The possibility now of losing Jon Knowl left her feeling numb, dazed, too paralyzed emotionally to release the secret chamber of her heart where the pain seethed. She had no prayers left.

They stayed with Jon Knowl for nearly an hour, but he never moved, never stirred or awakened, never showed the slightest sign that the strong-willed, gregarious brother she loved still resided inside that pallid shell of a boy.

They left the hospital around 6:00 A.M., as the early rays of dawn painted the sky with a wash of soft pastel pinks and baby blues. They grabbed a bite of breakfast at a local diner, then found a motel room close to the hospital where they could stay for a few days until they had a better idea of Jon Knowl's prognosis. They slept for several hours, then returned to the hospital about noon and sat by Jon Knowl's bed for an hour or so. He was still sleeping soundly. By evening Maggie's father pigeonholed another doctor, who told them Jon Knowl was holding his own, whatever that meant.

Maggie and her parents broke their vigil long enough for a tasteless dinner of meatloaf and creamed potatoes in the hospital cafeteria; then they promptly returned to her brother's room. Annie had brought the Gideon Bible from their hotel room, and now she sat beside Jon Knowl and read him the Scriptures.

At the sound of his mother's lyrical voice, Jon Knowl moved. It was just his hand at first, but then he turned his head in her direction and his eyelids fluttered. The family gathered around him with a sudden, desperate urgency, begging him to wake up and speak to them. His eyes opened halfway, and he gazed at them with a bewildered, lopsided smile. "Mom . . . Dad . . . what are you doing here?"

Once Jon Knowl woke up, he rallied quickly, although for several days his speech was slow and his memory foggy. It took him three days to recall the deadly clash between Kent State students and the National Guard. Even then, he had no recollection of the specific incident that had landed him in the hospital with a brain concussion. "Guess I got too close to some cop's billy club," he quipped dryly. He insisted on seeing every newspaper article on the riot; he had casually known the four students who were slain and, like everyone else, he was shocked and outraged by their deaths. But, lying in a hospital bed with his head bandaged, there was nothing he could do. He was too weak physically to protest or retaliate. Still, all he could talk about was getting out of the hospital and getting back to school and making the "pigs" pay for what they had done.

Maggie knew her parents were concerned about her brother's hotheadedness, but they admitted they could hardly blame him for his anger when half the world was incensed over the bloody Kent State confrontation. Maggie agreed, adding, "I just hope he doesn't take matters into his own hands and seek revenge."

"If he does, he could end up in jail like so many of his classmates," said her father. "I have no doubt that if he hadn't been injured, he would have been arrested and we would be here bailing him out of jail instead of visiting him in the hospital."

"It's not over, is it?" said Annie worriedly. "Jon Knowl won't let this be over. He's determined to change the world or die trying."

"We would all like to change the world," said her father, "but it's not going to happen with riots and violence."

Maggie shook her head. "What will it take?"

"Only heaven knows."

Within a week Jon Knowl was ready to be discharged from the hospital. Maggie's parents pleaded with him to come home with them, but he insisted on staying at Kent State and finishing the last few weeks of the semester. Reluctantly, after much haggling, they agreed. So on a warm Tuesday in mid-May Maggie and her parents drove home to Willowbrook without Jon Knowl.

A few weeks later, with the semester over, Jon Knowl arrived home on the train. Maggie's mother fixed a lavish dinner—all of her son's favorite dishes, plus a three-layer chocolate cake. But if they had expected Jon Knowl to enter into the spirit of celebration, they were dead wrong. Instead of showing gratitude for his mother's efforts, he expressed contempt for his family's foolish attempt to smooth things over when the world was self-destructing around them.

What Maggie had hoped would be a pleasant summer with her brother turned out to be a sweltering season of hot tempers and bitter estrangement. Jon Knowl walked around with a chip on his shoulder the size of a small house. No matter what anyone said to him, he took offense. He was moody, sullen, insolent, and seething with barely suppressed rage. All he could talk about was getting back to school and leaving his boring family and his antiquated hometown behind. He let it be known that if he were ever drafted, he would flee to Canada as a conscientious objector. And if the students at Kent State demonstrated again, he would be at the front of the pack. It struck Maggie that her brother had never been to battle, yet he had taken on the wounds of the war. She wondered what it would take for him to purge his inner demons . . . or would he die trying?

Jon Knowl's hot temper set off the rest of the family, especially their father, who had no patience for his son's impertinence. Maggie's mother became the peacemaker, vainly striving to arbitrate between father and son. Maggie herself kept her distance from the rest of the family, both emotionally and physically, for she was still struggling with her own issues of faith and her future. She felt as if she were foundering, treading water, spinning her wheels, accomplishing nothing.

As Jon Knowl raged outwardly, she raged inwardly, but she wasn't even sure at whom she was raging. She had stopped reading her Bible and praying, had dropped the choir and her Sunday school class, and found one excuse after another not to attend church on Sundays and Wednesdays. God seemed more and more like a distant acquaintance, someone she had once known intimately but hadn't visited for so long she wasn't sure she would recognize Him anymore.

Her only moments of joy came when she received an infrequent letter from Chad. They were newsy on a superficial level; rarely did he mention his feelings or inquire about hers. He was still in Southeast Asia working as a photojournalist for the *New York Times* and loved what he was doing as much as he hated the war that had brought him there. She saw his byline frequently and his trademark photos—distinctive, dramatic, telling a heartrending story without words. And she felt a wistful, grudging admiration that he had clearly found his calling in life.

In September Jon Knowl returned to Kent State, and as much as Maggie's parents hated to see him go, they were obviously relieved that their home would no longer be an armed camp with everyone on guard lest a verbal battle erupt.

As winter approached, Maggie threw herself into her work at Herrick House; she was promoted from an editorial assistant to fiction acquisitions editor, the one bright spot in an otherwise bleak season. On most days the "slush pile" of unsolicited manuscripts dwarfed the mahogany desk in her new office, but she was glad to be inundated with work. The harder she worked, the less time she had to brood about the gnawing emptiness in her life.

Early in November she received a mysterious missive from Chad, who announced he was on a special assignment, a secret mission, so to speak, about which he could divulge absolutely nothing. His tone was buoyant, yet puzzling. He said only that he had high hopes that their dreams might come true and he dare not say more, but that if all went as he hoped, she would be receiving some wonderful news by the end of the month.

Maggie had no idea what "secret mission" Chad was talking about until the last week of November when she picked up the newspaper and noticed one of Chad's syndicated articles. She eagerly scanned the story, and her heart sank as Chad's mysterious mission became clear. U.S. forces had raided Sontay in North Vietnam in an effort to free American prisoners of war, but they had found the prison camp empty. Chad had hoped to find Jordan, and his hopes had been dashed.

The impact of what had happened, or not happened, stunned Maggie. It was a dagger to her heart, the idea that Jordan might have been found, that he might still be alive . . . that he could have been freed by his own brother, no less! Dear Lord in heaven, her beloved Jordan could have come home to her!

Christmas of 1970 was the grimmest Maggie had ever experienced. It had been three years since she said good-bye to Jordan, three years since they kissed and vowed to always love each other. Each year got harder. The first year she was still young and idealistic enough to believe he would return; the second year she still believed, although her idealism had faded and her hopes grown a bit tarnished. This year her hopes were smothered under the bitter realities of a failed rescue attempt, an empty prison camp. It had been a desperate hope at best, the idea of Jordan being still alive, a prisoner of war rescued by his little brother. It was the stuff of fairy tales.

In spite of her dwindling hopes, Maggie still wore Jordan's locket around her neck, tucked under her clothes next to her heart. She refused to pack the necklace away, for it would be the same as admitting Jordan was dead. As long as she wore his locket, she carried in her heart the possibility that he was still alive, that he would come home to her someday.

There was little celebration in the Herrick household that Christmas for anyone. Jon Knowl refused to come home for the holidays, insisting he preferred to spend his time with friends. Maggie's father admitted he was afraid Jon Knowl was off plotting more mischief with his militant buddies. "What next?" he said, throwing up his hands in dismay. "What are these radical kids going to pull next?"

They found out several months later in April 1971, while watching the evening news on TV. The newscaster reported antiwar demonstrations in Washington, D.C., and in the accompanying film clip Maggie was sure she spotted Jon Knowl in the crowd of student protesters. Her father telephoned the school to inquire about Jon Knowl and was told that he and several other students had left the campus without permission several days before and that he was in danger of being expelled.

For nearly two weeks they had no idea what had happened to Jon Knowl. Then, on the evening of May 3, 1971, the phone rang in the

Herrick household and Maggie answered. On the other end of the line she heard a muffled, emotion-filled voice that at first seemed unfamiliar. "Maggie? It's me. Jon Knowl."

"Jon-Jon? Where are you?"

"Washington, D.C."

"You sound terrible. What's wrong?"

"I . . . I'm in trouble, Maggie."

"What happened?"

A long pause, then: "I'm in jail."

Maggie's breath caught in her throat. "Jail?"

"It's a long story, Maggie."

"Tell me! What did you do?"

"I'm not the only one, Maggie. They arrested thousands of us. We were protesting the war, like we've been doing for weeks. Students from all over the country. Only this time we figured we had to do something to show we meant business. So we decided to shut down the government."

"Oh, Jon-Jon, no!"

He rushed on, a note of excitement replacing his earlier distress. "We figured the only way we could keep the government from doing business was to stop traffic all over the city. So that's what we did. We had all the streets blocked, and nobody could get to their offices."

Maggie sank down in a straight-back chair beside the phone table. "And now you need help, is that it? Someone to bail you out?"

"Yeah, that's about it, Maggie. I'm sorry. I didn't want to get Mom and Dad involved in this, but I'm broke. If I don't make bail, I'll have to rot in this place until my court hearing."

"Okay, Jon-Jon, I'll get Daddy on the phone, but he's going to be livid. I know he'll be on the first plane to Washington, but you'd better pray he calms down before he gets to you."

As Maggie suspected, her father flew to Washington early the next morning, and as she predicted, he was seething with anger. And yet he would never let his feelings keep him from helping his children. The next night he flew home with Jon Knowl. The charges against him had been dropped. The turmoil in Washington was over, but Maggie had a feeling that with Jon Knowl back home, the turmoil was just beginning in the Herrick household. It was going to be another scorching, unbearable summer.

20

During the sultry summer of 1971, after Jon Knowl's participation in what came to be known as the Mayday antiwar protest in Washington, D.C., the Herrick household in placid Willowbrook became something of an armed camp. Jon Knowl was more sullen and uncommunicative than ever. Rather than being grateful for his father's efforts to rescue him from a possible prison sentence, Jon Knowl seemed to hold his father and the rest of the family in even greater contempt than before.

Jon Knowl, with his long, unkempt hair, his beaded headbands, leather vests, and frayed jeans, seemed a misfit in town and, more so, in his own family. Maggie suspected that he might be taking drugs again, certainly marijuana, if not LSD. He came and went like a shadow, rarely saying a word, not even hello or good-bye. He never divulged where he was going or what he was doing. To attempt even a casual conversation with him was to risk his scornful glance or sneer of derision.

Several times over the summer Maggie's father threatened to throw Jon Knowl out of the house, but each time he relented, fearing for his son's health and safety if he were to live off the streets. Often the two argued and nearly came to blows, until Maggie began to wonder how her father and brother could even be related, they were at such opposite poles on nearly every issue.

Maggie herself felt powerless to help her brother. Over the

months her faith had grown cold, and if she couldn't point Jon Knowl to God for redemption, what else did she have to offer him? If only Chad Barrett were around to take Jon Knowl under his wing as he had before, but Chad was still on his globe-trotting mission in Southeast Asia, capturing the war in his riveting black-and-white photographs for a world growing ever more battle-weary.

In September, Jon Knowl headed back to Kent State, and the entire family breathed a collective sigh of relief. Gone again, for a time, was the family's major source of stress and disruption. But somehow, as difficult as it was living with Jon Knowl, having him gone sent Maggie into a bog of depression. Gone again was her chance to reach out and help him, for surely there should have been something she could have done to make him see the error of his ways.

But at the moment Maggie was having a hard time keeping her own life in perspective. Everything felt muddy, clouded, heavy, as if she were, like Christian in *Pilgrim's Progress*, slogging through the Slough of Despond. In a far corner of her mind she recognized that her feelings of gloom and inertia were tied directly to her lack of communication with God. Before, when she was walking in step with Him, her life, in spite of its trials, seemed to purr along; she managed to ride the turbulent waves of everyday irritations and crises. She realized that she had let her love for God grow cold, but refused to articulate her transgression in a conscious act of repentance. She preferred to blame her ills on her less-than-perfect circumstances, or on the people in her life who didn't understand her, or on her own capricious mood.

One quiet autumn evening in late October—a chilly night with a brisk wind stirring the dry leaves—Maggie, her mother, and grandmother sat in the parlor, each absorbed in her own task. Maggie was writing a letter to Chad; Annie was reading over the galleys of her latest book; and Grandmother Anna was reading the newspaper.

Her grandmother broke the silence first. "Goodness gracious, listen to this. *Look* magazine won't be published anymore. They're losing lots of money. Says here they blame the soft economy and rising postal costs. My lands, no more *Look* magazine. Can you imagine?"

"That's a shame," said Annie, glancing up from her work. "*Look* has been a pillar in the publishing world for as long as I can remember."

"They published several of Chad's articles," said Maggie. "And lots of his photos."

"He'll be sorry to see them go," said her grandmother. "Matter of fact, so am I. It was always like a friend bringing the world to our doorstep."

"Now we have television to do that," said Maggie.

Her grandmother nodded. "I suspect that's part of the problem. Always some newfangled thing taking the place of the old, established ways." She continued reading the paper for several minutes, then let out an exclamation of disgust. "Well, I'll be!"

"What now, Grams?" asked Maggie with a bemused smile.

"Here's an article about a rock opera opening at some big theater in New York City. Called *Jesus Christ Superstar.* The way they describe it here, it sounds downright blasphemous."

"I've heard of it," said Annie. "It's created quite a stir. It has Mary—I suppose they mean Mary Magdalene—singing 'I don't know how to love Him,' meaning Jesus."

Grandmother Anna adjusted her wire-rim spectacles on her distinctive nose; even at her age she possessed a certain regal bearing with her square shoulders and her silver-gray hair forming a shiny wreath around her head. "Well, they may have hit upon a pertinent issue amid all their psychedelic folderol."

"Meaning what?" asked Maggie.

"Meaning . . . that's the confession we all need to make, if we take seriously God's command to love Him with all our hearts."

"I suppose you're right, Mama," Annie agreed. "It strikes at our very relationship with Christ. I don't know how to love Him."

"That's what I loved about the Jesus people," said Maggie wistfully. "They loved Jesus with such a pure, unblemished passion. It infused everything they did."

Grandmother Anna set down her paper and gave Maggie a sad, cryptic look. "Margaret, you had that kind of passion when you were writing their story. I marveled at it. You even inspired an old lady like me."

Maggie grimaced. "That was a long time ago, Grams. A lot has changed since then."

"Not God. He never changes. Christ is the same yesterday, today, and forever, child."

Maggie squirmed in her chair. "I know, Grams, but maybe I've just grown up. I've learned life isn't all black or white; there's an awful lot of gray in between."

"Growing up is one thing, Margaret. Growing away from God is something entirely different. Isn't that right, Annie?"

Maggie's mother raised her palms defensively. "Don't get me started on this, Mama. I won't have Maggie blaming me for interfering in her life the way Jon Knowl has."

"Mama, I'm not Jon Knowl," Maggie protested. "If you've got something to say to me, say it."

Several fleeting emotions played themselves out on her mother's face. At fifty-one, Annie looked a decade younger. She had pulled the pins out of her hair, and the soft, burnished ringlets hung loosely around her slim shoulders, giving her heart-shaped face a little-girl innocence. Maggie loved her mother with a deep ache of admiration and yearning; she had always wanted to please Annie, always wanted to *be* Annie. To her dismay, Maggie—two months short of being twenty-four years old—still felt an unshakable need to please her mother.

"Margaret, what I'm about to say isn't meant as a criticism, so please don't take it as such."

A small alarm went off in Maggie's head. She wasn't going to like what she heard. "Just say what you've got to say, Mama."

A long pause. "Margaret, dear, you know how worried we've been about Jon Knowl. Well, the truth is, we've been worried about you too."

Maggie's hackles rose. "Mama, how can you even compare me to Jon Knowl?"

Her mother's voice was quiet, gentle. "Your brother's has been an outward rebellion, noisy, explosive, full of frustration and rage. But yours, Margaret, has been silent and turned inward, so no one sees it except those who love you. Jon Knowl rages at the whole world, while you seem to have quietly shut the door of your heart on God."

Maggie felt the pressure of tears gathering at the back of her eyes, so hard her head ached. She refused to give in and cry; she would not be shaken by her mother's words. "I don't need a sermon, Mama," she said in a small, uneven voice.

"Maybe you do, Margaret," said her grandmother gently. "It's been a while since you've heard any."

"Grams, I'm old enough to make my own decisions about church."

Her grandmother's faded blue eyes were glazed with tears. "But you're never too old for God, honey."

Maggie's defenses crumbled. Large tears rolled down her cheeks. Her mother slipped over beside her on the sofa and embraced her, the sweet scent of cherry-almond lotion on her smooth skin. "Honey, your grandmother and I have been saying an awful lot of prayers for you. Tell us how we can help you."

"I don't know, Mama. I don't know!"

Grandmother Anna joined them on the sofa and handed Maggie her embroidered handkerchief. "The good Lord loves you just as He always has, Margaret."

"I know, Grams." Maggie wiped her wet eyes with the hanky. Suddenly the words came pouring out, broken, jumbled, heavy with regret. "But . . . don't you see, Grams? I—I don't feel close to God anymore. I wish I did. But I've lost—I've lost so many people I love—Jordan, Chad, in a way even Jon Knowl. I know I shouldn't blame God; I shouldn't, but I can't help it. I just wish I still felt the way I did when I was with the Jesus people. Everything was so big and powerful and dramatic with them. It was easier to keep on a spiritual and emotional high."

Her grandmother caressed Maggie's tousled hair. "Margaret, dear, lots of those folks you wrote about came from terrible, troubled, drug-filled lives. They needed a big dose of God's love to turn them around. But, honey, what God does for most of us in the extraordinary moments of our lives depends on what we've allowed Him to do in the ordinary, everyday moments. Our faith is forged in the routine, the drudgery, the commonplace, the mundane. The mountaintop experiences are wonderful, and we need them, too, but our walk with Christ is built on our daily habits of prayer and Bible reading, and sitting at the feet of Jesus and hearing His words, the way Mary, the sister of Martha and Lazarus, did. How long has it been since you've sat at the feet of Jesus, child, and let Him love you?"

Maggie hiccuped, her chest heaving. "A long time, Grams."

"Then maybe it's time you and your mother and I spent some time at His feet, worshiping Him and letting Him shower us with His love. Would you let us pray with you, Margaret?"

What started out as a peaceful, uneventful evening at home turned out to be a little slice of heaven as Maggie got down on her knees beside the sofa, her grandmother on one side and her mother on the other, and uttered a broken, halting prayer for forgiveness and restoration.

Maggie's closeness with God didn't return full-blown in that brief hour of prayer, but it came back gradually, day by day, as she spent time getting reacquainted with her Savior. Even on days when she didn't feel like praying or studying her Bible; when everything inside her resisted making the effort, she still made herself take that quiet time with God. And afterward she wondered how she could have made it through the day without her special time with Him. Even on days when her schedule was jam-packed, she disciplined herself to get up an hour earlier and spend a few peaceful moments with God before dawn colored the sky with bright pinks and oranges.

Why didn't I do this a long time ago? she wondered. *How could I have spent so much time feeling miserable when God was waiting here for me all along?*

By the Christmas holidays, Maggie had decided to start a new writing project—a devotional book based on three generations of women who loved the Lord. She would share the spiritual truths she was gleaning from her mother and grandmother, plus the lessons she herself was learning about developing a consistent, intimate walk with Christ.

When Jon Knowl came home for the holidays, she was ready, eager to share with him the way God was working in her life. At last, after her own wilderness experience, she felt she could genuinely help him; or more accurately, she had faith that God could reach him and change him.

But Jon Knowl wanted no part of any religious conversation. The moment Maggie broached spiritual matters, her brother made a fast exit. The week before Christmas, as the family gathered in the parlor to decorate the monstrous blue spruce Jon Knowl and Knowl had cut down in the woods, Maggie tried again. "Doesn't this time of year make you feel closer to God?" she said as they strung bubble lights and popcorn chains among the pungent evergreen branches.

Jon Knowl gave her a withering glance. "This time of year reminds me of the last time we saw Jordan, when we were all happy and didn't know the world was about to self-destruct. It was four years ago, Maggie. Four long years, and still no word about Jordan."

"I miss him too," said Maggie softly. "More than you'll ever know. But it's not God's fault that Jordan is gone."

"Isn't it?"

"No, Jon-Jon, it's not, and it's taken me a lot of years to really believe that myself. But I do. I finally do. And take it from someone who knows, you'll never be happy fighting God, or ignoring Him. He loves us and wants to be part of our lives."

Jon Knowl's lips curled in a sneer. "If God wants my attention, then let Him bring Jordan home! Until then, I want nothing to do with Him!"

On that frosty Christmas Eve of 1971, it wasn't Jordan Barrett who came striding up the snow-covered sidewalk to the Herricks' old Victorian homestead. But when Maggie, in her fanciest red velvet dress, heard the insistent knock and rushed to open the door, she thought she was seeing a ghost from the past as she gazed up into the ruddy, careworn face of Chad Barrett.

"Chad!" She drew back in amazement, convinced she was dreaming. "Is it really you?"

"It's me, Magpie." In his beige trench coat and dark blue suit, he looked taller and more imposing than she remembered. And older . . . and so much more sophisticated! And handsome! Had he always been this handsome, with his tanned, sharply chiseled features and that thick, curly chestnut-brown hair? And those warm, crinkly blue eyes that made her stomach tickle as he gazed at her.

"My goodness, Chad, don't stand out there in the cold. Come in."

"Thought you'd never ask," he said with a wry, twinkling smile. He stomped the snow from his heavy shoes and stepped inside the marble foyer; then in one sudden, graceful gesture he gathered Maggie into his arms. Caught unawares, she felt an avalanche of sensations bombard her at once: the scratchy fabric of Chad's overcoat, the wetness of snowflakes melting against her cheek, the solid encompassing warmth of his embrace, the fresh lime scent of his aftershave, the softness of his cheek against hers. Her head spun and her ankles felt weak, but he held her so tightly there was no way she could fall. Tears of joy and surprise welled in her eyes. Chad's lips brushed her forehead and cheeks and she prayed they would find her mouth, but just as she was ready to stay in his arms forever, he released her.

"You're as beautiful as ever, Maggie," he said, his gaze taking in her velvet dress, her upswept hairdo, her tear-stained face, and the familiar locket at her throat. "You're even more beautiful, if that's possible."

"What are you doing here, Chad?" she cried incredulously. "Aren't you still on assignment in Southeast Asia?"

He circled her waist with his arm as they made their way into the living room. "I told them I've had enough, Maggie. I've done what I set out to do. I let people see what the war is like firsthand. Now it's time for a change."

She looked up at him. "Does that mean you're coming home to Willowbrook?"

"Maybe so."

"For good?"

"That depends, my little Magpie."

"On what?"

His voice rang with a hint of mystery and merriment. "On whether you accept my proposal."

She stared up at him in bewilderment. "What proposal?"

He clasped her hand to his breast and drew his face down close to hers. "This proposal, Maggie, my darling. Would you do me the honor of becoming my wife?"

21

Before Maggie could reply to Chad's astonishing proposition, her family gathered around eagerly to welcome him home. Even the usually sullen Jon Knowl was bursting with excitement, pumping Chad's hand, then giving him a bear hug. As everyone greeted Chad and plied him with questions, Maggie was left wondering whether she had heard him right or only imagined his startling and very provocative offer. But it didn't look as if Chad would have a chance to mention the proposal again, and Maggie was too stunned to bring up the subject with everyone around.

From the moment Chad arrived, Grandmother Anna took him under her wing. "If you'd come earlier, you could have had dinner with us," she told him as she ushered him toward the dining room. "But there's some leftover ham. I could fix you a sandwich."

"No thanks, Mrs. Reed. I've already eaten. Sorry I couldn't make it any sooner. My folks would hardly let me sneak away as it was. I had to promise I'd be home in a couple of hours."

"Shame on them for not telling us you were coming."

"They didn't know. I surprised them just like I surprised you. I didn't want to get anybody's hopes up in case it didn't work out for me to leave 'Nam."

"Well, then, at least you've got time for dessert," said Grandmother Anna. "It just so happens I was ready to serve my homemade cherry pie. Don't suppose you'd like a slice."

Chad winked at her. "If it's the same cherry pie you used to bake when I was a kid, I'll have a real big slice, Mrs. Reed."

They all gathered in the dining room for dessert and took turns asking Chad about his work in Southeast Asia. But Maggie noticed he kept deflecting any serious questions about the war.

"This is Christmas Eve," he admonished. "Time to talk about happy things. There'll be lots of time later to catch up on all the news."

"Does that mean you've come home to stay, Chad?" inquired Maggie's father with a knowing smile in her direction.

"That depends, Mr. Herrick," Chad replied, giving Maggie that same knowing look.

"Well, we all certainly hope you're going to stick around, Chad," said Annie. "We've all missed you. Isn't that right, Jon Knowl?"

"Mama's right," Jon Knowl conceded. "There have been lots of times I wished you were around."

"I'm here now, Jon Knowl, so anytime you want to get together and talk, you give me a call at my folks' house, okay?"

"I sure will, man."

Shortly after they had finished dessert, Chad stood up and excused himself. "Like I said, I promised my mom I'd get home early and help her put the presents around the tree."

"Chad, why don't you and your folks come over for dinner tomorrow?" said Grandmother Anna. "If they don't have other plans, that is. I'll be fixing lamb, and as I recall it's your father's favorite."

"Sounds great. I'll tell them, Mrs. Reed. Good night."

Maggie walked Chad to the door, grateful to finally have a moment alone with him. As he opened the wide paneled door, an inrush of biting wind and whirling snow flurries bombarded them. They stepped back inside, laughing. Chad had snowflakes in his hair, and she touched them and felt them melt against her fingertips. Still chuckling, Chad reached for her hands and drew her into his arms.

He gave her a long, questioning look, as if to say, "What are you feeling now?"

She, too, had no words, only questions. The silence seemed to envelop them, a stillness as quiet as the snowfall. At last he tilted her chin up to his and brushed a warm kiss on her lips. "Maggie, my sweet Maggie," he whispered.

"Chad," she murmured, "what you said earlier . . ." She couldn't think how to put it, so she let her words drop away.

He smiled. "What I said when I arrived . . . I know I took you by surprise. I'm sorry. I didn't mean to shock you. The words just spilled out. Can we start over?"

"Start over?"

"Right. I don't expect an answer to my proposal. But I would like to make a date for tomorrow. Are you free?"

"You're already coming over for dinner, aren't you?"

"I intend to, if my parents have no other plans."

"Then I'll see you tomorrow."

Chad and Maggie spent not only Christmas together but nearly every day of the holidays. Either she was at his house or he was at hers, or they went ice-skating, or out to eat, or to church, or to visit friends. It seemed so natural for them to be a twosome. Maggie had never felt more content than she felt now with Chad. They could spend hours talking about everything and nothing; in fact, they could enjoy each other's company without conversing.

On New Year's Eve they attended the night watch service at church, then returned to Maggie's house for hot chocolate and some of her grandmother's delectable floating island pudding. They were both pensive as they sat facing each other across the kitchen table. The house was dark and silent except for one small hanging lamp over the table that gave Chad's sculpted features a rosy glow. "A penny for your thoughts, Chad," Maggie said softly as she sipped her steaming chocolate.

"A penny's not much these days," he quipped, warming his palms on the ceramic mug. He smiled wistfully. "I'm just thinking about this being 1972 already. A new year. Can't help wondering what's ahead. And can't help thinking about the past. My brother's been gone four years now. Hard to believe, huh?"

Maggie nodded, slivers of memory embedding themselves in her heart like lances. No matter how long it had been, thoughts of Jordan still brought lightning flashes of pain. "Have you given up hope, Chad?"

He shrugged. "I guess I'll never give up hope until they can prove he's dead. But if you're asking if I expect him to come home some-day, I don't count on it much anymore. What about you, Maggie? I see you're still wearing his locket."

Maggie touched the locket at her throat. "To take it off would feel like a betrayal, like accepting that Jordan's dead. I can't do that yet, Chad."

"Me neither, Mag. Sometimes it feels just like yesterday that he went away."

"And in all your travels through Vietnam, you never learned a thing about what had happened to him?"

"You'd be the first to know if I had, Maggie. A lot of false leads, of course. But that's all."

Maggie gave Chad a searching gaze. "You've been home almost two weeks, yet you still haven't talked to me about Vietnam. I have all your newsy letters, of course, but I want you to tell me in your own words now what it was like."

Chad was silent, his eyes downcast as he turned his mug between his palms. Finally he met her gaze, his eyes filled with something she hadn't seen before, an expression that made her wince. "I don't talk about it, Maggie, because I don't know what to say. Sometimes, when I think about Vietnam, my memories seem downright surreal. Here I was with my camera snapping photographs while war was being played out around me. Guys getting shot, bombs exploding, land mines blowing off guys' legs.

"Sometimes I had to put my camera down and help the guys in the field. Had to evacuate the wounded. Carry broken, bleeding men to the choppers. I saw guys die, Maggie, men who were making wisecracks one minute and lying in a pool of their own blood the next. I saw a lot of things that dug themselves into my soul, like a scar, things I'll never forget, never get over. I saw these men giving their all, putting their lives on the line, and then we'd hear talk about the riots at home and the demonstrations against the war, and the guys would wonder, 'What are we doing here? Why should we be dying for a war nobody wants, a war our country doesn't even intend to win?'"

"A lot of us are frustrated over that," conceded Maggie. "But what can we do? Become a protester like Jon Knowl? I feel we have to support our country, even if we don't agree with it; after all, it's the only country we've got."

"Yeah, I hear you, Maggie. But I'll tell you, there's a lot of anger and resentment over in 'Nam over our country's ambivalence. Do we want to fight a war or don't we? Do we want to win or don't we give a darn? While Washington and the Pentagon are doing their little dance between bombing raids and peace talks, a lot of guys are ending up facedown in the mud with a bullet in their brains or their limbs blown to smithereens by some land mine."

Maggie groaned inwardly. Had Jordan died like that?

"If a guy's going to risk getting blown away every day," Chad went on solemnly, "he expects folks back home to root for him, cheer him on, be proud of him. But that's not how it is. People just want to forget there's a war going on, and they want to forget the guys who are fighting. There are a lot of guys over there on drugs, Maggie. They want to block out what's happening, dull the pain. There's nothing pretty about it; most of what I saw turned my stomach. I saw examples of the greatest heroism you can imagine . . . and the greatest cowardice. I saw it all, Maggie. But I never saw Jordan. I never once saw my brother."

"Oh, Chad, I prayed so hard . . ."

"I know you did, Maggie. But maybe it's time to stop looking, stop waiting. Not give up hope, I don't mean that. But it's been four years. We can't keep our lives on hold any longer."

She studied him intently. "Is that what you think we're doing?"

"Aren't we?"

"We both have full, rewarding lives, Chad. I wouldn't call that sitting around waiting."

"All right, I agree. We both have busy schedules and successful careers, but what about our personal lives, Maggie? Don't you want someone to love, a home and family someday?"

Her voice caught on a jag of emotion. "You know I do."

"So do I, Maggie." He reached across the table for her hand and gently caressed her slim fingers. "You know how I feel about you, Mag. I'm no good at pretending. Man, the night I got home I popped the question on your doorstep, but I could see the shock on your face; I could see you weren't ready, so I've kept my mouth shut since then. Kept my feelings to myself until you got used to the idea of me being around again."

"Oh, Chad, I've been so glad to have you home . . ."

"It's good to be home. I've had enough globe-trotting, Maggie. I want a normal life for a change, where I don't have to keep looking back over my shoulder or wondering if my next step is a land mine or whether I'll still be alive by nightfall. I want to come home to Willowbrook and get my job back at the newspaper and maybe write a book of my own about the war." He paused meaningfully, his eyes glistening. "And I want to settle down with the woman I love and raise a bunch of kids."

Maggie's face grew warm. She lowered her gaze. "You—you'll

make a wonderful husband and father, Chad."

Still holding her hand, he got up from the table and drew her up beside him. "I want to be *your* husband, Maggie. No one else's. How about it? Will you marry me?"

"I . . . I can't answer that, Chad."

"Can't or won't? Are you saying you don't love me?"

"Love you? I guess I've always loved you as a friend. My dearest friend in the world. But marriage . . . ?"

"We're more than friends, Maggie." His resonant voice was filled with urgency and yearning. "Don't you feel it? I feel it whenever we're together. I feel it when I hold you in my arms, when we kiss. You love me, I know you do, just as I love you." He crushed her against his chest and brought his mouth down hungrily on hers, as if willing her to recognize the passion that flamed for both of them just beneath the surface.

In the sweet, smothering warmth of Chad's embrace, Maggie's emotions surged as they had the snowy night he greeted her on her doorstep. She kissed him back with an ardor and abandonment that startled her; his kisses, his caresses left her feeling lightheaded, breathless, weak in the knees. Yes, she did love Chad; she wanted him, needed him. And yet . . .

As her head cleared, she pushed him away gently. "Chad, please—"

He held her arms fast. "Say you love me, Maggie."

She gazed up into the deep blue wells of his eyes and felt herself drowning. "I do love you, Chad. I do."

"And I love you with all my heart." He cupped her delicate chin in his large hands. "I'll ask again, Maggie. Will you marry me? Become my wife?"

Tears glistened in her eyes. "Please, Chad. Give me time. Don't make me decide now."

His face fell. "How much time?"

"I don't know. Can't we just take things slowly? You've been gone so long. We're different people than we were when you went away. Don't you feel it too? We need to get reacquainted. Can't we just spend time together over the next few months and see what happens?"

He stepped back, releasing her. "You win, Maggie. I'll do whatever it takes to convince you we're meant to be together. But it won't be easy. I'm not a patient man. But I won't give up. Not ever. You wait and see. Someday you'll be mine."

If Maggie had expected the months of 1972 to drag by, she was greatly mistaken. So much was happening now in her life that the weeks raced by at breakneck speed. Chad moved back to Willowbrook, returned to his job at the newspaper, and settled back into his old life without missing a beat. And his life became Maggie's life, for what one did, the other did; where one went, the other went. When they weren't working, they were always together, as comfortable with each other as a pair of old shoes.

But what Maggie felt for Chad was more than mere contentment; her love for him was growing stronger every day, like a gnarled oak tree spreading its roots deeper and deeper into the soil, until it seemed that her life and Chad's were one and the same, grounded, wound together, inseparable.

As their romance blossomed, what happened in the rest of the world seemed somehow trivial, unimportant. President Nixon visited China and Moscow and ordered the mining of Haiphong harbor and other major North Vietnamese ports, then became embroiled in what came to be known as the Watergate scandal. In July, the Democratic National Convention nominated Senator George McGovern of South Dakota for president and Senator Thomas Eagleton of Missouri for vice president. This time no demonstrators rioted in the streets.

On August 12, the last U.S. ground combat forces were withdrawn from Vietnam, and later that month, President Nixon and Vice President Agnew were nominated for reelection by the Republican Convention. On November 7 Nixon won the election with the greatest Republican landslide in history. In December, one week before Christmas, after the Paris peace negotiations reached an impasse, the United States resumed full-scale bombing of North Vietnam.

Maggie was aware of all of these national and world events, but they seemed somehow remote in light of her blossoming relationship with Chad Barrett. Like Chad, she had distanced herself emotionally from the war; it had no relevance for her anymore.

On Christmas Eve of 1972, Chad and his parents once again joined the Herricks for a festive dinner of succulent lamb, boiled potatoes, creamed peas, and Grandmother Anna's homemade pumpkin pie. After dinner, as everyone was finishing dessert, Chad spoke up, a curious lilt in his voice. "Mom, Dad, Mr. and Mrs. Herrick, Jon Knowl . . . if all of you don't mind, I'd like to give Maggie her Christmas gift a few hours early."

"Go right ahead, Son," said Mr. Barrett with a wink at Maggie. "We'd all like to see what little surprise Santa has delivered."

"It's not from Santa," said Chad, "but I'm hoping you'll consider it your best Christmas gift ever, Maggie."

She pushed back her dessert plate and looked up expectantly. "Now you've really got me curious, Chad. What is it?"

He produced a small gold foil-wrapped package from his pocket and placed it in her open palm. She turned the tiny package over and examined it. "Whatever it is, I know it's smaller than a bread basket," she teased. She carefully removed the wrapping to reveal a velvet jewel case. The whole room was silent as she opened the lid. There, nestled inside was a resplendent diamond ring.

"Oh, Chad," she breathed.

Chad slipped out of his chair and knelt down beside her on one knee. With a jaunty smile, he took her free hand and gazed into her eyes. "Maggie, last Christmas Eve I asked you a question you weren't ready to answer. I'm asking you again now, with all our family as witnesses. Margaret Kate Herrick, I love you with all my heart. Will you marry me and make me the happiest man on earth?"

She laughed, her face flushing with a delicious warmth. "How could I possibly say no and spoil such a wonderful party?"

Chad hoisted himself up and drew her out of her chair. He held her in his arms, his face so close to hers she could feel the heat of his minty breath on her cheeks. "Is that a yes, my darling?"

A mirthful smile played on her lips. "Yes, Chad. Yes, yes, yes. A thousand times yes!"

Their families broke into spontaneous applause as Chad slipped the ring on her finger, then swept her back in his arms and kissed her soundly, like the swashbuckling hero of an old-time movie.

"When will the wedding be?" asked Mrs. Barrett. "We must start making plans."

Her head still spinning, Maggie gazed up questioningly at Chad. "I don't know. When shall it be?"

"The sooner the better," said Chad, holding her possessively. "Next month? Two months?"

"Oh, my goodness, no," declared Maggie's mother. "Margaret will need time to make arrangements. There'll be invitations to send and bridal showers to attend and rehearsal dinners to plan. And you'll need to think about where to live, although you're certainly welcome to stay here until you get on your feet."

"Or with us," said Mrs. Barrett. "We have plenty of room."

"Thanks, all of you," said Chad, "but I think Maggie and I will want our own little place, right, Mag?"

"Our own little place? Oh, yes, that sounds wonderful!" she said breathlessly.

Grandmother Anna spoke up. "Margaret, dear, I'd love to make your wedding dress for you, if you'd like."

"Oh, I'd love that, Grams. Thank you!"

"Does this mean I've got to wear one of those monkey suits?" said Jon Knowl.

"That's right, Jon-Jon," said Maggie. "No headbands, ratty sweaters, or hippie sandals. But you'll look great in a tuxedo. Especially if you get a haircut. All the girls will love you."

"Yeah? So there'll be a lot of girls there, huh?"

"Dozens and dozens," said Chad. "If I know our families, the invitation list will be a mile long. Besides, Jon Knowl, I'm hoping you'll be standing beside me when your sister comes down the aisle."

"Standing beside you?"

"Right. I'd like you to be my best man. What do you say?"

With a deep laugh Jon Knowl tossed back his mane of honey-brown hair. "I'll do it, man, but I can't promise I'll cut my hair."

"So okay, everybody, let's set a wedding date," said Chad. "How soon can you all be ready?"

"May . . . June?" suggested Mrs. Barrett, sounding nearly as excited as her son. "We should be ready by then if we all pitch in now to get things done."

"How about the second Saturday of June?" said Maggie, resting her cheek on Chad's solid chest. In his arms she felt wonderfully safe and protected and cherished. "Chad, darling, I've always dreamed of being a June bride."

He nuzzled her cascading curls with his chin. "A June bride it is, Maggie. In six months you'll be Mrs. Chad Barrett. I'll be counting the days until then."

Later that night, alone in her bedroom, Maggie slipped into her warm flannel nightgown, then stole over by the bay window and gazed out at the wintry, starlit sky. Snow flurries were falling softly on the mounds of glistening snow below, giving the world a magical, crystalline glow.

She gazed down at the dazzling ring on her finger, a symbol of the love she and Chad shared. She would wear it always as a reminder of their undying commitment. But as she fingered the gold locket at her throat, she realized there was one more thing she had to do. As if performing a ritual, she slowly unfastened the clasp and removed the heart-shaped locket from around her neck. She clenched it tightly in her hand for a long moment, her eyes glazing with tears. Looking out at the black velvet sky, she whispered, "I'm sorry, Jordan. I can't wait for you any longer. Wherever you are, know that I loved you once. But I have to believe Chad and I have your blessing. You wouldn't want us to grieve any longer. You'll always be in our hearts, Jordan. We'll never forget you."

As a tear slid down her cheek, she pressed the locket to her lips, then tucked it away forever in her top dresser drawer.

22

On a cozy winter evening on January 22, 1973, Maggie and Chad sat relaxed on the love seat in the parlor, half listening to the evening news on television while browsing through the "Houses for Sale" section of the newspaper. "I think we'd be better off with a new home in the suburbs, even if it's small," Chad was saying, "rather than a large, old home in a rundown neighborhood."

"But the old homes have such character and personality," said Maggie. "I love these old Victorians with all their cupolas and towers and wraparound porches."

"But most of them aren't in tiptop condition like this one. We'd probably end up spending a mint on renovations—repairing leaky roofs, shoring up sagging porches, scraping off yellowed, peeling wallpaper."

"I suppose you're right, Chad, but those modern homes we visited in that new subdivision seemed so cramped and boxy and completely devoid of personality."

Chad slipped his arm around her shoulder and drew her close. "I know, my darling girl. We'll just have to keep looking until we find exactly what we want. We still have time. But there's one thing I'm going to insist on."

She gazed up at his smiling, roguish face. "Exactly what will you insist on, my dear Mr. Barrett?"

He kissed the tip of her nose. "I must insist that we find ourselves a house with a number of bedrooms, three or four, at least."

"And why do we need so many bedrooms, my good man?" she asked in a lyrical, exaggerated voice. "After all, we can only sleep in one at a time."

His eyes crinkled merrily. "And I'll warn you now, my darling, I don't plan on getting much sleep for the first several weeks."

"And I'll warn you, my darling," she countered, "I'm an absolute bear without my beauty sleep."

He kissed her forehead and hair. "I'm sure we'll manage a satisfactory compromise. Meanwhile, about all those bedrooms . . . we'll need them for Henrietta, Abigail, and Eugene."

Her eyebrows shot up. "Who, pray tell, are Henrietta, Abigail, and Eugene?"

He broke into raucous laughter. "They're our children, my dear Magpie."

"Not with those names, they aren't! What's wrong with . . . with Mary, Sarah, and John?"

He was still laughing. "Nothing at all, if you don't mind boring our children to death with banal, obsequious names."

She was about to offer a clever retort when something on TV caught her attention. The newscaster had mentioned Vietnam. She sat up straight, quieting Chad with a finger to her lips. "Listen," she urged. "He's talking about the war."

Chad sprang forward and turned up the sound, and they both sat listening, no longer touching. "This just in," said the announcer. "A Vietnam peace agreement has been signed today in Paris by representatives from the United States, North and South Vietnam, and the Vietcong. These are the provisions all parties have agreed upon. There will be a cease-fire throughout North and South Vietnam. Within sixty days all U.S. forces will be withdrawn, and U.S. installations will be dismantled.

Within sixty days all prisoners of war will be released, including North Vietnamese, Vietcong, and U.S. prisoners."

All U.S. prisoners of war will be released . . . Maggie heard nothing else after that. *All prisoners of war!* Her heart pounding, she stared wide-eyed at Chad. "Do you know what this means? Jordan could be coming home to us at last!"

Frown lines furrowed Chad's brow. "Don't get your hopes up, Maggie. We have no reason to believe Jordan is a POW."

"But he could be," she insisted.

"And he could be dead."

"But what if he's alive? What if all these years he's been a prisoner and couldn't contact us?"

"Don't do this, Maggie!"

"Do what?"

Chad's temple throbbed. "Don't get our hopes up after all this time. I won't believe my brother's alive until the day I see him walk through my front door."

"It could happen," she said in a small, hushed voice. "We'll know whether Jordan's dead or alive . . . they said we'll know in sixty days! Oh, Chad, think of it. One way or another, we're going to know."

"All I know is, it would take a miracle for my brother to be one of the returning POWs, and I'm afraid I don't have that kind of faith."

"Maybe not, but I'm going to pray for a miracle anyway."

On a Friday afternoon less than two weeks later, Chad appeared at her front door, pounding insistently and shouting her name. "Maggie, open up! Maggie!"

She ran to the door and threw it open, breathless. "What's wrong, Chad? Is someone hurt?"

He burst inside, flushed, out of breath, swinging his arms as if unable to contain his energy. "You'll never believe—!" he began.

"What, Chad? What's wrong?"

"Nothing! Everything's right! Everything's wonderful!" He swung her up in his arms and whirled her around. "You've got your miracle, Maggie!"

She stared at him in confusion. "My miracle?"

Chad led her over to the green velvet sofa in the living room. "Sit down, Mag. You won't believe this."

They sat down, facing each other. "Tell me, Chad."

His ruddy face gleamed. Tears glazed his eyes as he choked out the words. "It's Jordan. He's alive. He's coming home."

Maggie covered her mouth with her hands. "Jordan? Alive?"

"The Pentagon telephoned my parents today. They said Jordan has been a prisoner of war for the last five years. They said he's okay. They have to run some tests and stuff at the military hospital, but after that he'll be home."

"Oh, thank God! Thank God!" Maggie couldn't hold back the convulsive sobs that heaved through her chest. She collapsed in Chad's arms and they both wept freely. Between sobs she said, "It's what we . . . what we've prayed for . . . all these years."

"We'll be together again like old times," said Chad, his voice riding a crest of excitement. "The Three Musketeers. All for one and one for all!"

"I can't wait," said Maggie. "When will he be here?"

"I don't know," said Chad. "From what the Pentagon told my mom, Jordan will be flying to Andrews Air Force Base outside of Washington, D.C., and then President Nixon will be throwing a big bash to welcome all the POWs home." Chad broke into a jovial grin. "And guess what, Maggie. We're invited to the party!"

"Us? Me too?"

"Sure, you're practically family. Can you believe it, Mag? My mom and dad and you and I will be flying to Washington to welcome Jordan home."

Two weeks later, Maggie found herself packing for her trip to Washington. Her grandmother and mother hovered over her like two anxious mother hens. "Do you have everything you need?" asked her mother for the hundredth time.

"I'm sure I do," said Maggie. "I've checked everything a dozen times."

"Do you have your new powder blue evening gown?" asked her grandmother. "You look absolutely regal in it. You must wear it when you meet the president."

"I will, Grams. It's already packed."

"And the matching pumps?" asked her mother.

"They're packed, Mom."

"And the matching handbag, Margaret?"

"It's packed, Grams."

Her mother clasped her arms and looked her square in the face. "Now, Margaret, if the hotel has a beauty shop, have your hair done in one of those fancy twists for the president's party, you hear me? I want you to look like the belle of the ball."

"Mom, no one's going to notice me. Everyone will be looking at all the POWs who've come home."

Her mother's voice softened with a sudden wistfulness. "One POW will be looking at you, Margaret. Jordan Barrett. After all these years, you want to look your best for him."

The ringing doorbell spared Maggie further interrogation.

She blew a kiss at her mother and grandmother, then ran downstairs and opened the door to Chad.

He was wearing a striking navy blue suit and looked taller and more handsome than she'd ever seen him. "You ready, Maggie? Our train leaves in an hour for Chicago. If we don't make it, we won't catch our afternoon flight to Washington."

"I'm all ready, Chad. My suitcase is upstairs."

"I'll get it. My folks are in the car. They're as excited as a couple of kids at Christmas."

"So am I!"

Chad grinned. "Now that you mention it, me too!"

He was about to head for the stairs when he paused and came back. He lifted her left hand, his eyes clouding. "Where's my ring?"

Her face grew warm. "I . . . I took it off, Chad. I didn't think Jordan should see it yet. We'll have lots of time later to explain everything to him."

Chad pressed her hand against his cheek. "It's not going to be easy for him, finding out we're engaged. But I guess he'll have a few months before the wedding to get used to the idea."

His gaze went to the hollow of her throat. "I see you're wearing Jordan's locket again."

"You don't approve?"

"I didn't say that. It's just . . . I'm surprised, that's all."

"I promised him I'd wear it always."

"But you didn't, Maggie. You took it off when you agreed to be my wife."

"I'm only wearing it until Jordan comes home. I want to do everything I can to make his homecoming special. Don't you?"

"Sure I do. He's my brother. I would've given my own life for him. You know that."

"Then right now we have to think about Jordan and his needs, not about ourselves. Agreed?"

Chad's expression was solemn, pensive. "Whatever you say, Maggie."

"Don't look so glum," she chided. "This coming week is going to be the best week of our lives. We'll have our Jordan back, and the whole world will be watching us celebrate at the president's party at the White House!"

As she anticipated, the next few days were a delightful, dizzying blur of activity as Maggie, Chad, and his parents flew to Washington, checked into a luxury hotel, and the next day took a taxi to Andrews Air Force Base, where they watched the gleaming U.S. Air Force transport swoop down like a great silver bird and land on the tarmac with a shuddering roar. This was the culmination of a long, grueling trip for the POWs. The American C-141 plane had picked them up at Gia Long Airport in Vietnam, flew them to Clark Air Force Base in the Philippines for a brief stay, and then flew them on to Andrews in Washington.

As Maggie stood in the cheering crowd, watching the released soldiers descending the ramp one by one, her heart pounded out the words, *My Jordan, my Jordan, my Jordan.* He was coming home to her at last.

Each soldier was met and embraced by eager, weeping loved ones—young sweethearts, wives with small children, stooped, gray-haired parents, laughing brothers and sisters. Some soldiers even bent down and kissed the ground. Maggie studied their faces, desperate for her first glimpse of Jordan. What would he look like? Would she even recognize him after five long years? Would he still think she was the most beautiful girl he had ever seen?

The questions tumbled in Maggie's mind until she spotted a tall, rangy man lumbering down the ramp, a man who resembled Jordan, with the same sturdy face, distinctive nose, and sculpted chin. And yet this man was pale, hollow-eyed, gaunt, his gait uncertain. A pitiable shadow of the man Maggie remembered.

"It's Jordan!" cried Mrs. Barrett over a sob. She broke into a run toward her son just as Jordan spotted the four of them in the crowd and came loping toward them, his lean face suddenly all boyish grin. Yes, the old Jordan. She recognized him now.

Maggie began running, too, arms open wide, her heart hammering in her ears. She had the sensation of moving in slow motion, her feet scarcely touching the ground; heaven help her, it was taking forever to reach Jordan.

Finally, as he caught her in his arms and kissed her; as his familiar voice whispered sweet endearments in her ear; as they all bear-hugged and wept and talked at once and wept some more, Maggie felt her head spin with a sweet delirium. She was dream-walking. Caught up in a rosy fantasy. This couldn't be real, couldn't be happening. She had played out this moment too often in her dreams for it to be real.

While TV cameras rolled and flashbulbs popped around them, Maggie and the Barretts (all of them at last!) made their way arm in arm in arm toward the limousine that would take them to their hotel. Jordan walked with one arm around Maggie and the other around Chad, leaning on them, his wide, eager smile in place, his expression dazed, as if he, too, was convinced he must be dreaming. "You look so good," he told Maggie over and over. "Everyone, everything looks so good."

In the limousine Maggie sat between Jordan and Chad. Her emotions were riding so high, her excitement at such a fever pitch, the sensation was painful, almost more than she could bear. She couldn't think rationally, calmly, couldn't contain the current of energy electrifying her senses. She kept reminding herself, *This is Jordan sitting beside me, my Jordan home from the war, my Jordan back from the dead!*

"Jordan, darling," said Mrs. Barrett, turning around in the seat ahead of them, "we're going to our hotel. You and Chad will be sharing a room together. You'll have several hours before the White House party tonight, so if you'd like to rest—"

"Do we have to go?"

"To the president's party? Everyone's going, Son."

"I don't like parties."

His mother's voice turned fretful. "But you always liked parties, Jordan. You were the life of the party, remember?"

Jordan's tone was distant, remote. "That was then."

"Jordan, you don't have to go anywhere, if you don't feel like it," said Maggie. "But a lot of your friends will be there. This might be your last chance to see them."

Jordan nodded. "You're right. I'll go. But I don't want to stay long."

"We can leave whenever you say," said Chad.

"That's right," said Mr. Barrett in his booming voice. "This is your night, Son. You let us know what you want to do, and we'll do it."

That night the POWs' welcome-home dinner party was held, not in the White House itself, but rather in an enormous two-story tent with broad red and white stripes and fancy hanging lights. As Maggie and the Barretts followed the other guests through the long receiving line, she felt as if she were still dreaming. Was she actually standing arm in arm with her beloved Jordan in his crisp navy uniform and meeting the President of the United States? As they reached the front of the line, President and Mrs. Nixon shook her hand warmly and thanked her and the Barretts for coming. Then Mr. Nixon gave Jordan's hand an especially firm shake. "Your country is proud of you, young man," the president said with a smile.

Jordan stood at attention and saluted. "Thank you, sir!"

As they made their way through the crowd, Maggie gazed around at the rows of lavishly decorated tables bedecked with candles and linen, crystal and china, and exquisite floral centerpieces. On one side of the tent was a stage where, in their stunning red jackets, the Les Brown Orchestra was spiritedly playing a popular jazz tune. Everywhere Maggie looked she saw celebrities—movie and television stars, eminent political figures, and legendary sports heroes— mingling with the returned prisoners of war and their families. Yes, this was going to be a breathtaking party, a once-in-a-lifetime event she and Jordan would tell their grandchildren about someday.

No! Not Jordan! She meant *Chad!* She and Chad would tell their grandchildren someday. After all, Chad was the one she was engaged to marry. But tonight, with Jordan by her side, her engagement to Chad seemed like part of another lifetime. And, for the life of her, she couldn't imagine breaking the news to Jordan without breaking his heart.

Throughout dinner, sitting between the two dear men in her life, Maggie couldn't get that worrisome sense of ambivalence out of her mind. *Chad or Jordan? Jordan or Chad?* To whom did she owe her loyalty, her love, her life? She loved them both. She had pledged her heart to Chad, had agreed to become his wife, but that was before Jordan had returned. Now everything was different. The old suppositions were gone; her former expectations had been dispelled by this new reality. Jordan was back, the man she had promised to love forever. But hadn't she promised the same to Chad?

Maggie had a hard time keeping her mind on the program, even though the irrepressible Bob Hope was on stage telling jokes and singing, and afterward the larger-than-life John Wayne, the Duke himself, got up and said a few words of welcome and praise, finishing with a heartfelt grin and a commendatory word to the POWs: "You're the best we have, and I'll ride off into the sunset with you anytime."

President Nixon spoke, too, flashing his broad grin and raising his hands in victory; this was obviously a triumphant moment for him as well as for the POWs. Several choral groups rounded out a program brimming with patriotism, pomp and circumstance, cheers and tears.

Afterward, Maggie and the Barretts mingled with the other guests. The mood of the crowd was upbeat, jubilant, everyone friendly and animated and in their best finery—the men in tuxedos, women in long gowns, the POWs in their respective uniforms. While the Barretts chatted with another couple whose son had come home, Maggie looked around and realized Jordan had disappeared. She turned to Chad. "Where's your brother?"

He looked around. "Beats me. He was just here."

Maggie felt a niggling worry. "Do you think he's okay?"

"I hope so. Just to be sure, I'll go check the restrooms."

"And I'll look outside."

She slipped away from the Barretts and made her way outside the sprawling, music-filled tent. Alone in the dark, she shivered and hugged herself. The night air was cold, the deep azure sky alive with stars. She looked around. No sign of Jordan. She was about to go back inside when she spotted a solitary figure sitting on a concrete bench near a twisted oak tree. Jordan! She walked over and sat down beside him. "Are you okay?"

He moved over, making room for her. "Yeah. Fine."

"What are you doing out here? The party's inside."

"I'm not much for parties."

"You said that before, but you used to love them."

He sat forward and lowered his head. "Not anymore. Too much noise. Confusion. Commotion. Everyone pressing in on you, smothering you. It's too warm, too close. Makes a guy feel claustrophobic."

"I guess it is a lot to handle after . . ." She let her words drift away.

Jordan stood up and paced back and forth, his breathing ragged. "I just want this evening to be over."

"But it's for you," she argued. "Everyone wants to welcome you home, let you know how much they care."

Jordan's voice rose and his gestures grew more agitated as he swung his arms and pounded his fist against his palm. "I didn't ask for this, Maggie. I just wanted to go home. I don't need presidents and celebrities giving me big, fancy speeches. Just let me get on a plane and go back to Willowbrook."

"You will, Jordan. We're all flying home together tomorrow."

He sat back down beside her on the bench and reached for her hand. "Thank God, I've got you, Maggie. You're what kept me going . . . you and God." He swiveled his torso toward her and drew her into his arms. He felt thinner, less muscular than she remembered, but the warmth of his embrace and the closeness of his lips stirred buried memories. Not memories exactly, but sensations and emotions she hadn't felt in five long years.

"No matter what they did to me, Maggie," he said in a husky whisper,

"I just kept telling myself that someday I'd be back home with you. You gave me strength. And hope. I knew you were praying for me. I knew you were waiting. A lot of guys found out their girls, even their wives, didn't wait for them. It kills me thinking how they must feel now. Thank God, you waited for me, Maggie."

Guilt twisted inside her. What would he say if he knew she hadn't waited? If he had come home a few months later, he wouldn't have encountered Maggie Herrick, but Mrs. Chad Barrett, his brother's wife!

Jordan turned her chin up to his. "Did you hear me, Maggie? You're the reason I made it home. Every day in the camp I would play out in my mind what it would be like when we were together again. After so many years of thinking about it, I've got the scenario down pat. I can picture you in your wedding gown walking down the aisle to meet me. I can imagine what our first home will be like. I can even visualize what our kids will look like. A boy and a girl. They'll look just like us."

Maggie forced a little laugh. "Jordan, aren't you rushing things?"

He tightened his embrace. "Rushing things? Our lives have been on hold for five bitter, long years, Maggie. How can you say I'm rushing things?"

She struggled for words. "So . . . so much has changed, Jordan. We're different people now. We hardly know each other anymore."

With his index finger he traced the heart shape of her lips. "I know we're different, sweetheart. And I know the world has changed. But deep inside, where it really counts, we're the same people, Maggie. The love we felt for each other is still there."

Before she could protest, he tilted her head back and brought his mouth down hungrily on hers. Maggie's head reeled, until a deep, familiar voice brought her back sharply to the present. "Maggie!"

Jordan released her, and they both stared up into Chad's glaring eyes. "What's going on here?" he demanded.

Maggie jumped up, her heart pounding, her face prickling with an uncomfortable warmth. "Nothing, Chad. We were just—"

"Just making up for lost time, old man," said Jordan with a hint of his old droll whimsy. He got up and slapped his brother on the back, but his bravado seemed forced, thin. "By the way, if I didn't say it before, I want to say it now, Chad. Thanks for keeping an eye on Maggie while I was gone. It looks like you've taken good care of my girl. I owe you one for that."

Maggie could see that Chad was fuming inside, but he ground his jaw and remained silent until he got control of his emotions. With a furtive glance at Maggie, he said, "Don't thank me, man. She's an easy girl to keep an eye on."

Jordan circled her waist with his arm. "Yeah, you can say that again. Now maybe you can help me convince her that the two of us can pick up where we left off."

Another furtive glance from Chad. "She needs convincing?"

"Seems so. She has this idea that we're different people now."

"Maybe she's right," said Chad. He gave his brother's shoulder a comradely squeeze. "Listen, man, we'd all better get back inside. The folks are going to wonder what happened to us."

Jordan scowled and seemed to shrink back. "You go ahead, Chad. I'm staying out here."

"Chad's right," prompted Maggie. "We should go back in. It's not every day you get to party at the White House."

Jordan stiffened. "No. I can't. I'm sorry."

Chad studied his brother with concern. "Are you feeling okay? You didn't eat much dinner."

"It's the rich food," said Jordan. "Guess my stomach can't handle it after five years of rice and swamp weed soup."

Maggie clasped Jordan's arm solicitously. "Listen, maybe we all should go back to the hotel." She looked knowingly at Chad. "You two wait out here, okay? I'll go back inside and get your parents, and we'll call it a night."

Chad nodded, his hand protectively clasping Jordan's shoulder. "Sounds like a good plan, Magpie."

Before returning to the party, she took a quick glimpse back at Jordan standing shoulder to shoulder with Chad, and what she saw made her heart wince. There was little in this haggard, tentative man to remind her of the vigorous, top-of-the-world Jordan she once loved.

23

Jordan's homecoming stirred a media blitz Willowbrook hadn't seen since the end of World War II. Television and newspaper reporters descended on the Barrett household like swarms of hungry bees, wanting an interview, insisting on a story. During Jordan's first week home, Maggie found herself spending most of her time at his home helping his mother take the barrage of phone calls and sorting the deluge of mail.

Most of the time Jordan kept to himself, spending long hours alone in his room. When a news anchorman from a Chicago television station called and asked for a live interview that would be syndicated to other stations across the country, Maggie was ready to turn him down. She wasn't sure Jordan was up for such a strenuous undertaking, nor whether he would be distressed by the probing questions. But, to her surprise, Jordan agreed to the interview. "Maybe if I get it over with once and for all, people will see it and stop asking me questions."

The next day the anchorman, Les Broderick, a tall, swarthy man in a shiny black toupee, arrived with his crew and a truckload of television equipment—cameras, cables, lights—enough paraphernalia to clutter Mrs. Barrett's spacious living room. Chad and Maggie made a point of sitting in on the interview, like sentries, one on each side of Jordan.

It took the crew nearly an hour to set up. Meanwhile, Jordan sat and fidgeted, then got up and paced, obviously wishing he hadn't gotten himself into this. Maggie tried to calm him, as did Chad, but Jordan wouldn't be calmed. By the time the blazing lights went on and the anchorman sat down beside Jordan and began pelting him with questions, Jordan looked as if he were being interrogated by his Vietcong captors.

"Lieutenant Barrett, tell our viewers how you were captured by the North Vietnamese five years ago," said Broderick.

Jordan, looking stiff and uncomfortable in his navy uniform, cracked his knuckles nervously and avoided looking directly into the camera. "I was flying a bombing sortie north of Hanoi," he said, so quietly everyone strained to hear.

"Could you repeat that, Lieutenant?"

Jordan looked perturbed. "I said, I was flying a bombing sortie north of Hanoi, taking out a large expansion bridge." He paused, kneading his knuckles. "Just as I released my bombs, a surface-to-air missile took off the left wing of my aircraft. It must have hit somewhere else, too, because smoke started billowing up through my instrument panel."

As the memories returned, Jordan's voice grew deeper, more resonant. "I knew I was going down, so I ejected from the plane. But I flew out so hard and fast I thought I was going to rip my limbs off. I couldn't believe I was going down. I landed in a rice paddy amidst a swarm of armed peasants who started kicking and punching me and hitting me with their rifle butts and trying to stab me with their bayonets. Man, they were mad as hornets. I didn't think I was going to make it out alive.

"One guy stole my boots; my uniform was in shreds. They tied my hands behind my back and paraded me through their village. The women and children threw stones at me."

"Where did they take you, Lieutenant?"

Jordan blew into his palms and rubbed them together, as if he were cold. "They took me to a prison camp called Hoa Lo Prison. We dubbed it the Hanoi Hilton."

"And what happened to you there?"

"They threw me into a cell in the interrogation wing, a section called Heartbreak Hotel, where they had built-in leg irons. They left me in solitary confinement for days. I lost track of time. Didn't see anyone except two guys who came in every day to beat me up and try to get me to sign some propaganda documents saying I was against the U.S. aggressors. I refused, so they beat on me harder."

"Were you able to communicate with other American POWs?"

"Shortly after I got there, I found out the guys were communicating with one another through a special code of taps. Not the Morse code—it was too slow. They'd tap out words and sentences on the walls of their cells. We'd listen with a tin cup. The letter C was the call for church, so when guys tapped the letter C from wall to wall through the camp, everyone would stop for silent prayer. It drove the guards crazy. They didn't want us communicating with one another.

"But we did anyway. We had secret committees for everything. Entertainment committee, morale committee, education committee, escape committee. We memorized the names of every man in camp—those who arrived, those who died—so someday whoever got out could call their families back home."

Les Broderick sat forward and adjusted his microphone. "Lieutenant Barrett, what was it like being a prisoner of war?"

Jordan rocked back and forth on the sofa, his gaze downcast, his jaw tightening. "It was like falling into a black hole with no way to climb back out; it was five long years of torture, deprivation, and starvation. I tried to escape at least a dozen times, but each time I was captured, brought back, and beaten."

"What did you wear? Surely not your uniform."

"No, they confiscated that right away." Jordan paused and drew in a deep breath. "In the winter we wore plain, loose uniforms that looked like long-sleeved pajamas, with a number on the back. Mine was 381. In the summer we wore baggy shorts and short-sleeved shirts and sandals made from rubber tires."

"Did you ever try to communicate with your family back home?"

Jordan stole a glance at Maggie. "I could have written a letter home, letting my family know where I was, but it would have meant cooperating with my captors and feeding into their propaganda. My interrogators tried to get me to write propaganda messages, but I wasn't willing to do that, so I never got a chance to write home. But I figured everyone at home knew where I was, knew I'd been captured."

"No," said Maggie. "We knew nothing at all. We thought you might be dead, but we never gave up hope."

Broderick broke in. "Lieutenant, would you describe your prison camp, the Hanoi Hilton, for us?"

Jordan cleared his throat. "It was a huge concrete structure with a high arched, heavy paneled door. Utilitarian looking. A smattering of trees. They kept five hundred prisoners of war there. You couldn't escape because the wall was too high, and broken glass was cemented to the top of it. But you kept trying anyway."

"What was a routine day like for you?" asked Broderick.

Jordan heaved a sigh and cracked his knuckles nervously. "I slept on a concrete pallet for a bed, in a small cell, alone, except for the rats and roaches. At 5:30 in the morning the VC would beat on gongs, and we would get up and go outside to wash and bathe. We had ten minutes. The only bathroom we had was the honey bucket in our cell. We ate twice a day: a little rice and soup made from swamp weed, sometimes moldy bread. Some guys got down to skeletons because they couldn't eat the food."

Broderick moved closer to Jordan, as if attempting to probe deeper. "What about the interrogations, Lieutenant? The beatings? How often were you forced to endure them?"

Jordan flinched visibly. He was rocking back and forth, clenching and unclenching his hands. "Every day the guards would interrogate us mercilessly. They wanted to know all kinds of personal stuff about us, and if they didn't get what they wanted, they beat us with strips of rubber or bamboo or put us in solitary confinement. They tried to force us to make tapes and write statements denouncing the war and the U.S. government. They wanted us to tell young GIs they had no business fighting for the American Imperialists."

"What other vivid memories do you have of your captivity, Lieutenant Barrett?" asked Broderick.

Maggie spoke up. "I think Jordan has told you enough. He's very tired—"

Jordan reached over and squeezed her hand. His palm was ice cold, his face blanched white, his eyes shadowed. "It's okay, Maggie. I'll talk about it just this once. Spill my guts and get it over with. Then maybe I can put the whole horrible nightmare out of my mind once and for all."

"Thank you," said Broderick. "Now about those memories—"

"I have too many memories," said Jordan darkly, as if looking inward at the secret screen of his mind. "I remember the fetid odor of open sewers on humid nights. The 'reeducation' camps where I had to hoe the rice paddies until I dropped. I recall the dysentery, the gnawing hunger pains, my body a mass of bruises, welts, and lacerations from the beatings. I recall the mosquitos, the hard labor, the exhaustion. The torture devices where my body was stretched until my bones popped out of their sockets. I remember the numbing monotony. But in solitary, in the darkness, a guy's mind knows no limits, no bounds. You can imagine anything and everything. It's incredible how the mind compensates for deprivations. I spent a lot of time praying and going over Bible verses I'd learned as a kid. I'd mentally reconstruct the life of Jesus, starting with His birth and going right up to His resurrection. Then I'd put the events of the Old Testament in order—Creation and the fall of Adam and Eve right up through Noah, Moses, and all the rest."

"Yes, that's very interesting." Broderick looked suddenly ill at ease and changed the subject. "Did you ever hear any news from the outside world?"

"Only what the Vietcong wanted us to hear. There was a loud-speaker in the courtyard area, and every morning and afternoon they would play an English propaganda broadcast with Hanoi Hannah, who would berate and scold us. When she criticized us for the Christmas bombing, she inadvertently let us know an American had landed on the moon. She asked how could a coun-try that placed a plaque on the moon saying 'We come in peace for all mankind' kill and maim and strafe so many innocent people?"

"That's an interesting issue you've brought up," said Broderick. "Are you aware, Lieutenant, that a vast majority of your countrymen are against the war? They feel we're fighting an immoral war, that we have no business being in Vietnam. What is your take on that?"

Jordan bristled and his face darkened. "Yes, I've heard about Americans being against the war. We heard the rumors over in 'Nam, in the prison camps. It tore us up. The guards loved to rub our faces in it. In fact, I heard directly from a Vietcong guard that it was the protests against the war going on here in America that gave them the encouragement they needed to fight harder against us."

Jordan paused, rubbing his chin. His eyes were dark, solemn, intense. "I don't have all the answers, sir. I can just tell you that the South Vietnamese desperately want our help fighting the Communists. They want to live free like we do, and if we don't help them, I predict it's just a matter of time before the whole country will be living under Communist rule."

"What is your opinion of the way the war has been fought?" asked Broderick.

Jordan thought a moment. "The guys I know have given it their best, their very lives. But I admit a lot of us had the feeling we were fighting with one arm tied behind our back. There were times when our pilots were told to bomb bridges and worthless targets, but were forbidden to strike the real targets, the missile installations, the harbors, the antiaircraft sites. We could have fought a winnable war if we'd used all our power and resources, if we had gone into Hanoi and Laos and Cambodia right away. Why are we giving up? Why can't we maintain a permanent presence in South Vietnam like we have in South Korea?"

"I'm not sure even our administration has an answer to that one, Lieutenant," said Broderick.

Maggie patted Jordan's arm. "You look tired," she whispered with concern. "Do you want to stop?"

"Please, just a few more questions," Broderick broke in. "Lieutenant Barrett, you sound like a man who feels your country has betrayed you. Is that true?"

Jordan stiffened warily. "No, sir, not exactly." He hesitated, gathering his thoughts. "Okay, yes, I feel hurt and disappointed that people here at home consider the war a mistake when so many of us have given all we have, our lives, our blood, our souls, for our country. I'm not the only vet who feels like, while we were over there spilling our guts, our country abandoned us. Nixon talks about 'peace with honor.' What peace? What honor? It's a travesty! So, to be honest, yes, I feel like this administration has given the war away."

Broderick paused meaningfully, then cleared his throat. "One more question, Lieutenant. You've been gone five long years. What do you think about the world you've come home to?"

Jordan flashed a grim smile at Maggie. "I haven't been home long, sir, but from what I've seen so far, I feel like I've come back to another planet. Everything feels different—the music, the lifestyles, the clothes, the culture, even TV, with all this crazy, wild, psychedelic stuff. And the clothes—man, are they ugly. I see men going around with this foppish long hair and wearing paisley shirts and checkered bell-bottom trousers. What happened to men being men?"

Mr. Broderick flashed a wry grin. "You're not the only man who's wondered that, Lieutenant. Anything else you've noticed?"

Jordan nodded. "This new militancy in the air . . . all these groups—women, minorities, students, just about everyone—demanding their rights, sometimes with violence. We guys in 'Nam didn't have any rights; we laid it on the line, every right we ever had, for the good of our country, because that's what our country asked of us. How have these other groups earned the privilege of demanding their so-called rights?"

"That's something only they can answer, Lieutenant. You've talked about how the world has changed in five years. How have you changed?"

Jordan sat back and heaved a sigh. "I don't know if I can answer that, sir. Time will tell. I guess I'm more serious, more cautious, more impatient, more introspective. I'm not the happy-go-lucky guy I was, the guy who was convinced he could win any battle. Now I'm a guy who just feels lucky to have survived."

"And what about the future, Lieutenant? Is it going to be a rosy one for you?"

Jordan gave Maggie a searching glance. "I hope so, sir." He slipped his arm around her shoulder. His voice came out light, wistful. "I have the girl I love by my side, sir. She waited for me all these years. Not many guys are that fortunate. I'm hoping she'll agree to be my wife as soon as we can throw together a wedding. And I hope we can fill a house of our own with a bunch of happy kids. That's my dream, the one that kept me alive through five years in the prison camps."

Maggie stole a quick glance at Chad and winced at his pained expression. Guilt plagued her. How could she talk with Jordan about a wedding when her wedding to Chad was just three months away? They were living a lie that was breaking their hearts, but the truth would break Jordan's heart, and that was a risk neither of them was ready or willing to take.

24

In the weeks following Jordan's homecoming, Maggie noticed a disturbing phenomenon. Jordan seemed to be getting worse instead of better. Rather than settling back into his life and making the necessary adjustments, every day he seemed to feel more disenfranchised from his past and at odds with the present. He was becoming increasingly morose, remote, moody, a man Maggie wondered if she even knew anymore.

After his interview with the Chicago anchorman was aired on national TV, Jordan received a flood of invitations to share his story with churches, civic groups, and colleges, but he refused them all. "I said what I had to say, and that's the end of it. Why don't they leave me alone and let me figure out where I belong in this insane world?"

"People care about you," Maggie told him. "They're interested in what happened to you and what you have to say."

"They look at me like I'm a freak," he stormed. "I don't fit in anywhere. I look at other guys my age and I feel like a misfit, a pariah. I don't know them; I don't understand them. Man, I don't even like them—these pantywaist guys going around with their 'Make love, not war' mentality."

Often when Maggie stopped by the Barrett house to see Jordan, she found him sitting alone in his room, staring out into space. It unnerved her, the way he could sit for hours doing nothing, tuned out to her and everyone around him. "What are you doing,

Jordan?" she asked one day as he sat staring out the window for what seemed forever.

He stared at her as if he had forgotten she was in the room. "What, Maggie? You said something?"

She repeated her question, and he seemed irritated that she would even question his behavior. "I was just thinking. Anything wrong with that?"

"Of course not. But thinking about what?" she persisted.

"Nothing. Everything. What does it matter?"

Only when Jordan was talking about their future did a glimpse of the old irrepressible Jordan return. "When are we going to set our wedding date, Maggie?" he asked one sunny April afternoon as they sat together on her front porch swing.

She felt her whole frame grow tense, guarded. "Is there any hurry, Jordan?" she hedged.

He clasped her hand, intertwining their fingers. "I just think . . . I don't know . . . maybe once we're married, I can get back on track with my life. I just feel so . . . so aimless. I don't know what to do with myself, Maggie. I don't have a job, a career. I don't know what I'm going to do with the rest of my life."

"Then maybe it's too soon to talk about marriage."

He looked at her, his clear blue eyes narrowing in his lean face. "You still love me, don't you, Maggie?"

Her heart lurched. "Oh, Jordan, of course I love you. Only . . . only—"

"Only what? I'm not the man who went away five years ago? I know that, Maggie. I keep looking for that man, but I can't find him. I guess I've got to settle for the man I am now, and to tell you the truth, I'm not quite sure who that fellow is." He lifted her hand to his lips. "But one thing I know. The man who loved you then loves you now."

Maggie laid her head on Jordan's shoulder and gazed out at the sunset sky, ablaze with a bright orange crimson. Her thoughts churned. She seesawed between telling Jordan the truth about her engagement to Chad and setting a wedding date with Jordan just so the issue would be settled. "But you have so much to get used to, Jordan," she ventured. "Adjusting to a marriage right now is too much to ask of you."

"You're not asking; I'm telling. I'm saying marriage is just what I need to get me inspired, motivated. Having a wife to support— and kids someday—will get me off my duff and force me back out into the workplace."

She smiled up at him. "You really don't have to support me, Jordan. I have a wonderful editorial position at Herrick House. And I'm still receiving modest royalties from the book I wrote with Chad about the Jesus people."

Jordan frowned. "That's well and good for now, Maggie, but it'll be different after we're married. You'll be staying home with the kids."

She stifled a sudden spurt of laughter. "Jordan, there are no children, and there might not be for years. Surely you're not suggesting I give up my job the minute we're married!"

She felt him grow cold, distant. He gazed off toward the horizon. After a long, discomfitting moment he looked back at her, his eyes glinting with moisture. "I'm sorry, Maggie. I spent so many years in the prison camp imagining what our marriage would be like, living it in my mind day after day, that I forget you weren't there with me planning it out. But it was so vivid . . . so perfect . . . You don't understand what I'm talking about, do you?"

"I'm trying, Jordan. I know you had lots of time to think."

"It was more than that, Maggie. To keep my sanity, I had to turn inward to my mind. I had a whole other life going on in my imagination. I pictured you, Maggie, and I imagined what our life would be like together. I played out the days thinking about our wedding, the house we would build, the kids we would have, the things we would talk about. Man, I even imagined the things we would argue about. I got so good at visualizing this whole other life that sometimes I almost forgot where I was."

"But that life wasn't real, Jordan. It has nothing to do with reality, with our lives now."

"I know that, Maggie. But it's hard to let it go."

Maggie gazed down at her hands. "Jordan, sometimes I'm not sure you really know me anymore. I've changed just like you have. That's why I think we should wait before we talk about marriage." She gazed up at him, silently entreating him to understand. "Who knows? Maybe if you knew the real me, you wouldn't even want to marry me."

He slipped his arm around her and drew her against him. "Not a chance, Maggie." He kissed the top of her head. "I'm confused about a lot of things in this crazy, mixed-up life, but not that. You'll always be the only girl for me. So what will it be? A June wedding?"

Her breath caught in her throat. For an instant she was convinced he knew about her wedding date with Chad and was trying to rub it in, but then she saw the innocence in his expression and realized he didn't suspect after all. "A June wedding?" she gasped at last. "I don't think I could possibly be ready by then."

"Well, just think about it, Maggie. I don't want a big wedding. The fewer people the better. No fuss, no muss, you know. Just our families, a cake, and a preacher. Nothing fancy, okay?"

She was stunned, her mind a blank. No words came.

"Think about it and let me know in a few days."

A few days later, Maggie returned home from work to find Chad waiting for her in the parlor. He was pacing the floor, and his countenance was as dark as a storm cloud. "What's this about you and Jordan setting a wedding date?" he demanded.

She stared at him, dumbfounded. "We didn't . . . I haven't . . . Chad, I just told him I would think about it."

"Well, that's not the message he got. He's ready to reserve the church. So it looks to me, Maggie, like you're scheduled to marry two guys in June. Me and my brother! Tell me how you're going to get yourself out of that one!"

She sat down on the love seat and put her head in her hands. "Chad, I don't know what to do. Jordan seems so fragile, so vulnerable emotionally, that I can't bear to hurt him after all he's been through."

Chad sat down next to her and slipped his arm loosely around her shoulder. "I don't want to hurt him either, Maggie, but this whole business of keeping our engagement a secret is killing me. What's worse, we've got half the town in on the conspiracy. Every time I see somebody we know, I have to warn them not to mention our engagement to Jordan. We can't go on this way."

She looked searchingly at him. "What do you want me to do?"

He cupped her face in his palm, his tone solemn, entreating. "I don't know, Mag. Just tell me one thing. Is it still me you love?"

Tears welled in her eyes. "Of course it's you I love. Did you doubt it?"

His lips tightened. "I was beginning to wonder. You've been spending an awful lot of time with Jordan."

"Because he needs me, Chad. You know I love him, too . . . as a friend."

"Just as a friend?"

"Yes, my darling," she assured him, her lips curving in a faint smile. "The Jordan I loved five years ago is gone, just as the girl who loved him then is gone. We're different people now. I keep hoping Jordan will realize that, but he seems so tied to the life he created for us in his imagination during his years in captivity. But one of these days he has to realize we don't belong together."

Chad gently rubbed her arm. "You're fooling yourself if you think he'll ever come to that conclusion on his own."

She met his gaze and felt the tickle of excitement that always stirred when she looked into those luminous blue eyes. "What do you want me to do, Chad? Tell me."

His fingers tightened on her arm. "I can't, Maggie. It has to be your decision."

"Why? It involves you too."

"Because you know what I want. I want you. I want us to be together. But maybe that's not the right choice for you."

She fingered Jordan's locket that still nestled in the hollow of her throat. "It's not that I would hate being married to Jordan. I do love him. I want him to be happy. I want to do everything I can to make him happy." She gazed back at Chad and her voice caught on a crest of emotion. "If only I hadn't fallen in love with you, Chad, if only I didn't know what we have together, the way our minds think alike, the way we both feel impassioned about the same things, the way we work so well together. Look at what we accomplished with our book on the Jesus people. Our minds, our feelings, our hopes and dreams . . . we fit like hand in glove. You're the one I want to spend my life with."

"Then we have to tell Jordan."

"Can we risk it? Is he strong enough emotionally?"

A shadow crossed Chad's eyes. He drummed his fingers on Maggie's arm. "I don't think he's ready, Maggie. The truth is, you only see Jordan at his best. I live with him. I see him every day, at his best, at his worst."

"His worst? What are you saying?"

"I'm saying he's not the brother I remember. I don't know him. I can't predict him. He won't open up, won't let me in. He spends most of his time alone in his room. He doesn't want the radio or TV playing—he doesn't like any kind of noise. It's as if he feels bombarded by so many sensory images that he can't cope; he withdraws into himself and shuts out the world. He stays like that for hours. Just sits and stares into space."

"I've seen him like that," Maggie conceded. "It scares me because I feel as if he's somewhere so far away he might never come back."

"And when he does do something, he gets impatient if it doesn't go the way he expects, whether he's trying to use the electric can opener or play chess or figure his checkbook. He's always on edge emotionally. He flies into a rage if things don't go right, or if he makes a mistake, or if he feels someone is putting him down. You know how he and I used to joke around and tease each other. Well, now he's always dead serious. If I try any rough and tumble stuff, he stares me down like I've violated his rights somehow."

Maggie shook her head. "I guess we should have known there would be a period of adjustment."

"It gets worse, Maggie," said Chad solemnly. "The nights are awful. The pits!"

She stared at him. "What do you mean?"

"I mean, Jordan paces the floor like a caged lion. He can't sleep. He hates the nights. I hear him prowling the house long after I've gone to bed. Sometimes I hear him pound his fist into the wall, and in the morning his knuckles are bruised."

"I've seen them like that, but he wouldn't tell me what had happened."

"And most nights—usually in the dead of the hour—I hear him cry out or scream."

"No!"

"He makes an ungodly sound, Maggie, worse than a scream, bloodcurdling, as if he's reliving the torture he experienced in the camps. The first few times I tried to go in and comfort him, but he was oblivious to me. Then one night he nearly attacked me; I think he thought I was one of his North Vietnamese guards. I had to wrestle him to the floor. So now I don't go in; I lie there in my own room and listen and pray that God will get him through the nightmares."

Maggie choked back a sob. "He never talks about his nightmares, or his trouble sleeping, or his temper tantrums."

"I'm sure he doesn't want you to know. He doesn't want you to worry."

"But I do worry. My heart aches for him."

"Mine too."

"He has big chunks of his life that nobody knows or understands, and he doesn't know how to share them."

Chad drew in a long, ragged breath. "One of the strangest things, Mag . . . maybe I shouldn't even tell you this. But when I go in his room in the morning, I find him curled up on the floor in a corner asleep."

"The floor?"

"He sleeps on the hardwood floor, Maggie. Sometimes with a blanket, sometimes not. He surrounds himself with a few items of clothing, his sandals, his Bible, his flashlight, and a photograph of you."

"Have you asked him why he sleeps that way?"

"Yeah. He says the bed is too soft. He's used to sleeping on a cement pallet in a small place with his stuff around him. That's all he's comfortable with now. So, you see, Maggie, he doesn't need a wife. He needs a . . . a keeper!"

Maggie inched closer to Chad and laid her head on his shoulder. "What are we going to do?" she asked quietly. "We both love him so much. How are we going to help him?"

Chad shook his head. She could feel his chest rise and fall heavily. His voice cracked as he said, "I honestly don't know, Maggie. I pray for him day and night. I want so much to have the brother I knew and loved back again. But I don't know what it will take."

In a whisper she said, "He sacrificed so much for us, for our country. Maybe it's time we sacrificed something for him."

Chad turned slightly and raised her chin to his. "What are you saying, Maggie?"

Tears glazed her eyes. "Maybe I need to go where I'm needed most. Chad, you're strong and whole. So capable. So talented. You can make it on your own. You don't need anyone . . ."

His blue eyes filled with a wrenching melancholy. "I need you, my sweet little Magpie. Don't you doubt it for a moment."

She caressed his face with her palm. "I know you do, my darling, and I need you too. But both of us could survive without the other if we had to. We've already given one another so much. We've shared such a precious love, enough love to last us for a lifetime."

A tear slid from the corner of his eye. "Are you saying what I think you're saying?"

Her own salty tears spilled out. "I'm not sure what I'm saying, Chad. I don't know how to put it. I just feel—we prayed for so many years for Jordan to be alive, and God gave us that miracle. Jordan has come home to us; he's survived against incredible odds, and now the two of us have to do everything we can to ensure that he makes it the rest of the way."

"And if we told him we were getting married, it would be like cutting him off from us, leaving him stranded in deep water to swim alone."

"You say it so well," she agreed. "I don't think either of us is willing to risk setting him adrift."

Chad pulled her closer and said huskily, "Then there's only one thing we can do."

She gazed up earnestly at him. "But only if you agree. I've pledged you my love, my very life; I've promised to marry you, and I won't break that promise unless you release me from my commitment."

"Oh, Maggie, Maggie!" He gathered her into his arms with a fierceness that startled her. Holding her so close she could feel his thundering heart against her own, he smothered her face with kisses, leaving her cheeks wet with his tears. His passion left her weak, breathless, dazzled.

"I release you, my darling," he whispered against her parted lips, "but I will never stop loving you."

"Nor I you," she murmured.

At last he broke the embrace and stood up. He straightened the cuffs of his shirt and smoothed back his hair. He stared down at her with desolation in his eyes. "Do what you have to do, Maggie," he said with a raw edge in his voice. "If that means marrying my brother, I won't stand in your way. I'll find a way to get over you, even if it means leaving Willowbrook, leaving Indiana, leaving the country, if I have to."

She stood and held out her arms to him. "No, Chad, don't go away. I couldn't bear it."

He seized her wrists and held her at arms' length. "And I couldn't bear to stand by and watch you marry Jordan."

"Then I won't. I couldn't."

"You must, Maggie. It may be his only hope."

"Oh, Chad, pray to God there'll be some other way."

"I'll be praying every hour of my life. But if you find there is no other way to help my brother, then . . . then marry him . . . with my blessing."

Before Maggie could go into his arms one last time, Chad pivoted sharply and strode out of the room, his shoulders straight, not looking back. She heard his heavy footsteps going down the hallway, then heard the door shut with a jarring finality. She was alone in the darkened parlor, more alone than she had ever been in her life. A torrent of sobs broke in her chest. She collapsed on the floor, laid her head on the love seat, and wept brokenly. Dear God in heaven, she loved Chad more this moment than she ever had in her life.

25

During that spring of 1973, Maggie found herself planning a June wedding, but it was Jordan Barrett she was engaged to marry, not her beloved Chad. And as Jordan had promised that Christmas Eve so long ago, he placed a diamond ring on her finger in exchange for the gold locket she had worn around her neck all these years.

As the weeks of May slipped by, Maggie tried to convince herself that she had made the right decision, for certainly she had never seen Jordan happier. He talked of nothing but the wedding. It had become his obsession. It would be a small event with just their immediate families—intimate, elegant, beautiful. Yes, he had every detail planned out, right down to the vows they would exchange (he wrote them himself), where they would honeymoon (Hawaii), and where they would live afterward (a small rented bungalow on the north side of town until they could afford the down payment on a ranch-style home in the suburbs).

He knew it all so well, had their entire future perfectly orchestrated, for he had had five interminably long years to dream and plan. And after five years of subsisting with absolutely no control over his destiny, Jordan now seemed determined not to relinquish control of even the slightest detail of their lives.

But for all his happiness, Jordan still displayed behavior patterns that worried Maggie. He hadn't found a job, hadn't even ventured outside to look for one. With a degree in industrial arts, he could have taught at the local high school, but he insisted he wasn't about to face a classroom of long-haired hippie antiwar activists.

All too often he lost his temper over minor problems. His tolerance level was low; the slightest frustration set him off. When he went to renew his driver's license, he failed the test and was so enraged he drove the car over the curb and clipped a stop sign.

And, unlike the gregarious Jordan that Maggie remembered, he was now very much a loner. Preferring the isolation of his room to fraternizing with others, he seemed painfully uncomfortable with anyone outside the family. He even resisted going to church because "those people are always asking me stupid questions and poking their nose in my affairs."

Perhaps the most troubling news about Jordan came from Chad, who informed Maggie that Jordan still slept on the floor in a corner of his room, tucked in a fetal position, surrounded by his favorite possessions. And he still had horrifying nightmares that prompted hair-raising screams in the dead of night.

It struck Maggie as a sad paradox that, when they were growing up, Jordan had been the strong one, the natural-born leader, the one who invariably took charge and knew exactly what he was doing, while Maggie and Chad, struggling to keep up, had been no match for him. Quiet cowards at heart, they had thrived on his energy, his passion, his boldness. They were only pale moons to Jordan's rising sun.

But now, incredibly, Maggie felt like the strong one, the one upon whom Jordan leaned; she was the one with a firm grip on her life, who was spurred by a passion for God and her work and had already accomplished many of her heart's desires. During Jordan's absence she and Chad both had learned to swim on their own, to break through the constraints of their own cautious, introspective personalities. Chad had found himself in his photojournalism just as Maggie had found herself in her writing. Now it was Jordan who was floundering, rudderless, treading water. It was Jordan who was in danger of drowning in the nightmares, the very atrocities he thought he had survived.

But while Jordan had his nightmares, Maggie had plenty of her own as their wedding drew close. She would awaken in the middle of the night in a cold sweat, convinced she was spiraling madly down the wrong road, headed for destruction. She realized her dreams were a thinly veiled metaphor of her relationship with Jordan. She had to be crazy to be marrying him out of pity, simply because she felt sorry for him. How could she build a future with a man who seemed so needy, so broken, so different from the man she once loved?

And yet in the light of day, Maggie saw no other course but to marry Jordan. At rare moments when he laughed at her jokes or picked her flowers from his garden or allowed himself to become vulnerable enough to reveal horrific details of his captivity, Maggie almost believed they could make it work; they could have a future together. But at other times she looked at him, truly stopped and saw him as he was now, and felt a ripple of terror go down her spine at the prospect of spending her life with a man who was virtually a stranger to her.

In her prayers each night, Maggie entreated God to give her His answer, for surely He was not the God of confusion. And didn't He promise to work all things for good to those who loved Him and were His chosen ones? And yet she had never felt more baffled and bewildered. Was she exemplifying Christ's unconditional love by marrying Jordan? Or was she showing a lack of faith in God's redemptive power by trying to save Jordan on her own? The more she tried to view her life with some perspective, the more muddled everything became.

One day early in June, less than two weeks before her wedding to Jordan, Maggie experienced what she could only call an epiphany of the soul. The truth struck her one morning as she sat reading her Bible. She had spent so much time wrestling with her decision to marry Jordan that she had ceased to keep her eyes focused on the Lord. In fretting over her own future, she had allowed her passion for Christ to slip away.

"God, forgive me," she whispered tearfully. "My soul feels dry, my heart cold as stone. I'm so wrapped up in myself and my problems; I've lost sight of my love for You, Lord. Help me to love You the way I used to, when I felt joy just sitting in Your presence. And, Father, help me to leave my circumstances in Your hands. If You want me to marry Jordan, I will, and I'll trust You to make it work. But if You don't want us together, make Jordan see the truth, because I can't bear to hurt him myself."

That very afternoon Jordan stopped by with news. "I've got a job, Maggie."

"Really?" she said, pleasantly surprised. Getting a job was an enormous step for Jordan. "Where? A school?"

"No," he said as he followed her into the living room. "A small furniture factory on the south side of town."

"Furniture?"

"Yeah. You know I love working with my hands. I'll be putting together and finishing tables and chairs. Solid oak. The finest furniture. Quality stuff."

"But what about teaching?"

He shrugged, looking disappointed over her lack of enthusiasm. "Maybe I'll teach someday, but I'm not ready yet. I'd go nuts in a roomful of rowdy kids. At the factory I can work alone, at my own pace. It'll be good for me, Maggie."

She went into his arms and hugged him. "I'm happy for you, Jordan. I know you'll do beautiful work."

"It doesn't pay much," he conceded, "so we'll still need your income for a while."

"That's fine. I love my job. I have no plans to quit."

His brow furrowed slightly. "That's fine for now, Maggie, but one of these days I'll be the breadwinner and you can stay home and take care of the children, just like we planned."

Maggie's ire rose. "Jordan, we've had this conversation before. I like having a career, and I'm in no hurry to have children."

Jordan's expression darkened. He was angry with her and trying not to show it. "You're letting these Women's Libbers influence you, Maggie. All this talk these days about women's rights, it's not good. How can we have a real home if we're both out working?"

She almost said, "Chad and I had no problem planning a home with both of us working," but she caught herself and turned away before Jordan saw the frustration in her face.

"You're not going along with all this stuff, are you, Mag? Women wanting to act like men? The Supreme Court's even saying women can have abortions now. Surely you don't approve of that, do you?"

"No, of course not, Jordan," she said impatiently. "That has nothing to do with me wanting to continue my career. Why are you trying to force the issue?"

His shoulders sagged slightly. "I don't know, Maggie. I just want you home with me after we're married. I want us to feel safe and protected. I don't want any surprises."

"Surprises? What are you talking about?"

He sat down on the sofa and cracked his knuckles loudly. "I don't know what I mean. Nothing, I guess. I don't know why I even said that. Forget it, okay? Just forget it." He reached into his shirt pocket and brought out a folded envelope. "Look, Maggie. I got a letter from one of my buddies in the camp. Fred Logan. Remember him? You met him at the White House party."

"Fred? The tall, thin man with the scar across his forehead."

"Right. He was in the cell next to me. A Green Beret."

Maggie sat down beside Jordan. "Fred wrote you a letter?"

"Yeah. Short and sweet. Or maybe I should say . . . bittersweet." He handed it to her. "You can read it if you want to. Fred and his wife split up. Now he and another guy I know are at a V.A. hospital in Washington. Says they're getting help. Therapy. Counseling. They say it's helping."

Maggie looked closely at Jordan. "Is there a reason you're telling me this?" she ventured softly. "Jordan, do you think counseling would help you too?"

He crushed the letter in his fist, and his face reddened. "I'm not talking about me, Maggie. I'm just saying I got a letter. It has nothing to do with me. What's the matter? You think I'm crazy because I want you to quit work? It's not my problem, Maggie. It's yours. Don't blame me."

"I'm not," she said quietly, her gaze downcast. She felt herself shrinking inside, closing in on herself, erecting a silent, impenetrable wall, the way she always did these days when she and Jordan clashed. Why was it they could never talk to each other anymore without one or the other misunderstanding and feeling hurt?

She shuddered, a chill of apprehension sweeping over her. In less than two weeks Jordan would become her husband—God forbid!— yet each day he became more of a stranger, someone she wasn't even sure she wanted to know!

After a minute she composed herself and took the crumpled letter from Jordan's hand. She read it silently while he stared off into space. After a minute she handed it back to him. "Your friend invited you to come visit him at the V.A. hospital, Jordan. Maybe you should think about it. You'd be with someone again who knows what you've gone through, who lived it with you."

He stuffed the letter back in his pocket. "Sure, I'll just up and go, with our wedding two weeks away. Be reasonable, Maggie. There's no way I can go to Washington. Besides, Fred makes it sound like he thinks I need counseling too. Well, I don't. All I need is for the two of us to be together as husband and wife, and you'll see a world of difference in me."

She wanted to argue with him, tell him marriage wouldn't change anything, that if anything, it would only complicate matters further, but the words wouldn't come, so she pressed her lips tightly together and sank back against the sofa in mute defeat.

"Come here, Mag." Jordan drew her into his arms and pressed her head against his shoulder. "We're not like them, Maggie, like Fred and his wife. That's not us. We're going to be fine, better than fine. We'll have a wonderful life, starting the day you walk down the aisle to meet me. You wait and see."

Maggie looked up at Jordan's sturdy face and noticed the blazing intensity in his clear blue eyes. So much was going on inside him, so much that Maggie couldn't begin to comprehend. It was as if they were speaking different languages or as if they were sojourners from vastly different planets. Somehow she had to find a way to span the gulf between them.

She reached up and touched his face and gathered all the courage she could muster. "Jordan," she plunged in shakily, "you know I love you. I care deeply about what happens to you. And I have to say I think Fred is right. You may need help. Counseling of some sort. It would make our marriage better, stronger."

He drummed his fingers on her arm. "What is this, Maggie? You two ganging up on me?"

"Of course not. But I know you've had trouble sleeping since you got home. And there are the nightmares. Chad has told me about them. You need someone to talk to who knows about these things. I'll be glad to listen, Jordan, but I'm no professional."

"I don't need a professional," he snapped.

She ran her fingers over his cheek, her boldness growing. If she didn't speak now, perhaps she never would. "But you're not the Jordan I remember. Surely you can see that. Don't you want him back—the man you were then?"

He removed his arm from her shoulder and sat forward, his head in his hands. He made a low, guttural sound, not quite a sob. She ran her hand over his back, his starched cotton shirt coarse against her palm. "Jordan, talk to me, please!"

He shook his head miserably, his face still buried in his hands. "I don't know what's wrong with me, Maggie. In the prison camp, I was strong; I stayed focused; I knew who the enemy was. I steeled myself for survival 100 percent, twenty-four hours a day. They beat me, tried to humiliate me, and messed with my mind, but I wouldn't let them win. Wouldn't let them steal my pride, my self-respect."

"Oh, Jordan—"

"I kept thinking, *If I can just get home alive, I'll be okay; if I can just get home alive! I'll do all the things I dreamed of in captivity; I'll be better than ever because I know how much my freedom cost; I know how much it's worth. I'll make up for lost time; I've conquered the worst there is, so everything after this will be duck soup, easy as pie.*

"But now here I am, Maggie, home, alive, no enemy, nothing stopping me. I'm home with the people who love me, and I feel aimless, unfocused, powerless; I don't know who the enemy is anymore." He drew in a deep, ragged breath that convulsed his entire frame. "Dear God in heaven, Maggie, sometimes I think the enemy is *me!*"

"Jordan, dear Jordan, it's okay." She rubbed his muscled back, his knotted shoulders, and found herself pouring out words of comfort she hadn't expected to say. "It's going to take time. And prayers. And love. And we have all three. We'll get through this. God will show us the way."

Three days before the wedding, Maggie received a phone call at work from Jordan's mother. Her voice was edged with hysteria as she cried, "Maggie, it's Jordan. Something's happened. I don't know what—"

"Is he hurt? An accident?"

"No, not an accident. He's locked himself in his room and won't come out. I hear him banging things around. He's angrier than I've ever seen him."

"Angry? Why?"

"I have no idea, Maggie. Please come over. Maybe you can reason with him. I can't reach his father—he's at a business meeting in Fort Wayne, and Chad is out somewhere on a photo assignment. Please hurry!"

"I'll be right there."

All the way over, as Maggie accelerated her late-model sedan, she wracked her brain, wondering what could have set Jordan off. He should have been in a chipper mood with the wedding just days away. She parked at an odd angle in front of the Barrett house and ran up the walk to the sprawling porch. Mrs. Barrett opened the door before Maggie knocked and wordlessly stepped aside to let her enter.

Maggie took the stairs two at a time and arrived at Jordan's door breathless, her heart pounding like a jackhammer. "Jordan!" she called as she tried the knob. "It's me, Maggie. Let me in!"

"Go away!" he shouted, the words muffled.

"What's wrong, Jordan? Please, open the door!"

"I said, go away!"

"No, not until you tell me what's wrong."

Dead silence.

"Jordan, do you hear me? I can't help you unless you let me in."

His voice erupted thick with antagonism. "You can't help me, Maggie. Nobody can. Least of all you!"

"Why, Jordan? What have I done?"

Silence again.

"I'm not leaving until you open this door, Jordan!"

"It's too late, Maggie. Just go. Get out of here."

She leaned against the door, a weakness spreading through her limbs. What terrible thing had happened to make Jordan so distraught? "I'll sit outside your door all day, Jordan, if that's what it takes."

More silence, and then finally she heard the lock click and the door opened a crack. She caught a glimpse of Jordan's reddened, tear-stained face. She slipped her hand inside the door so he couldn't close it again. "Jordan, please, tell me what's wrong."

Slowly he opened the door and let her enter. He was wearing a rumpled tee shirt and grey sweat pants. His honey-brown hair was mussed, several strands straying across his high forehead. His usually clear blue eyes were bloodshot, red-rimmed. Instinctively she reached out to touch him, to offer comfort, but he shrank from her touch as if he'd been burned.

Maggie sat down on the unmade bed and gazed around the room. Everything was in disarray—clothing, books, records, toiletries, photographs. A table lamp had been overturned, and Jordan's old high school mementos had been knocked off the desk. A framed photograph of Maggie lay on the floor by the bed, the glass shattered. Alarm spiraled through Maggie's chest. "Jordan, why?"

"Don't you know?" he demanded.

"How could I? I just got here. Please, tell me. What has you so upset?"

He handed her a newspaper clipping.

The moment her eyes settled on the familiar photograph, everything clicked into place. Above the picture of a couple embracing was the headline, JUNE WEDDING PLANNED FOR LOCAL COUPLE, MARGARET HERRICK AND CHAD BARRETT.

Maggie let the paper flutter from her fingers. Her stomach

somersaulted, and her mouth turned to parchment. She tried to speak, but no sound came.

Jordan grabbed up the engagement announcement and crumpled it in his hand. "Why, Maggie?" he demanded, his voice half accusation, half lament. "Why didn't you tell me?"

"I wanted to," she managed weakly.

Jordan waved his hand at her. "What was it? You and my brother figured I'd be too ravaged by the war to figure out what was going on? Too stupid? Too blind? Is that what you thought?"

"Of course not, Jordan."

"Then what? Why didn't you tell me from the beginning that you and Chad planned to get married? Did you think I was too weak, too fainthearted to accept the truth?"

She shook her head miserably. "We didn't want to hurt you."

"So you made up this elaborate charade to fool me? You pretended to love me, to want to be my wife? You must have had half the town in on this ruse. And our families! My own parents went along with you. Great Scott, Maggie, how far were you going to take this? Our wedding is on Saturday!"

"It wasn't a charade," she said, tears gathering. "I do love you, Jordan. You know that. I've always loved you."

He stared her down. "But you love my brother a little more! Is that it?"

Tears streamed down her face. "I . . . I love you both."

Jordan's voice broke with anguish. "Is it love, Maggie? Or do you just feel sorry for me? The poor, battle-scarred POW?"

"I . . . I don't know."

He raked his fingers through his mussed, wheat-colored hair. "Well, at least you're honest, maybe for the first time since I got home." He paced the floor, pummeling his fist against his palm. "How could I have been so stupid not to see it? You and Chad. It all makes sense now, the way you two are so comfortable together. The best of friends, right? What did we used to call ourselves? The Three

Musketeers? All for one and one for all? Well, looks like it's really the Two Musketeers, and I'm the odd man out."

Maggie wrung her hands as tears made rivulets down her cheeks. "I'm so sorry, Jordan. We wanted to tell you, but we couldn't."

He glared down at her. "What would it have taken, Maggie? A little courage? I had to work up courage to endure five years of hell on earth. Surely you and my brother could have summoned enough courage to tell me the truth. You could have left me with some shred of dignity instead of letting me humiliate myself in front of you and half the world. I guess I was good for a laugh, though, right? I bet you all had a real good laugh at my expense. You and half the town. What a joke!"

"It's not funny, Jordan," she protested tearfully.

He waved his finger under her nose. "You bet it's not funny, Maggie. You say you didn't want to hurt me. Well, you just tore out my heart. Are you happy?"

She covered her face with her hands and wept. Never before had she felt such anguish, such shame. Jordan was right. She had betrayed him in the worst possible way. "How did you find out?" she asked.

He didn't look up. "I was going through some of my mom's things, looking for pictures of us as kids for a wedding display. I found the article tucked away with some old photos and mementos."

"I'm sorry. Terribly sorry. I don't know what else to say."

He sat down on the opposite end of the bed and put his head in his hands. He looked suddenly exhausted, as if all the fight had gone out of him. "Maggie, there's nothing you can say that will make any difference now."

They sat for several minutes in a discomfiting silence, Maggie weeping quietly, Jordan with his head lowered in his hands. Finally she got up and helped herself to a tissue on the bureau and wiped her tears and blew her nose. A thought came to her: *Jordan has told the truth as he sees it; now you tell him the truth as you see it.* The idea baffled her for a moment, but suddenly the words were coming.

She sat down beside Jordan and put her hand on his arm. He recoiled slightly, staring at her with a mixture of suspicion and bewilderment. She kept her hand on his arm and spoke quietly, with a surprising measure of calm. "Jordan, I can't change what's happened, and I understand why you're angry. You think Chad and I betrayed you."

"Think? I know!"

"But you don't know. You know part of the truth, not all of it."

He gave her a chilly sidelong glance. "What more is there? It looks pretty black and white to me."

She drew in a deep, shuddering breath. "Listen to me, Jordan. Please let me explain."

"Forget it, Maggie. I don't want a bunch of lame excuses."

She tightened her hand on his arm. "If you really care about me, you'll listen."

She felt the tension in his arm relax a little. "Okay."

"Chad and I didn't plan to fall in love. It just happened after years of being best friends. We didn't fall; we grew in love. We found we had so much in common; we thought alike, looked at the world the same way. We had this sense of harmony between us, like we were marching to the same drum beat."

Jordan snorted. "And this is supposed to make me feel better?"

She reached up and turned his face toward hers and waited until he met her gaze. "For years, Jordan, we grieved together, Chad and I. Grieved for you. We both loved you and missed you. Finally, after so many years, we began to accept that you were dead. By that time, we discovered our friendship had grown into love. So, yes, we were going to be married."

"And then I came home and put a crimp in your plans."

"We didn't think of it that way," said Maggie. "We were overjoyed to learn you were alive. Your homecoming was the answer to our prayers. We wanted to do everything in our power to make life good for you again. Don't you see? You had given so much and been so terribly wounded. We loved you so much, we would have done anything for you."

"Even marry me when it's my brother you wanted?" he said grudgingly.

She lowered her gaze. "Yes, Jordan, even that." She looked back at him. "Please try to understand. I agreed to marry you, Jordan, because I love you in so many ways. Even the best way."

"The best way?"

"The Bible calls it *agape* love. Unconditional, sacrificial love. The kind of love Christ has for us. I'm not pretending I can love with that kind of love on my own, Jordan; I can't. But I can let Christ pour His love through me. That's the love I feel for you, Jordan. And that's the kind of love your brother feels for you. Together we agreed to put our love for each other aside so we could focus on you and do whatever was necessary to make you happy. Even if that meant Chad and I would never be together."

Jordan's eyes narrowed. "I never would have asked that of you."

"I know. It was our choice. And we still feel that way, Jordan. Chad is willing to stand at the altar as your best man and let you become my husband. He's willing to put aside his claim to me because that's how much he loves you. So you see, Jordan, this isn't about betrayal or lies; this is about love and sacrifice. Maybe we didn't handle it well. Maybe it backfired in our faces, and we ended up hurting you more than we would have otherwise. But please believe me, what we did we did out of love."

Jordan was silent for a long minute. He rocked a little, lost in his own thoughts. The knots of anger had left his face. He looked weary, careworn, and older than she had ever seen him.

"What now?" she asked in a small, tentative voice.

He didn't answer right away. Finally he turned the question back to her. "You tell me, Maggie."

She shrugged. "I don't know."

"There's a wedding scheduled," he said simply.

She nodded, rubbing her hands nervously. Her fingers were ice cold. "What should we do?"

He sighed heavily. "It's up to you."

She massaged her clammy fingers. *Dear God, help me to know what to do! Let me do the right thing!* "I promised to marry you, Jordan."

He made a low, scoffing sound. "Do you think I would hold you to your promise now?"

"I don't know."

He tilted her chin up to his. "Are you saying you're still willing to marry me on Saturday?"

Somehow she found the words. "If that's what will make you happy."

He straightened his shoulders, a new buoyancy in his voice. "Okay, Maggie, you've got a deal. The wedding goes as planned. No matter what the world thinks, on Saturday you become my bride!"

26

Maggie's wedding day dawned clear and balmy, a perfect day except for one glaring detail: She was marrying the wrong man. Privately her parents and the Barretts gently inquired whether she was making the right choice. Mrs. Barrett hugged her and said, "I'm so happy for Jordan, but my heart breaks for my other son."

Maggie knew all about broken hearts, for hers was breaking right along with Chad's. When she encountered him in the church's all-purpose room an hour before the wedding, it took every ounce of self-control to keep from rushing into his arms. She was already dressed in her satin and lace bridal gown, a tiara of gold and sheer organza accenting her plaited hair.

Chad was there as Jordan's best man; he carried Jordan's tuxedo over his arm and the wedding ring in his pocket and would be standing beside Jordan when Maggie marched down the aisle.

"Where's Jordan?" she asked, feeling suddenly self-conscious under Chad's scrutinizing gaze. "I don't want to run into him before the ceremony. It's bad luck, they say."

"Don't worry. Jordan's still at home. He said he had some last-minute things to do. Jon Knowl is with him, and he'll be driving him over. The two have become good buddies."

"I've noticed that," said Maggie. "Jordan even went with us last week to Jon Knowl's graduation from Kent State. I was so proud of Jordan for making the trip with us."

"Me too," said Chad. "He's mixing better with people. Seems less withdrawn."

"Is he still angry with you?" she ventured.

"You mean about keeping our engagement a secret?"

"Yes. He was so infuriated with me at first."

"Same here. But he seems better now. Still quiet and remote, but not angry. In fact, he seemed genuinely touched that I was willing to be his best man."

"So am I, Chad. Thank you. You don't know how much it means to me."

Chad's eyes grew moist. "It's not easy, Maggie. In fact, standing at the altar with the two of you will be the hardest thing I've ever had to do." He paused meaningfully. "Are you still going through with it?"

"With the wedding? Of course. I've come too far to back out now. Did you think I would?"

"I guess I was still hoping."

"I can't forsake Jordan, Chad. He needs me."

"So do I."

"I know, but it's . . . it's different. His very life—his well-being, his future—is at risk."

"And mine isn't? It's killing me to stand by and watch you marry my brother."

She clasped his sturdy hand. "But we agreed!"

"I know. And, don't worry, I'm a man of my word."

"At least now everything is out in the open. No more secrets or pretenses."

He took her hands in his and held them tightly. He looked strikingly debonair in his tuxedo and pale pink cummerbund. "Maggie, you're the most beautiful bride I've ever seen. May I have the first kiss?"

She wanted to say, *The first, the last, and every one in between.* Instead she flashed a demure smile. He gathered her gently into his arms and kissed her lips with exquisite tenderness. For a moment she forgot where she was or that another man would be waiting for her at the altar.

Chad released her and stepped back unsteadily. Incredibly, he was as flustered as she! "I'd better let you go get ready, Maggie. I hear organ music playing. It won't be long now."

She nodded, tears starting. "Everyone will be arriving. Grandmother Anna, Aunt Catherine, and Uncle Robert. Even my cousin Jenny and her husband Danny cut their concert tour short to make the trip home so she could be my matron of honor."

"Even with just our immediate families, it'll be quite a little gathering," Chad noted.

"And Uncle Todd must be here already," she rushed on. "It makes it nice having a minister in the family at times like this."

Chad nodded. "Yes, Reverend Marshall is a terrific man."

Maggie's face grew warm. "We're . . . we're just rambling, you know. Silly small talk."

He smiled grimly. "I know. I'll talk about anything to keep you here with me. After the wedding, when you truly belong to my brother, it'll be different between us."

She stared at him in alarm. "But why? It doesn't have to be. We'll always be friends."

"Yes . . . friends. But not close. Not like this."

She swallowed a sob. "I don't want to lose what we have, Chad."

He swept her into his arms and held her close for a long magical moment, nearly crushing her satin gown with his powerful embrace. In the sweet, enveloping warmth of his caress, she could feel their hearts beating as one. "I'll never stop loving you, my darling little Magpie," he whispered, his voice raw, full of agony. "Never!"

Tearfully she broke free and pushed him away. "No, Chad, I won't . . . I can't! It's Jordan now, only Jordan!" She pivoted, picked up the lacy folds of her gown and fled back to the dressing room.

Minutes later a gentle knock sounded on the door, and her mother slipped inside. "Everyone's here, darling. Jenny's in the next room putting on her gown. Catherine's helping her. And the organist wants to know when to start the Wedding March."

"Jordan and Jon Knowl are here, too?"

"I haven't seen them, but I'm sure they must be. It's almost time."

Maggie smoothed out her gown and adjusted her veil. "I'm ready, Mama."

Her mother looked her full in the face. "Are you sure, Margaret? This is what you want? To marry Jordan? It's still not too late to change your mind."

Maggie spoke over a wave of surging emotion. "No, Mama. This is my choice. God has given me a peace about it."

"Well, then, there's nothing else to say, is there?" A tear formed at the corner of Annie's eye. "I'll check on Jenny, and as soon as she's ready, I'll come get you and we'll all go to the vestibule. You remember the sequence Reverend Marshall explained. Mrs. Barrett and I will be seated, the wedding march will begin, and Jenny and Chad will go down the aisle together, taking their places as matron of honor and best man. Then your father will escort you down the aisle. Remember to move with the music, not too fast, not too slow . . ."

"Mama, I know. Don't worry. It'll be perfect. Jordan has made sure every detail goes like clockwork."

Minutes later Maggie, moving slowly in her graceful, flowing gown, met her father and Chad and Jenny in the vestibule. She and Jenny exchanged brief hugs and complimented each other on their dresses. Maggie smiled faintly at Chad and he nodded back, with more a grimace than a smile.

"Ready, honey?" her father whispered, his eyes crinkling with a wistful smile behind his glasses. He looked dapper in his black tuxedo, surely as handsome now as he had been when he married Maggie's mother.

She nodded and tightened her fingers around her bouquet of pink roses. They stepped forward to the entrance of the sanctuary, first Jenny and Chad, then Maggie and her father. Maggie saw Reverend Marshall step forward to the altar, but where was Jordan? Surely he had arrived by now.

Maggie heard a rustling sound behind her and looked around to see Jon Knowl striding toward her in his crisp black suit. His hair was shorter, and he had lost that radical look of his rebellious years. He had settled down quite nicely at last. "Where's Jordan?" she whispered.

Jon Knowl was out of breath, his face ruddy. He smoothed back a thatch of flyaway hair and inhaled sharply. "Jordan said when the wedding march starts, the procession should begin."

"But where is he?" she persisted.

Jon Knowl managed a lopsided smile. "Don't worry, Sis, your groom will be there by the time you get to the altar."

Maggie had no more time to question her brother, for the wedding march had begun, Chad and Jenny were already moving down the aisle, and the congregation was standing, waiting for her. She hugged Jon Knowl and he kissed her cheek and whispered, "Be happy, Sis!" She nodded, fighting back the tears, then tucked her arm around her father's and began her cadenced walk toward the altar, toward her future with Jordan Barrett.

When she reached the altar, she cast a sidelong glance at Chad, as if to ask, *Where's Jordan?* Chad looked puzzled too. They both looked at Reverend Marshall, who returned a quizzical glance. What happened next stirred even greater confusion in Maggie's mind. Jon Knowl came striding down the aisle, approached the altar where she stood, and handed her an envelope. "Jordan asked me to give you this," he whispered.

"Where is he?" she asked with concern.

"The letter explains everything."

She looked questioningly at Reverend Marshall and he nodded, as if to say, *Go ahead, take your time; we'll wait.*

A low murmur of whispers rippled over the congregation as she tore open the envelope and removed the gold locket Jordan had given her that Christmas Eve so long ago. Along with the locket was a single sheet of stationery. She unfolded the flimsy paper.

Yes, she recognized Jordan's distinctive handwriting with the strong, slanting letters and the graceful loops.

My darling Maggie,

By the time you read this letter I will be on a plane for Washington, D.C. and you will be standing at the altar with the man you were meant to marry. I hope you'll forgive me for orchestrating your wedding day in such a peculiar way, but I knew if I released you from your commitment in any other way, you would have gone on with the wedding to spare hurting me.

I admit I was stunned to learn that you and Chad loved each other and had planned to marry, and for a while I was a pig-headed boor, full of anger, jealousy, and resentment. But after our talk a few nights ago I began to realize the sacrifice you and my brother made for me. You showed me what unconditional love is all about. You were both willing to put aside your love for each other to give me my heart's desire.

But you're not the only ones who can show what sacrificial love is all about. You two have given me the strength and courage I need to admit I still have a long journey to go before I'm whole and my own man again. But I have no doubt that day will come, in part thanks to you.

I've decided to take my buddy Fred up on his offer to visit him at the V.A. hospital in Washington. Maybe the people there can help me the way they're helping Fred. Anyway, it's worth a try. Please thank Jon Knowl for helping me with my little conspiracy and for delivering me to the airport in one piece. I'm sure he broke all speed records trying to make it back to the wedding in time.

One of these days, when I'm ready, I'll return to Willowbrook. Who knows? Maybe one day I'll even come home with a girl who loves me as much as you love Chad. Meanwhile, my dear Maggie, remember, in my heart we'll always be the Three Musketeers. You, Chad, and me. All for one and one for all.

Give my parents a kiss for me and tell that brother of mine he'd better treat you right or he'll have to answer to me. Now have yourselves a glorious wedding!

Love, Jordan

Maggie was weeping now, large warm tears that rolled unhindered down her rosy cheeks. She didn't even know when the tears had started. She felt a hundred emotions exploding inside her chest at once. Shock. Amazement. Wonder. Love and gratitude to Jordan. Excitement and love for Chad.

She opened the familiar heart-shaped locket that she'd worn so faithfully for years. But this time, instead of her picture and Jordan's, the locket contained her picture and Chad's. She pressed the locket to her breast, closed her eyes, and whispered, "Thank you, Jordan, for loving me enough to let me go!"

Chad stared down at her, baffled, ill at ease, and whispered, "What's going on, Maggie?"

She smiled and handed him the letter and watched the same emotions she'd just experienced play out on his face, one by one. As comprehension finally swept over him, he stared back at her, wide-eyed, a smile playing on his lips. "Does this mean—?"

She brushed at her tears. "I don't know. What do you think?"

"Jordan says . . . is he serious? He seems to be giving us his blessing."

She smiled tearfully. "Yes, he does, doesn't he?"

Reverend Marshall stepped forward and broke in with his deep, sonorous voice. "Well, how about it? Is there going to be a wedding today or not?"

The small crowd broke into vigorous applause.

Maggie's lips curved in a dazzling smile. "What do you say, Chad? Am I destined to be a bride left standing at the altar?"

He chuckled. "Never that, my darling."

"Then . . . will you marry me?"

He grinned back mischievously, enjoying the witty repartee. "Why not, my darling Magpie? I have nothing else planned today." He took the bouquet from her hands and gently enfolded her in his strong arms. "Will you do me the honor, Margaret Kate Herrick, of becoming my wife?"

Her words rose on a sigh. "Yes, Mr. Chad Barrett, I would love to."

With his arm circling Maggie's waist, Chad turned to Reverend Marshall and with a triumphant little nod, declared, "Let the wedding begin!"

About the Author

CAROLE GIFT PAGE, an award-winning novelist, has authored more than forty books. She is a frequent speaker for conferences, schools, churches, and women's ministries. Carole has taught creative writing at Biola University and received the C.S. Lewis Honor book award. She has been nominated for several Gold Medallion awards and the Campus Life Book of the Year award.

She is the author of five other books in the Heartland Memories Series—*The House on Honeysuckle Lane, Home to Willowbrook, The Hope of Herrick House, Storms Over Willowbrook*, and *A Rose for Jenny*. Carole and her husband, Bill, have three children and live in Moreno Valley, California.

OTHER BOOKS IN THE HEARTLAND MEMORIES SERIES

The House on Honeysuckle Lane (Book One)

It's 1932, and Annie Reed and her best friend, Cath Herrick, share dreams of the future at Annie's house on Honeysuckle Lane. But never could they have imagined how troubles brewing in the world around them would reach into their lives and change so much.

0-8407-6777-3 • Trade Paperback • 288 pages

Home to Willowbrook (Book Two)

When Catherine Herrick awakens from a coma after a car accident, she must rebuild her shattered life. As old memories come back, Catherine begins to learn hard lessons of acceptance and renewal. Set just after World War II, this is a compelling story of faith, mercy, and the power of love to heal wounded hearts.

0-8407-6778-1 • Trade Paperback • 252 pages

The Hope of Herrick House (Book Three)

When a devastating fire kills her mother and destroys her home, Bethany Rose Henry comes to live with her half-sister, Catherine Herrick. Resentful and frightened, Bethany contends with a new world as she gets to know the family she never knew she had. Soon she learns that her mother was murdered, and clues to the murderer point to a member of Catherine's family. Will Bethany speak up, or will she push everyone away, including the handsome young minister who has fallen in love with her?

0-8407-6780-3 • Trade Paperback • 288 pages

Storms Over Willowbrook (Book Four)

It's 1951, and Alice Marie Reed has finally become a success as host of a popular TV show. Then comes an urgent message summoning her to a Chicago hospital, bringing her face to face with her long-lost husband who deserted her so many years ago. When reunion turns to loss and an unexpected pregnancy complicates her life, Alice Marie realizes there is only one safe place for her in the world—her old home in Willowbrook and the family she has been estranged from for so long. There she meets a handsome stranger whose mysterious mission could cost her everything, even her life.

0-7852-7651-8 • Trade Paperback • 288 pages

A Rose for Jenny (Book Five)

It's 1960, and eighteen-year-old Jenny Wayne is ready to conquer the world. Embittered by the circumstances of her birth and her inability to feel close to her own mother, Jenny has never truly felt a part of the family in Willowbrook. So when Danny DiCaprio offers her the chance to run away with him and join a rock 'n' roll band, the temptation is too hard to resist. This fifth book in the Heartland Memories series is a touching story of a young woman's search for love and her personal journey of faith.

0-7852-7671-6 • Trade Paperback • 288 pages